I0596028

IN ORDER OF APPEARANCE, A. F. STEWART, PAUL MICHAEL, MICHAEL CHANDOS, TJ O'HARE, THOMAS ROGGENBUCK, CRYSTA K. COBURN, JACY SELLERS, TIM KIDWELL, SARAH VAN GOETHEM, PHOEBE DARQUELING, K. A. LINDSTROM, AND DREW CARMODY

Cogs, Crowns, and Carriages

A Steampunk Short Story Anthology

Copyright © 2019 by In order of appearance, A. F. Stewart, Paul Michael, Michael Chandos, TJ O'Hare, Thomas Roggenbuck, Crysta K. Coburn, Jacy Sellers, Tim Kidwell, Sarah Van Goethem, Phoebe Darqueling, K. A. Lindstrom, and Drew Carmody

All rights reserved. No part of this publication may be reproduced, stored or transmitted in any form or by any means, electronic, mechanical, photocopying, recording, scanning, or otherwise without written permission from the publisher. It is illegal to copy this book, post it to a website, or distribute it by any other means without permission.

This novel is entirely a work of fiction. The names, characters and incidents portrayed in it are the work of the author's imagination. Any resemblance to actual persons, living or dead, events or localities is entirely coincidental.

In order of appearance, A. F. Stewart, Paul Michael, Michael Chandos, TJ O'Hare, Thomas Roggenbuck, Crysta K. Coburn, Jacy Sellers, Tim Kidwell, Sarah Van Goethem, Phoebe Darqueling, K. A. Lindstrom, and Drew Carmody asserts the moral right to be identified as the author of this work.

First edition

ISBN: 978-1-7347298-1-8

Editing by Crysta Coburn
Editing by Phoebe Darqueling

This book was professionally typeset on Reedsy.
Find out more at reedsy.com

Contents

Foreword ~ Crysta K. Coburn

One of the things that I love most about a genre like Steampunk is how everyone brings something unique to the table. People who aren't familiar with the term often ask me, "What is Steampunk?" I can never adequately answer this question, even after being involved with five Steampunk anthologies! With every new project and each new author and creator that I meet, I find something new. Still, we do have some hallmarks. Cogs and gears. Fantastical gadgets. Unconventional modes of travel. Monsters, both real and conjured. Within these twelve stories, you will find it all from authors and stories that span the globe.

"Secrets and Airships" by A.F. Stewart, "Peregrine Rising: A Skies of Fire and Lightning Story" by Drew Carmody, and "Treason in the Sky" by Jacy Sellers all take us on soaring adventures with intrepid sky pirates (the two former) and a brave young wartime mechanic (the latter). The radical spirit continues in "Regicide and Prejudice" by Paul Michael, in which an inventor of a surprising nature is called on to protect Prince George, and "The Last Automaton of Doctor Jubal Varva" by K.A. Lindstrom, with the warmachine automaton to end all wars.

But it isn't all fun and games. The unscrupulous inventor in "Gho-Power" by Michael Chandos revolutionizes the power industry with horrific results, while the asylum doctor of Phoebe Darqueling's "The Mobius Trip" abuses his power, shattering his patient's soul. In "Monster of the Deep," Thomas Roggenbuck warns about the hazards of sea travel. The gargoyle hunter of Tim Kidwell's "Catchin' Gargoyles" learns not to become overconfident.

Some long for love and mourn its loss. A post-mortem photographer in "The Last Sleep" by Sarah Van Goethem discovers the high price of saving her beloved, deathly ill brother. The characters of my own story "Where the Light Enters" struggle with when to hold on and when to let go. In "Nihon Daitan'na" by T.J. O'Hare, the Emperor's devotion to his people and his country lead him to take drastic action when the Americans arrive to force open Japan's borders.

A project of this worldwide magnitude should never be undertaken lightly. Everyone involved has made it worth every moment for me. I am glad to have gotten to know these diverse authors and their stories, and I think I speak for all of us when I say how thrilled we are to be sharing them with you. If you are new to Steampunk, enjoy this broad introduction. If Steampunk seems like old hat, I hope you find something new, as I did, that inspires you.

Secrets and Airships by A. F. Stewart

Allison leaned forward in her hard-backed chair, the hum of the airship fading into background noise as her fingers turned the page of the diary. Under the flicker of the gas lamp, she read the faded, ink-scratched words on the yellowed page again.

I found it. After all these years, I thought it was only legend, but Skull Island truly exists. And now the island and its treasure are all mine...

A loud knock sounded on the door of her quarters, breaking her focus and sending a twinge of angst through her mind. She hastily stuffed the diary into her satchel, scurried across the room, and opened the door.

Roland Whitlock, second-in-command of their airship, *Windlass Bluebell*, stood there. "Your father wishes to see you. He awaits you on the bridge."

Allison's stomach knotted, but she smiled and followed the airman to the bridge to see her father, the great Lord Leopold Everett, scion of the skies and master of the Pirate Guild.

He turned to her and beckoned her forward with his hand. She moved with reluctance to his side.

"I'm glad you decided to be an obedient child today instead of indulging that stubborn streak of yours. As my sole remaining heir, you must be witness to such events as those that will unfold today."

Allison gritted her teeth at his reminder of their loss. She wanted to slap him for even daring to refer to her as his "heir."

Jeb was your heir, not me. So eager to please it got him killed. I won't make that mistake.

Oblivious to her mood, Lord Everett continued, "Pay attention, Allison.

Today, I demonstrate how to deal with rogues and how to enforce the fealty of your subjects. At all times must your subjects show their loyalty, know their place, and always obey their master."

Allison tried not to glare, ramming her hatred deep inside and wondering what poor fool had incurred her father's displeasure.

Loyalty? What do you know of loyalty? You abandoned your own son. You let Jeb hang.

She repressed a shudder at the thought of her brother's fate, momentarily turning her eyes from the ship's windscreen. The memory of the newspaper headline bubbled to the surface. *Infamous Son of the Pirate King Hanged!* it declared. A worse remembrance, the horrific photo that accompanied the article: her brother's corpse swinging from the gallows. That's when she knew she would never forgive her father for Jeb's death. These days she could barely stand to be in the same room with him.

The ship-to-ship vocal telegraph crackled, interrupting her musings, and a deep, male voice resounded through a tinny speaker on the bridge. "Captain Julius Blaylock of the *Raven Zephyr* reporting to the *Windlass Bluebell,* along with my convoy ships *The Wayfarer Crown* and *Star Storm.* As requested."

Lord Everett smiled, a gesture that turned Allison's stomach and sent a shiver to shake her skin. He glanced at her and remarked, "Always know your duty, Daughter, and learn to obey your betters. This one needs to be brought to heel, and today will be his first lesson."

Allison clenched her jaw, fighting back a retort and a tiny shard of fear. She nodded instead, having learned the hard way not to defy or question her father in front of his men.

Lord Everett seemed satisfied with her response and waved a hand at his vocal telegraph operator. "Send an acknowledgment, Ensign Philpott. And give Captain Blaylock his new orders. I want to see how he reacts."

Allison frowned, and watched carefully as the crewman flipped some switches. The ensign tapped code into the machine and spoke sharply into the transmitter mouthpiece. She quietly shifted her stance as the man relayed the message to be broadcast to the other ship.

"*Windlass Bluebell* to *Raven Zephyr.* Transmission received and acknowledged. Proceed to Spring Haven Island to offload your spoils. You and your ships are grounded until further notice."

Static crackled as the operator's voice faded, and a few minutes of silence settled over the bridge. Allison fidgeted, unease prickling up her spine. The quiet broke as another snap of static sounded, and then Blaylock's voice echoed out of the speaker.

"I don't think so."

Allison inhaled sharply, and shock reverberated around the bridge at the defiance. Then a crewman's voice shouted, "They're manning guns, sir! All ships!"

Allison took a step back, wanting to flee the bridge, but she felt a hand on her shoulder. Roland Whitlock's presence kept her in place as her father jumped to his feet and shouted, "Ready all weapons!"

But the boom of the other ships' guns and the slam of weapons fire rocked the *Windlass Bluebell* before any crew made any significant countermove.

As the *Bluebell* listed, someone yelled, "Main guns aren't responding, sir!"

Allison's gut churned as more shouts rang out over the barrage of attacking guns.

"Secondary guns are not responding!"

"Flight control is damaged!"

"Rudder control is gone!"

Metal ripped through metal and the ship lurched. As Allison smelled smoke, she fought down her fear and struggled to keep her footing. Her father shouted at his men, but she shut out his words. Visions of plummeting from the sky chased through her head.

Then the sounds of bombardment stopped. The vocal telegraph buzzed again in broken static, and the slightly distorted voice of Blaylock could be heard.

"We've crippled your ship, Everett. Surrender, and we won't drop you from the skies."

For a moment, Allison thought her father would doom them all to a fiery death and let the ship be destroyed. His jaw tightened and his fingers curled into fists, yet he only walked over to the vocal telegraph and relayed his answer.

"You have my surrender. The *Windlass Bluebell* is yours."

A reply crackled back almost immediately. "A wise choice. Your ship will be towed by my convoy to Spring Haven Island. Your days as Master of the Pirate Guild are over."

Relief flowed over Allison until she saw the smile on her father's face.

As Blaylock's coup included personnel within the pirate sanctuary, the *Bluebell's* company were taken prisoner upon arrival at Spring Haven Island. Allison watched nervously as she and her father were separated and the dispirited crew led off in chains. Men clamped shackles on her and on her father's wrists, but she noticed one mutineer whispering to him. Before she had time to question, they were taken away to see Julius Blaylock.

Sitting behind Lord Everett's mahogany desk, Blaylock waited for them in her father's office, his boot-clad feet propped up on the corner. Bits of mud from the soles scattered over the wood, and her father's lip curled in distaste.

Blaylock smiled. "How does it feel to finally be bested, Lord Everett? To have someone else issuing the orders?"

Allison's father matched Blaylock's smile. "I wouldn't know. Because you've won nothing."

Blaylock's boots thumped to the floor, and he leaned over the desk with a sneer. "Still defiant? Even now?"

"Of course." Lord Everett chuckled, and it sent a quiver along Allison's skin. She suppressed a gasp as a horrid thought sprang in her mind.

Dear heavens, he's planned something. He knew.

Fear crept up her throat, threatening to gag her as she listened to the rest of her father's words.

"Did you think I wouldn't find out about your little rebellion? And those disgruntled men you recruited, did you really think they were all your followers? Most were mine, Blaylock. By now, your pitiful band of malcontents will have been rounded up by Roland." Lord Everett stamped his heel three times, and a number of clicks sounded along the back wall. Secret panels slid open, revealing armed men, their guns pointed at Blaylock.

Lord Everett stepped forward and added, "You didn't actually think you had won, did you?" He grinned at the now stricken man. "It's your turn to surrender, Blaylock."

Allison held her breath, but Blaylock raised his hands and hung his head in defeat. Her father's men shackled Blaylock while releasing her and her father from their chains.

She rubbed her wrists as she watched Blaylock be led away, cursing the man under her breath. She stiffened when her father laid a hand on her shoulder.

"You see, Daughter, the man needed a lesson."

She nodded, seething, and the words slipped out, "Did that lesson have to include us nearly being killed aboard the *Bluebell*?"

Lord Everett's hand slid from her shoulder. "That was a miscalculation. Blaylock moved sooner than I anticipated. I assumed he would wait until he arrived at the island, not attack and commandeer the *Bluebell*."

Allison turned and looked at her father. His face revealed nothing of what she sought to see in his expression. "How long have you known he was moving against you?"

"Two months now. Long enough to infiltrate his ridiculous coup."

"I see. Two months." The knot in her shoulders tightened as she asked her last question. "Do you think you found them all? All of his conspirators?"

Lord Everett grinned. "Indeed. Not to worry, our position here is secure. Blaylock and his ilk won't be bothering us again."

Lord Everett brushed past her, striding out the door of his office. Allison watched him go with a sigh of relief.

Allison stepped quietly through the underground passage, her night-view goggles allowing her to see in the darkness. She crept forward until she reached the hidden entrance to the island's prison and held her breath as she turned the knob. When she gave the door a gentle push, not a hinge or mechanism squeaked to betray her. Allison slipped into an alcove and closed the entrance. Pressed back against the stone and shadows she peered into the blackness with her goggles. She saw no sign of guards.

As I hoped. Topside. No doubt drinking.

She still moved forward slowly, staying in the shadows until she reached the cell and the prisoner she came to find. On the wall a gaslight sputtered and Allison pushed up her goggles. She stepped forward into the dim light, her silhouette casting a shadow into the cell.

The suspicious voice of Julius Blaylock echoed into the silence. "Who's there?"

Her harsh whisper whipped out with contempt. "Who do you think, you fool?"

"Allison? Allison, is that you?" Blaylock scurried forward, peering out through the bars. Allison moved closer. "It is you." He grinned. "Hurry up and get me out."

Allison stared at Blaylock through his cell bars, shaking her head in disgust. Then she hissed, "I'm not here to help you escape, you idiot. As far as I'm concerned, you can rot." She spat on the ground. "What the hell were you thinking? I told you to drop that stupid plan of a coup. I told you not to openly make a move against my father." She scowled at him in the muted light. "Now you've forced my hand sooner than I wanted. I'm lucky I made sense of the diary before you made this mess, or the trouble you caused would be even worse."

Blaylock inhaled sharply. "You deciphered it? Owen Bicker's bloody diary? Hell, woman! I know you said last month you were close, but I never dreamed... Now you have to get me out of here so we can go after the damn treasure."

"Why should I? You are of little use to me now. Why shouldn't I leave you to my father's mercy?"

"After all we used to be? Come on now, you know you still have a soft spot for me." He slid his best charm into his words and dipped them in sweet honey.

"Maybe." Allison admitted, frowning, not liking that he might be right about her feelings. "But not enough to risk springing you. Besides, you betrayed me. No way I'd trust you."

"Don't be like that. I can still be useful," Blaylock wheedled. "And I didn't betray you. I never told your daddy all the secrets of my ill-fated overthrow, did I? That you were in on it." Blaylock grinned, arrogance plastered over his face. "At least not yet. You wouldn't want me to confess all, would you? Get me out, and your secrets stay hidden."

Allison grinned back, ready to disabuse the man of his conceit. "You are a fool. As usual, you overplayed your hand. I was never a part of your coup. My plan was to find the treasure and set up my own empire." She moved a step closer, her voice full of scorn. "So why should I care about what you say to the great Lord Everett?"

"Daddy wouldn't like what you've been doing, either way. He'll put a stop to all your plans if I tell."

Allison snorted. "You can confess what you like. Father will let you stew here overnight, we both know that, and I'll be gone by morning. I hoped to have your ships at my back, but I'll make do without them."

Blaylock chuckled. "You won't leave me behind. You'd miss me too much."

"Of all the arrogant…" Allison raised her chin and snapped, "Maybe I did come tonight just to see you, thinking to help, hoping you'd join me again, but now I see that was foolish. This is goodbye. We're done." Allison stalked away from the cell, eager to leave.

Blaylock surged forward against the bars and hissed, "Wait. I still have airships."

Allison turned back and retorted, "My father has your ships. I don't fancy stealing them back."

"Not those ships. A few I never reported or turned in to your dear daddy. Plus crew." Blaylock softly chuckled. "Always have a reserve. One of your father's lessons I took to heart."

Allison frowned. "You could be lying."

"I could." Blaylock grinned again. "But it's a risk worth taking, ain't it?"

She pursed her lips and stared him down. The man's face didn't show anything but arrogance. Allison was a heartbeat away from believing him when she saw the twitch of his right shoulder.

She let out a breath and replied to his question, "No it's not. Because you're lying. I told you to work on that tell of yours and stop twitching." Allison grinned. "And without ships, you are useless to me. See you around, Julius. Or maybe not, once my father's done with you."

She melted back into the shadows, followed by Blaylock's curses and pleas.

Allison pulled the shawl tighter around her face and lowered her head, avoiding eye contact with those she passed. She had escaped Spring Haven undetected, and it wouldn't do to have someone recognize her now.

Not when I'm this close to my dream.

She glanced up briefly, stepping past a man with a mechanical hand. After three days of skulking about dealing with other business, she finally arrived safely at Blackheart Cove, a known sanctuary port for pirates, rogues, and other scoundrels.

She made her way through the narrow cobblestone streets, chased by the drone of airship engines, ignoring the sounds of the tinkers hawking parts to those come to buy at the marketplace. Allison breathed in the steam and the smell of grease, secretly smiling as she heard the hiss and whir of the mechanics working on gadgets or automatons, and the clanking and grinding of gears. She wished she could stay and just wander every nook and cranny, but she'd come on business.

Allison turned her last corner and slipped into an alleyway. She headed straight to a doorway at the end and crept inside a building, a lowly dive bar that catered to black marketers and pirates. She waited in the shadows until she saw the man she came to meet. Then Allison hurried across the floor and slid onto the bench across from him. She leaned on the knife-scarred wooden table and grinned.

"Hello, Jack."

The thin-faced man looked up, his demeanor a mix of ease and anxiety. "Hey, Alli. Glad to see you made it. Everything's still on then, I take it?"

"It was touch and go for a bit, but the plan's in place. We're going, and nothing will stop us."

Jack sighed, his whole body relaxing. "I thought maybe you wouldn't show."

Allison frowned. "I'd never cut you out. You came to me with your father's diary. Just because I figured out his clues, doesn't mean I'd exclude you. This is your hunt as much as it is mine."

"I know, but with Blaylock and all, I thought maybe…." Jack averted his eyes.

"Blaylock." Allison scrunched her nose and scowled. "He nearly ruined everything. Stirred up trouble for nothing. I'll have to stay out of sight more than ever. My father's spies are out in force. Can't have the great Lord Everett interfering now."

"Probably best, considering." Jack fidgeted in his seat. "Lot of cutthroats around here be willing to cash in."

Allison narrowed her eyes. "Considering what? Cash in on what?"

Jack gaped, and a low whistle of surprise passed his lips. "You don't know?" He bent down and scrounged through a rucksack at his feet. When he straightened, he slid a folded and slightly crumpled sheet of heavy paper across the table. "These are posted all over the port. Ripped down as many as I could without being spotted, but the word's out."

Allison unfolded the paper carefully and ground her teeth. "A reward? He posted a reward for my return?"

Jack nodded. "Keep reading. It gets worse."

She pulled the paper in closer, bending over it to read it without possible prying eyes. "What?" The word came out as a hiss. "He's saying Blaylock kidnapped me? I left that fool back on the island in prison to rot. What the hell is my father playing at?"

Jack inhaled sharply. "Blaylock's not with you? Damn! I thought for sure you sprung him."

"He escaped?" Allison crumpled the paper in her fist, shock running through her body. "How?"

"Don't know." Jack shrugged. "Like I said, I thought you got him out, but if you didn't…. The only story I heard was what's circulating from your father. That Blaylock escaped by overpowering a guard. He then kidnapped you and disappeared."

"What a load of damn bollocks!" Allison thumped her palm on the table and leaned forward. "Father's up to something. We'll have to be more careful. Did you get the supplies? I have the transport."

Jack nodded. "Ready and waiting. Shame we had to go with the backup plan, but can't be helped, I suppose. I'm just glad I got the message you sent."

"Yeah, damn Blaylock messed up the whole scheme. If I hadn't needed him to pilfer Wilson's strongbox for the missing pages…." Allison scowled.

Jack patted her hand. "It was the only play. If he had stuck to the plan, we'd be golden."

"Aye." She glanced over to the door as more scruffy airmen wandered into the dive. "But we'd best be out of here and off this island."

Jack nodded again, and the two slipped out of the bar.

They wandered down poorly lit streets to a crumbling, dockside store-house in a seedier part of town—if that was even possible in such a disreputable port. Jack pulled a key from his pocket and let them in a side door. Inside stood a peculiar contraption, a steam-powered contrivance of a wagon piled high with crates.

Jack walked over and patted one of the metal sides. "All loaded and ready to roll out to where you need her to go. We can offload the crates to an airship or boat, whatever you found to take us there."

"Airship," Allison muttered absently. "Will this thing run the back roads? I'm moored in one of the outer hideaways."

Jack grinned. "Course she will. I built her. She goes anywhere on this island."

Allison matched his grin. "Then let's go."

"Hop in."

Allison did as she was bid, climbing into the high passenger seat in front of the crates. Jack winched open the main doors before sprinting back to the wagon. He fed the coal hopper, cranked the steam engine into life, and jumped into the driver's seat where he eased down the brake stick and pushed the throttle steering forward. The wagon lurched and then jounced through the doorway at a slow clip. Jack eased off the steam power, yanked up the braking, and jumped down to lock up the storehouse.

Then they were on their way, catching speed as they travelled. They bounced over old roads, slightly overgrown and rutted, but the wagon took it all, though jostling and rattling its passengers. After fifteen minutes, Allison gave Jack the last of the directions, and they rolled up to a clearing where an airship hovered, moored and waiting.

Jack pulled the wagon to a stop near the ship. A soft breeze blew, but everything else was quiet. He craned his neck, staring at the ship. "Nice size, if a bit old."

"Yeah, but beggars can't be choosers." Allison shrugged. "She runs well, and I have a good crew." She smiled. "And I had her modified a bit. I'll show you when we're aboard."

"That sounds interesting. Where'd you find a crew?" Jack climbed down from the wagon and started unfastening the restraints holding down the crates. "They inside the ship? Wouldn't have thought any man would cross your father now, not after what happened with Blaylock."

"See for yourself." Allison grinned and shouted, "Ahoy *Nightwind Moon*. We got cargo to load."

At her words, figures crept from the underbrush, and lines and nets dropped from the airship. Jack looked around from face to face as several members of Allison's crew approached.

"Blimey. They're women. You recruited a crew of women. That's brilliant!"

Allison nodded. "Sisters, daughters, wives of pirates, who all want out of Lord Everett's fold like me." She frowned as they got closer. "But they don't look happy." She rushed forward. "What's wrong? Has something happened?"

A tall and slightly stout, dark-haired woman wearing a red bandana on her head and a scar on her cheek answered. "We found a stowaway! Blighter jumped aboard at our last stop. Don't know how he located us or stayed hidden for so long on board, but he did."

Allison stood very still. "Who? Who's the stowaway?"

"That would be me!" A cheery male voice hailed from a short distance away. Allison peered through the foliage at a man tied to a tree.

"Blaylock! You rat bastard!"

"Hello to you, too." He cocked his head and smiled as she strode to his side and glared at him, inches from his face. "And no hard feelings for leaving me in that cell. As you can see, I managed to get out all on my own and join you for the hunt."

"I see that." Allison spat on the ground. "Despite my saying I didn't need or want you along. How in the world did you escape?"

"Skill and good fortune mostly."

Allison scowled. "You always did have the devil's own luck. Though it may have run out. My father seems to be under the mistaken impression you kidnapped me. You've somehow gone and made a dangerous situation even worse."

Blaylock shifted in his bonds, the smile fading from his face. "I had nothing to do with that. Your father's ideas are his own. We did disappear together. Perhaps he jumped to erroneous conclusions."

"My father?" Allison snorted her derision. "More likely he used you as a scapegoat to cover the fact that his daughter and only living heir ran away. Your disloyalty is one thing; mine is something quite different."

"Bah. You give him too much credit."

"And you not enough. He saw through your mutiny and foiled your stupid grand plan, didn't he?"

"My stupid…? Rash, perhaps, but not stupid. And he may have foiled me as you said, but he couldn't keep me prisoner." Blaylock puffed out his chest against the ropes tying him to the tree and smirked.

Allison rolled her eyes and walked away a few steps. The echo of his voice followed her.

"Come now. Aren't you impressed that I escaped? Just a little?"

Allison twisted back to look at him. "You know, I am." She grinned as she watched Blaylock's smirk widen. "Impressed you kept your mouth shut long enough to reach this island without being discovered."

Then Allison turned to her first mate, the scarred woman who went by the name Rothschild. "Get this cargo loaded and prepare to cast off. I want us in the air and on our way as soon as possible."

Rothschild nodded. "Aye aye, Captain. What about him? Do we leave him here?"

Blaylock grunted in protest.

As tempting as that prospect was, Allison shook her head. "Load him on the airship as well, in the brig. He's better off where we can keep an eye on him." Then she grinned. "Besides, we may have to use him as a bargaining chip if my father tracks us down. Won't that make a story: Pirate King's daughter foils her own abduction and delivers the villain to her father for punishment."

Blaylock gasped. "You wouldn't!"

Allison snorted. "Try me. Neither you nor my father will get between me and Owen Bicker's treasure!" She marched over and stared him right in the eyes. "And if you try, or cause any more trouble for me, I'll toss you overboard into the sea."

Blaylock swallowed hard and turned pale as Allison walked away.

A half-hour out from Blackheart Cove, they were flying through clear skies over open waters and heading west. Allison sat in the captain's chair, studying her charts.

A young lass—a new recruit to the navigator's chair—cleared her throat. Allison looked up, noticing her restless and nervous movements.

"Something wrong, Ensign Wilde?"

The fidgety woman glanced back at her captain. "No, ma'am. I mean, well, we're headed into the Indian Ocean to a place I never heard whisper of before. How do we know it ain't some fairytale spun out of this diary bloke's imaginings?"

Allison smiled. "A fair point, but Skull Island is real enough. It was a pirate haven for the Ghost Brotherhood long before either of us, or even Owen Bicker, was born." Then a touch of avarice crept into her grin as she added, "The Brotherhood met a terrible fate, but neither their vast treasure nor Skull Island were ever located until Owen Bicker. And now us."

The ensign stared wide-eyed and open-mouthed, but before she could reply, an alarm blared. Wilde snapped her attention back to her console and barked, "Instruments showing another ship headed this way, Captain."

Allison's gut tightened. "Increase speed and prepare for evasive maneuvers. We want to avoid contact with other ships at all costs."

She gripped the arm of the captain's chair, hoping the approaching craft was merely a pirate vessel avoiding the regular airship lanes and possible patrol zeppelins. Her instinct prickled against the back of her neck and warned her otherwise. She didn't want to be right.

"Is the ship still headed our way?"

"Yes, Captain. It seems to have picked up speed as well and is headed straight towards us. Should we try to evade?"

"Aye." The prickling on her neck worsened. She bit her lip as the *Nightwind Moon* banked away from the ship closing in on them.

"Are they veering off?"

"No, ma'am, keeping pace with us and closing the gap fast."

"Ready the weapons and sound the alarm. And signal Jack in the engine room we're preparing for a fight." Allison closed her eyes for a moment as the klaxon alarm shrilled throughout the ship.

Damn. At best, it's pirates looking for an easy target, at worst...

Confirming her fears, the vocal telegraph crackled, and her father's voice echoed across the bridge.

"Time to come home, my wayward daughter."

For a second, Allison froze. Then anger crept up her spine. She calmly gave an order to her vocal telegraph operator. "Send a reply." She paused for a breath, collecting her thoughts. "I have no home with you, not anymore."

In the quiet of the bridge, the clack of the telegraph and the voice of the operator resounded. Then came the answering crackle and the voice of Lord Leopold Everett.

"You can't win this game, you know. It's only a matter of time before you fold. Save yourself the trouble, and stop pursuing foolish dreams. Surrender now. Don't make me chase you."

Allison gritted her teeth, wanting to spew venom at her father. She didn't get the opportunity, as soft footfalls padded behind her.

"He is persistent, I'll give him that."

Allison spun halfway around, twisting in her chair at the sound of the voice behind her. "Blaylock! How the hell and blazes did you get out of the brig?"

The man flashed his trademark smirk and replied, "I know a few tricks." Then he shrugged his shoulders. "You better know a few, too, or we will both end in the fire. Your father will haul your pretty ass back to Spring Haven, and he'll probably toss me overboard."

"Sit down and shut up!" Allison yelled and shot him a dirty look. Blaylock remained standing, but closed his mouth.

Allison stared out the windscreen, her father's ship growing larger in view with each passing second. Blaylock was right. The great Lord Everett wouldn't give up, and he would never let her go. Not until she was a good little subject of the all-powerful Pirate King.

Just like Jeb.

Something broke free in her mind and soul. "I'll never be like Jeb. I'll never be yours to command." Allison compressed her anger into a cold hard decision. She barked another order to Wilde. "Swing her about! No use in running. We'll take the fight to him! Blast him out of the sky. Or die trying."

"Are you mad?" Blaylock screeched.

"Activate the forward guns and target the enemy ship's weapons. And signal the engine room to fire up the power on the star spinner. I want that cannon up and ready for a full out attack."

"Star spinner?" Blaylock grabbed her arm. "What are you playing at? That weapon went down with your brother's ship."

Allison sneered. "Fat lot you know. Only *his* prototype was lost. Not mine. And who do you think designed the weapon in the first place?" Allison shook off his grip and pushed him away. Blaylock sank down into an empty deck chair, shock distorting his face.

Full speed ahead and fire when in range!

The airship lurched forward, speeding towards her father's ship, the vessel that only moments before she had wished to leave behind. Her gut churned, her feelings conflicted but her resolve strong. Either she or her father would be left standing.

"A long time coming, Father, this showdown." The whisper rode into the ether on tension and anxiety.

Despite the shiver of her skin and cold lump in her belly, Allison refused to acknowledge the fear and tuned out Blaylock's whines and whimpers. The clack of gears and the hum of the engines were the only sounds she let herself hear.

Her breath came fast, and her fingers tightened on the arms of her chair as the distance between the two ships closed. She recognized the vessel and markings of the *Winged Fury*, her father's second-best ship. She smiled. It had ample guns, but less maneuverability than the *Windlass Bluebell*.

"Coming up on gun range, Captain, but it looks like the enemy ship is aiming its weapons." Wilde spat out the words. "And we have power on the star spinner."

"Target the side gun arrays and fire forward weapons! Then evasive maneuver Falcon Feint. Bring her around to top port side and target her envelope with the star spinner."

The boom and echo of the *Nightwind Moon*'s guns ripped through the sky, and its bullets shattered into the *Winged Fury*, whose own forward guns answered back moments later. But the *Moon* had already veered away, and only the outer hull off the gondola was raked by the enemy's weapons. She banked around, pulling into position to the *Winged Fury*'s port side as that ship's side guns cranked about, ready to launch a volley.

"Fire!"

The skinny, pigged-tailed weapons officer yanked the lever, and a loud boom and whoosh reverberated from the front of the ship, followed by a sharp, noisy succession of rapid clacks and pings. The bridge crew held a collective breath as the race between which ship would fire began. The seconds ticked off as one cannon powered up and the other guns moved to target.

The star spinner won.

A burst of explosive rounds flew across the sky between the ships and tore into the envelope of the *Winged Fury*, shredding its metallic fabric like paper and lighting it on fire. It lurched at the sudden decompression, gases and pressure screaming into the air. The *Fury*'s guns fired, but thrown off target, they went wide. The *Nightwind Moon* swung broadly to starboard, escaping harm. Then she veered about to watch the demise of her enemy.

The *Winged Fury* fell fast, her structure deflated and collapsed. She left a fiery trail as she plummeted from the sky, projecting a flickering orange glow against the clouds. Dry-eyed and without a word or a regret, Allison watched her take all her crew to their death.

Her father was gone. Finally gone.

Rest in peace, Jeb.

A cheer rose on the bridge, and Allison let it fade before speaking. "Resume course to Skull Island."

She glanced over to Blaylock, who remained oddly silent. He stared, his expression an odd mix of awe, fear, and distaste.

She returned her gaze to the horizon as the *Nightwind Moon* flew onward.

"Was this really necessary?" Blaylock complained from a cramped position in the scout craft. "Couldn't we have flown in with the *Moon*? Why take the smaller craft? And why bring him?" Blaylock nudged Jack with his elbow.

"You're the one we should have left behind," Jack sneered.

"Shut up, the both of you," Allison barked from the pilot's chair. "Jack has a right to be here, and I don't trust *you* out of my sight."

"Why does he have the right to be here?" Blaylock whined. "I earned my spot. What did he do?"

Allison clenched her jaw, wondering if she shouldn't have tossed Blaylock overboard when she had the chance. "Jack is Owen Bicker's son, you ninny. That's why he's here.

"Oh. Sorry." Blaylock scuffed his foot against the floor. "But that still doesn't explain why we're flying there stuffed like rats in a trap."

Allison sighed. "We are going inland with the scout craft because it's safer to navigate the Skull Island terrain. I don't want to risk the ship or more of the crew." Allison banked the scout craft, then continued, "And that means, with only the one smaller ship, it's just the three of us."

Jack voiced his concern. "About that. What happened to the second scout ship? A vessel of the *Moon*'s size should have two."

Allison hesitated, choosing her words carefully. "Out on another mission. Couldn't be helped."

Jack lapsed into silence and Blaylock into grumbles. Allison flew on until they arrived at their destination and moored the scout ship in a large clearing.

On the ground, Allison pointed to the northwest. "The treasure should be that way. Along this trail." She waved at a path through the underbrush and forested landscape.

"How do you know?" Blaylock sneered at her.

She pulled the diary out of a bag she had slung over her shoulder and waved it in front of Blaylock's face. "This is how I know. It's all written down in here. Remember?"

Blaylock tried to grab for the book, but Allison snatched it away. "Oh no, you don't. Nobody but me sees what's inside." She moved the journal to her left hand and placed her right on the handle of her pistol. "Unless you want me to shoot you."

"That won't be necessary." Blaylock retreated a step and waved a hand. "Lead on."

Allison consulted the diary, then shut the book and slipped it into her bag. She led them on a short trek through overgrown trails, though still surprisingly well marked. They ended the walk at a large cavern carved into the side of a mountain.

"That's what the diary leads us to, this cave." She looked over at Blaylock while placing a restraining hand on Jack's shoulder.

Blaylock grinned and rubbed his palms together. "Look at the size of this place. I'm betting it's full to the top with treasure!" He pushed past Allison and rushed inside. Then she and Jack followed at a more sedate pace, if with excitement in their step, only to nearly run headlong into Blaylock. He stood still as death just inside the cave entrance.

"There's nothing. There's nothing here." Blaylock's sad voice echoed off the hollow, empty interior.

Damp, rocky walls surrounded them, dripping with water and stained with moss. The inside of the cave stretched out into a gaping blackness, but the only sign of treasure were two medium-sized chests fastened with rusty locks and sitting in an alcove near the entrance.

Blaylock whirled and glared at Allison, disgust marring every inch of his face. "This is Owen Bicker's great treasure? Two paltry chests? Maybe coin and jewels if we're lucky?"

Allison kept her face solemn, but let the tone of disappointment bleed into her voice. "It appears so. I hoped… The diary made it sound… But whatever he supposedly found and hoarded away—if there ever was anything to begin with—isn't here."

"It has to be! It has to be. Maybe there are more clues." Blaylock rushed over to the chests and grabbed a nearby rock. He smashed the locks and flung open the lids. Gold coins and some jewelry glittered, but nothing pointing to more treasure. Allison watched him closely and saw him scoop something into a coat pocket.

He stood and turned to face her. "So we did all this for nothing?" Blaylock's voice edged higher, snuggling closer to a whine.

"Not for nothing." Allison shot a quick glance at Blaylock's hand as it reached into his pocket. "We took down my father. I can still claim his empire, and you'll have a place there. For what we once were to each other." She paused, waiting to see what he would do.

"Will I now?" he asked, arrogance and scorn in his voice. "A place." Blaylock took a few steps forward, then pulled out a small pistol, holding it towards Allison and Jack. "I don't want a 'place'; I want it all." He waved his gun. "At least old Bicker left this handy weapon. Care to test whether it still works?"

Jack made to move, but Allison stepped in front of him and shook her head. "No need to shoot. You're in control."

"Smart." Blaylock smiled. "Now, you two haul those chests back to our scout ship and load them aboard. Any false moves, and I'll shoot you."

Through gritted teeth and protests, Allison and Jack lugged the chests back to the ship and loaded the treasure on board. Blaylock climbed into the ship as well, then leaned out the hatch with one last taunt.

"Good thing your airship is on the far side of Skull Island. I'll be clean away before you hike back to tell them of what happened and halfway to claiming your dear father's empire. It may not be much, but at least Bicker's treasure should bribe enough men to my side." Blaylock grinned.

Jack moved forward waving his fist. "You blackhearted rogue!"

Allison caught him and dragged him back as Blaylock raised his pistol. The gun lowered.

"I'll forgive the outburst, young Bicker. It must be such a disappointment to come so far and lose." Jack snarled and Blaylock chuckled. He turned to Allison. "This is the end of our partnership, my dear, and I win."

He slunk inside the ship and slammed the hatch shut. A few moments later, the scout ship was airborne and flying from Skull Island.

"And he just gets away! After all our work?" Jack shouted at the treetops, fuming and hopping like a madman. "We have to chase him, fight him for control of the pirates, something!"

"Don't worry, Jack." Allison's amused voice cut through his ranting. "Blaylock did exactly what I expected him to do, though I had hoped he would join us. He might be a backstabbing rogue, but he's a good pirate, and I thought we meant something to each other." At Jack's confused look, Allison grinned. "This was all a ruse, the empty cavern, 'finding' the treasure, and the conveniently placed gun—empty by the way."

"What? Why?"

"To test his loyalty after all his shenanigans. And to have a little fun with the arrogant bastard." Allison grinned. "I'm not so stupid as to tell my plans. The one good thing the great Lord Everett did teach me." Emotion caught in her throat, but she stuffed it down.

"How did you pull it off?"

"I located your father's secret base a month ago, and I've had a post here for all that time. Had my crew set it up while I kept Father and Blaylock distracted." She chuckled at Jack's gaping stare. "I'd hoped to have Blaylock's support in all this, or steal his ships out from under him, but he ruined that plan with his mutiny. So a bit of improvising was needed. And when I found out Blaylock stowed away, I had Rothschild send the *Nightwind Moon*'s other scout ship off to Skull Island to prepare this bit of theater. Just in case."

Jack swung his head around, looking toward the cavern. "So that wasn't the treasure?"

"Heavens, no. Come along, I'll show you the real thing."

Allison led Jack back down the trail and further into the cave, where a crewwoman waited with lanterns.

"Everything's all down the left-hand tunnel there." Allison pointed to another branch of the cavern. "Heaps of large trunks filled with gold coins and other valuables, and plenty of chests of jewels tucked away. All Blaylock got away with was a small portion of the gold and jewels. And he left the real treasure behind."

Jack frowned. "Real treasure?"

"Aye. Follow me." Allison picked up an extra lantern, lit it, and walked off, Jack tagging at her heels like an eager hound. She led the way through a labyrinth of tunnels, exiting onto a chamber with a stone staircase. She led them up the steps to an enclosed grotto, open to the sky. At the far end rested a large derelict airship.

Jack stared. "Is that…?"

Allison grinned. "It is. *The Nimble Buccaneer*. Your father's ship. She's busted up a bit, but fixable. Figured you'd want to be the one to get her airborne again."

"Would I ever!" Jack's smile nearly split his face.

"Excellent. She'll be our flagship, Jack. The start of a great fleet. With the gold and jewels of the treasure, we'll get more ships and crew, maybe even some of my father's men. No doubt Blaylock will attempt to take over the Pirate King's empire, but he's not well liked. I suspect he'll find it more difficult than he imagines. We will give him a run for his money."

Jack gave a whoop. "The Pirate King is no more! Long live the Pirate Queen!"

About A.F. Stewart

A steadfast and proud sci-fi and fantasy geek, A. F. Stewart was born and raised in Nova Scotia, Canada and still calls it home. The youngest in a family of seven children, she always had an overly creative mind and an active imagination. She favours the dark and deadly when writing—her genres of choice being dark fantasy and horror—but she has been known to venture into the light on occasion. As an indie author she's published novels, novellas, and story collections, with a few side trips into poetry.

She is fond of good books, action movies, sword collecting, geeky things, comic books, and oil painting as a hobby. She has a great interest in history and mythology, often working those themes into her books and stories.

Regicide and Prejudice by Paul Michael

"Please," muttered the man, eyes closed, a look of terror on his countenance. "Please…"

The face opposite loomed forward in the candlelit gloom. The pale skin and fog grey eyes pressed closer to the man. A smile formed, revealing two sharp canines, unnaturally long.

"Come on now, it's not that bad," said the creature. "It will be over soon."

The man whimpered and opened his eyes. He tugged at the leather straps that kept him bound to the chair.

"That's for your protection," said the vampire opposite him. "After last time…"

"Please, no, not like last time," he said.

The vampire had a cheery tone to his voice. "Let's start!"

A whirring sound started from behind the man strapped into the chair, and he gibbered lightly. Mechanical arms from behind slammed a plate in front of him, causing the man to jump. The vampire opened a book and made little scratching notes. A fork slammed down next to the plate by the arms, then a knife, which came in at a strange angle and stuck into the table. The vampire tutted and scratched some more. A steaming leg of chicken was deposited on the plate, and then a spoon tumbled potatoes and peas onto it as well. The two hands reappeared with a pepper grinder and gave three sharp twists of pepper. Finally, a salt cellar appeared in one mechanical hand. It was shaken vigorously and the lid fell off, depositing a pile of salt upon the food. The arms disappeared, and the man sighed with relief.

"Too. Much. Salt," said the vampire, writing in his book. Phlebotemous

Bosch looked up at the man. "Well then, Mr Gribble, let's get you out of your chair. As you can see, the automaton butler is nearly ready for use."

"Thank you, thank you, Mr Bosch," said Mr Gribble, as the straps were undone. "Thank the Lord, too."

"I told you that was just an unfortunate accident last time," said Phlebotomous. Mr Gribble rubbed his right ear, feeling for the missing chunk as the vampire continued, "I'll just take the automaton back to my workshop, make some final adjustments, and we can try again."

"Oh Lord."

"One thing. Could we use something other than a chicken? Since I'm a vegetarian, I don't really like to use it."

"Whatever you say, Mr Bosch."

"I don't really want to force my opinions on anyone, but it would make me happy if we could…"

"I really must hurry you along, Mr Bosch," said Mr Gribble. "The staff will be home soon from their evening off."

"Oh! Is the automaton a surprise for them?"

"I suspect it will be."

"Well, best not spoil their special surprise!" Phlebotomous packed up the machine.

A few minutes later, Phlebotomous flagged down a hackney carriage in the smart London street where the Gribbles lived. As the carriage pulled up, Phlebotomous dragged the heavy case containing the automaton into the cab. He sat down and was about to call the destination when a woman jumped in.

"I'm sorry," said the woman, "but I have something very urgent to attend to. May I possibly share your cab?"

"But you don't know where I'm going," said Phlebotomous.

"Where are you going?"

"Fulham."

"Exactly where I need to go." The woman called the destination to the driver.

The cab started off, and she smiled at Phlebotomous. He glanced at her, then looked awkwardly out of the window.

"Veronica Herringay," said the woman.

"Pardon?"

"Veronica Herringay?"

"No," said Phlebotomous, "Phlebotomous Bosch."

"I mean, I'm Veronica Herringay." .

"I see." Phlebotomous continued to stare out of the window.

"You seem very comfortable with strange women jumping into your cab without explanation."

Phlebotomous looked back at the woman with a look of apprehension. "Are you somehow dangerous?" he asked.

The woman giggled coquettishly, then made one gloved hand into a claw. "Rarr!" she growled. "Wouldn't you like to know?"

"Yes." Phlebotomous fidgeted in his seat. "That's why I asked."

"How will you ever find out? I know, why don't you ask me to dinner?"

"Because I don't know you?"

"Isn't that the point?" purred the woman. "When you don't know people you have dinner with them."

"But, for example, I don't know the cab driver either. Should I invite him for dinner, too?"

Veronica smirked a little. "Don't you usually?"

"I usually just pay the fare. I didn't realise you had to go for dinner as well."

"We're here," called the cab driver from above.

"Let's say tomorrow, eight at the Ritz, shall we?" said Veronica.

"Tomorrow, eight at the Ritz," Phlebotomous said.

Veronica smiled, then disappeared into the night.

"That's two and six," said the driver. Phlebotomous handed over the money.

"Are we supposed to have dinner as well?" he asked. The driver shot him a look and rode off.

"I presume that's a no." Phlebotomous dragged his heavy case down the street.

Back in the comfort and safety of his home, Phlebotomous prepared himself some dinner. Vampirism had not been easy on him and had certainly not been a choice. An unfortunate misunderstanding had led to his current condition, and Phlebotomous, who had been a vegetarian as a human, was certain he wasn't about to start eating animals just because of it. As an avid scientist and inventor, he had instead concocted a blood-like beverage made from plant products involving nuts, seeds, mushrooms, and tomato for a little effect. As he took a container of his invented drink, he mused on the events of the day.

One thing puzzled him, and his mind refused to let it go. Why had the top come off the salt cellar? He had vigorously tested the strength of salt shaking before the demonstration and had ensured the salt cellar itself was of requisite strength. Never mind, he thought, these sorts of minor mishaps always seemed to occur. And it was rare that anyone was seriously injured.

He sat down by his self-igniting fireplace and turned it on. The flames shot up and Phlebotomous automatically used the fire extinguisher when the mantlepiece caught fire. He was used to that little problem by now, and it seemed easier to use the extinguisher than to fix the fire.

He started to make plans for the next day when he realised he had a dinner appointment with the woman he had met in the hackney carriage. Phlebotomous was not a master of the social arts, or even an apprentice. Decades of vampirism had reduced his social circle until it had become a mere point. In truth, he hadn't been much of a social butterfly when he was fully human.

Nevertheless, even to him the dinner request had seemed unusual. He was vaguely aware that sometimes people told a "white lie" in these circumstances in order to avoid this kind of appointment. However, he couldn't think of a reason not to go as his diary was free, so he felt compelled to attend. He did, though, prepare a "white lie" to allow him to leave quickly if necessary. Then he turned back to the problem of the salt cellar.

The next day, Phlebotomous turned up at the Ritz at 8 p.m. He easily found Veronica in the restaurant and went to the table. She was dressed in a glamorous and low-cut gown.

"Please, Mr Bosch, sit," said Veronica.

Phlebotomous sat. "I may have to leave at any moment to attend to a sick cat," he said.

"You have a cat?"

"No," said Phlebotomous.

A confused look quickly passed across Veronica's face before a charming smile re-asserted itself. "Mr Bosch, I must confess I know rather more about you than I have let on," she said.

"Oh. I'm glad then I didn't lie about the cat. About having one I mean."

"Yes, yes. Trust is so important. But I mean something else." Her voice dropped to a whisper. "I know what you are."

"Say it!" said Phlebotomous, feeling excited. "Say it!"

"You're a..." said Veronica, looking left and right, "vampire."

Phlebotomous sat back, deflated. "Oh that. Everyone knows that," he said. "That's not special, that's just annoying. I thought you meant the other thing."

Veronica raised a quizzical eyebrow.

"I'm an inventor!" said Phlebotomous, grinning.

"Really?" Veronica's eyes widened. "How fascinating. Why don't you tell me more?"

Phlebotomous then spent a happy hour regaling the lady with stories of the inventions, occasional mishaps, intermittent hospital visits, and persistent lawsuits that had accompanied his career. He noticed how interested she was, which was an unusual experience for the vampire. He barely noticed the vegetable soup and extremely similar vegetable stew that he ate during the meal. Finally, as dessert arrived, he stopped talking.

"But enough about me," he said. "Have you invented anything?"

"No," answered Veronica. "I'm not as clever, nor creative, nor brave as you are. But you know what? I think I may be able to help."

"Oh, are you good with spanners? My wrists are a bit weak for them, and I notice you have quite big hands."

"No, not like that." Veronica looked mildly put out. "You see, I work for the Home Office. My boss, Mr Quigley, may be interested in some of your ideas."

"Really?"

"I'll arrange a meeting for tomorrow. I imagine evening would be best."

"Oh yes, please," said Phlebotomous and took a big drink of his glass of milk.

The next evening, just after dusk, Phlebotomous found himself in King Charles Street, armed with a briefcase filled with plans, and brimming with optimism. He was admitted to the building and brought into an ornate office. Behind a desk sat a middle-aged man with a jowly face along with Miss Veronica Herringay, wearing formal business attire.

"So, Mr Bosch," said Quigley. "Miss Herringay tells me you have quite some prowess at inventing."

"Yes."

"Would you care to elaborate a little?"

"Yes," said Phlebotomous, then paused. "Do you mean now?"

Quigley nodded, and Phlebotomous began.

"Well, I am an inventor of many different devices, mostly for household use. I have created many patents for my inventions, and there have only ever been minor injuries resulting from them. Apart from poor Mr Croup who was, to be fair, gravely unwell even before the incident. I have been invited to numerous conferences, most of which I have been unable to attend due to my situation."

"You can't afford them?" said Quigley.

"No sir, I'm a vampire, so travel is rather complicated."

Quigley looked disturbed.

"Oh, don't worry Mr Quigley," said Phlebotomous, "I'm a vegetarian."

"I see," said Quigley. "Well, Mr Bosch, that's very impressive. Let me explain our situation. I must ask you, though, to sign this piece of paper, which acknowledges that what I am about to tell you cannot be shared with any living soul."

"Technically," said Phlebotomous, "I'm not a living soul."

"Hmm. Let me cross out living and then you may sign."

The large man amended the document and passed it over. "Mr Bosch, our king, George III, is gravely ill. He is unwell in his mind, as he has been before. This time there is a push for a regent to take control."

"I see," said Phlebotomous. "And you want a mechanical regent?"

"No," said Quigley. "No. The regent is likely to be his son George, the Prince of Wales. But there are objectors to this plan. Objections, in fact, to the man himself."

"His detractors say he is a drunk," said Veronica, "a letch, a feckless, fickle halfwit. A man that can be swayed by the opinion of a trained monkey. A man without the moral fibre of a blade of grass and even less intelligence than that. A waistral, a fop, a dandy, and an embarrassment to all who hold Britain dear."

"So they don't want him to be regent," said Phlebotomous, just to be sure.

"Just so," said Quigley. "Thus there is a plot, nay, a multitude of plots, to eliminate him." Quigley gave Phlebotomous a meaningful glance.

"To eliminate him..." said Phlebotomous uncertainly.

"Precisely!" said Quigley. "And this is why we seek your help. We need some device, some mechanism to keep him safe no matter what the assault is."

"Oh, I see!" They want to kill the Prince!"

"Shh!" hissed Quigley and Veronica in unison.

"Oh, I have just the thing," said Phlebotomous. "I have been working on a cloak that has a plethora of defensive devices. I thought it might be useful for the man about town, but it sounds perfect for you."

"Excellent!" exclaimed Quigley, clenching his fist. "We shall dispatch you to Brighton on the morrow with this garment, to keep his majesty safe."

"I shall pack at once!" said Phlebotomous, excited. "Oh. One thing. I can only work when it is dark, you know, because—"

"That will not present a problem at all," said Quigley. "In fact, I suspect that you and the Prince will find you keep similar hours."

"Hurray for Harry, England, and Prince George," said Phlebotomous. "I'll go at once." With this, the vampire headed out, full of enthusiasm.

Quigley turned to Veronica.

"Well?" she said.

"Well, well," said Quigley. "Well done indeed. This buffoon's crazy invention is bound to backfire. We can then eliminate the moronic Prince…"

"And the vampire takes the blame," said Veronica with a smile.

Quigley chuckled, then laughed, then broke into great big guffaws.

"You know," said Veronica. "You should probably see an alienist about that."

"Could you have made it any less fashionable?" sighed George, Prince of Wales.

Phlebotomous stroked his chin, then walked around the prince, who was dressed in an enormous and rather bulky cloak. "Possibly," Phlebotomous said, "but I may need some help with the details. I'm not a keen follower of fashion."

"That was a rhetorical question!" snapped George.

"What's that?"

"It's a question you aren't supposed to answer. You mean to say you haven't heard of a rhetorical question before?"

The vampire shuffled from one foot to the other for a moment. "Is that a rhetorical question, too?" he asked.

"Yes! No!" said George.

Phlebotomous opened his mouth, then shut it when he saw Veronica placing a finger over her mouth.

"I don't know why I have to wear this ridiculous thing," said George.

"Sir," said Veronica, "we believe there is a plot to end your life. We have asked Mr Bosch to provide us with this cloak for your protection."

"Who would want to harm me?" said the Prince. "What a nonsensical notion."

"There are those abroad who believe you are unfit to become regent," explained Veronica. "They believe you to be a vain, ignorant, selfish, incompetent, and drink-addled dandy."

"Yes, all right. But I have, you know, whatsit and whatsit to look after me." George indicated two burly men with enormous moustaches.

"Parker and Davis," said Veronica. "Yes indeed, but they can't be with you all the time."

"Neither can this awful cape," said George. "Some of the clubs I attend have rules you know."

"You are the Prince of Wales and soon to be the Prince Regent," said Veronica patiently. "I am sure they will bend the rules in return for your patronage."

George went quiet at this and studied his reflection in the mirror.

"Do you remember everything I told you about the cloak?" said Phlebotomous.

"Not a word of it," said George. "I was too distracted by the hideous cut. You'll have to accompany me when I go out so I can use it."

"Um… That may not always be possible," said Phlebotomous.

"Oh, so you have something more important to do than protecting the heir to the throne?"

Phlebotomous looked awkward. "Is that a rhet—"

"I don't know!" snapped the Prince.

"The problem, sir," said Veronica, "is that Mr Bosch is not able to go out during daylight."

"Why ever not?" asked George.

"I'm a vampire," said Phlebotomous.

"You're a vampire? Well then, you simply must accompany me. Between you, this horrendous cloak, and thingy and thingy, I'll be perfectly safe."

Several hours later, Prince George, Phlebotomous, Parker, and Davis were all strolling along the seafront at Brighton. The sun had just set, and the Prince had decided he wanted a constitutional to start his day. Phlebotomous had noticed some strange winking and nodding between the two guards and Veronica, but couldn't work out what it meant.

"This thing weighs a tonne, Bisch," said George.

"Actually, it's only eight pounds," said Phlebotomous.

"Feels like a tonne," said George. "Oh blast, that's Lord Hollingbury coming. He's bound to pass comment on it."

"Good day, Your Royal Highness," said a tall man dressed in high fashion. "Is that the latest London look?"

"Indeed," said George. "I'm surprised you don't have one yourself."

Lord Hollingbury smiled condescendingly at the Prince, winked at Phlebotomous, and then continued walking.

"Oh, this really is too much," said the prince. "Turn about, we're going back."

"Sir," said Parker. "I find myself unexpectedly caught short, and I notice there is a public facility just a small distance ahead. Would you mind if I…"

George waved him on in a bored manner.

"Sir," said Davis. "I find myself in a similar predicament and I…"

"Go, just go. "I'll be safe here with Basch."

The vampire and the prince stood together for a moment when suddenly a bearded man dressed in a long black overcoat rushed up to them.

"I am a dread anarchist and terrible enemy of the state!" said the man theatrically. "Death to His Royal Highness Prince George!"

George gasped as the man produced a pistol and fired it straight at him. But before the bullet could hit, a metal hand shot out of the cloak and caught it. The anarchist gaped for a moment before pulling out a large sword and swinging it at the prince. Before the vicious blade landed, a large shield sprang out, causing the sword to clatter to the ground. The anarchist then swiftly produced a large bottle with a skull and crossbones printed on it. He threw the deadly contents at the prince, but an umbrella snapped open out of the cloak, deflecting the poison. Finally, the anarchist extracted a round black bomb from his coat. With shaking hands, he lit the fuse.

"What now?" said George to Phlebotomous.

"This." The vampire delved into the cloak. There was a clicking sound, then a loud boing, and a huge spring appeared at the bottom of the garment. George and Phlebotomous flew into the air and landed 500 feet away. The two royal guards appeared from the public convenience and approached the anarchist.

"Well Gillespie?" asked Davis. "Did we get him?"

The anarchist shook his head and indicated the black fizzing ball.

"Oh…" started Parker.

"Bang," said the bomb.

"Well," said Quigley, sitting behind his desk, "all I can say is that the Prince and the people of Britain can't thank you enough."

"Enough!" said Veronica, standing beside the desk and on the verge of hysteria.

"It was nothing, really," said Phlebotomous. "The cloak worked nearly perfectly, although the spring release was a bit too much. Lucky for me I suppose."

"Lucky!" agreed Veronica. Her eyes were quite red, and she was staring at Phlebotomous.

"Did they find out who that mysterious anarchist was?" asked Phlebotomous.

"We shall never know I suspect," said Quigley. "He was blown up in the explosion like those poor loyal guards who gave their lives for the Prince. Mr Bosch, Prince George has asked that we bestow upon you a gift of no small monetary value, for saving his life and for providing him with the cloak. He intends to wear it always."

"Always," said Veronica. "Always!"

"Um, Miss Herringay," said Quigley. "You seem overwrought by these terrible events, perhaps you should… retire for a while."

"Retire," she agreed, backing out of the door. "Retire, retire."

"She has been quite touched by this situation," said Quigley. "She feels it deeply. But as I was saying, we owe you a debt of thanks, and the Prince has promised, uh, a princely purse in recompense."

"Happy to be of service," said Phlebotomous. "If you need any more—"

"No!" snapped Quigley, then said softly. "No. You have done…quite enough."

Phlebotomous left the office, and Quigley sighed.

"There is one thing we can take from this sorry mess, though," he muttered to himself. Rising, he walked to the door.

"Miss Smith, can you please come through? I wish to dictate a memo."

Promptly, a smartly dressed young lady appeared in the office.

"This is to Lord Montague at the Admiralty, please," he said. "Dear M, I have some ideas to discuss for our espionage department, Q."

"Well, I'm sure there'll be no trouble this time, Mr Bosch," said Gribble, sitting in his chair with the automaton behind him.

"Fingers crossed!" said Phlebotomous. "Actually, don't cross them, just in case the calibration is off."

Gribble gulped, and the machine went through its serving process as before. Phlebotomous was pleased to see the knife land correctly on the table, to the right of the plate, and not at all in Mr Gribble. The cauliflower cheese and potato were served perfectly, a triumph given how thin the cheese sauce was. Finally, and disappointingly, the salt cellar again fell apart whilst shaken, and a pile of salt deposited on the food. Both Phlebotomous and Gribble sighed in unison.

"Mr Gribble," said Phlebotomous, "have you considered the many health benefits of a low sodium diet?"

About The Benthic Times

'Jennings and Jennings, Paranormal Investigators, available for hire in the Home Counties. Are you plagued by supernatural goings on or troubled by fantastical events? We can help, using the most modern scientific advances, to rid you of even the most ancient of terrors. 3 pence an hour, double on Sunday.'

So ran the advert and soon came the requests for our husband and wife team to help out in these 4 gothic comedy stories. Gasp, laugh, and be generally titillated as you encounter:

A haunted house, a strange case of mesmerism, a murderous fiend, and mysterious theft of alchemical artefacts.

Find out more at https://thebenthictimes.com/

Gho-Power by Michael Chandos

"Your machine is crap, sir," roared the chief inspector. The massive policeman leaned over Jimmie's working desk like a dynamited skyscraper. His scarlet face contrasted vividly with the silver braid on his midnight blue uniform. "The Lothian and Borders Police missed the certain arrest of a known murderer and bank robber this afternoon, solely due to your slow and unreliable steam-carriages. They're noisy, and the lights are useless. Take them back."

"Chief Inspector, perhaps you didn't keep the steam up to pressure," said Jimmie Wattnott, inventor and factory owner. Loaning steam-carriages to the police was supposed to promote his business, not destroy it. "You know you have to—"

"We waited for the murderous bastard to strike at the East Lothian Bank, hiding for six hours in the cold rain. Three times we had to run for water. Three times we had to borrow coal from houses and pubs. The hyena appeared, and we pursued him, but then the carriages ran out of steam, and we had to stop. The bastard got away in a hansom cab pulled by a single horse. Hear that? *A single horse cab.*" The chief inspector pulled himself to attention for his final pronouncement. "No more, Mr. Wattnott. I will not miss another dangerous criminal due to ill-conceived, malfunctioning, so-called 'modern' inventions."

The chief inspector banged his sizable fist on Jimmie's oak desk. The full ashtray bounced across the desktop and knocked over the little statue Jimmie's daughter had made in school. Ashes went everywhere. Workmen in the Velociter steam-carriage factory stopped to watch the angry scene through the long window between the factory and the owner's office.

"Thank you for the use of the steam-carriages in this trial run, but the experiment failed. Good day, sir."

The chief inspector and his equally massive sergeant tramped out of the workshop and slammed the heavy street door behind them. Jimmie, apparently, was disposable to the Lothian and Borders Police. The workers turned back to their tasks, but they kept an eye on the owner's office.

"Oh my God, Abernethy, we're ruined," said Jimmie. "I expected an endorsement, not a condemnation." He slumped into his desk chair and turned away from the blueprints of the new model. Cigarette ashes hung in the air and dusted his coat sleeves, the diagrams, and his University of Glasgow tie. He absentmindedly dusted the ashes off his daughter's artwork and swabbed his rectangular eyeglasses.

"The Wattnott Velociter Company is still strong, Mr. W," said his chief mechanic in his workingman's brogue. Angus Abernethy was Jimmie's first employee. He sat at a long workbench next to the factory door wearing a beige lab coat, tweed pants, and a white shirt buttoned to the top. Wires, tools, and Velociter subassemblies covered most of the surface of his workbench. Drawings covered the walls. "We make the best steam-powered commercial carriages in Scotland." He turned on his steel stool and pushed his round goggles up on his forehead. He wore his Scottish driving cap backwards, as always. "Perhaps we should increase our efforts on the new electrical motor."

"No. The Sprague DC motors are promisin', but they're far too heavy for dirigibles or swift runabouts. Who in a hydrogen airship wants a hot, sparkin' motor on board? What pleasure driver escorting a beautiful and finely dressed lady wants a vehicle with battery boxes full of fuming sulfuric acid beneath his bottom?"

Jimmie looked at the ceiling, but it was too late for divine intervention. He rubbed his face and smoothed back his receding black hair. "This is the Age of Invention, of great machines and visionary men. Am I mentally bankrupt already?" He brushed the ashes off the blueprints. "I know my designs can change the world. I can clear our dank skies of coal smoke and bring prosperity to the working man. I'd do anythin' to succeed."

Jimmie got up from his desk and paced in front of the wide window that overlooked the Velociter factory floor. The window muffled the factory noises and kept most machinery odors from the office. Teams of men and women were hard at work on his newest steam-powered carriages, building the cabs from Scottish poplar wood, upholstering the seats with deep red leather, and pin-striping gold details on brilliantly polished black lacquer. Were the workers building vehicles with little or no commercial appeal? His shoulders slumped and his fingers twitched.

"I've built up this company from a two-man garage to a ninety person manufacturin' business. We got here by thinkin' and designin' things no one else could do. We know how to make things happen. My employees and their families depend on me for their futures."

One fist slowly tightened and Jimmie turned to the coat rack next to the factory door. He put on his long, wool overcoat and his bowler, and wrapped a dark blue scarf around his neck. "We must make fast and reliable steam-carriages that anyone would be proud to own. We just need a technology breakthrough."

He paused at the street-side office door and turned to his assistant. "I'm goin' out, Abernethy. Please send everyone home and close up for today."

"But, sir. We have orders to fill."

"Meet me here in the mornin', lad. We'll chart our way out of this. You'll see."

Jimmie sat alone with a glass of golden ale at a small cast iron table outdoors at the White Hart Inn and examined his fading options. Oil-gas street lights faintly illuminated the two broad cobblestone lanes of Grassmarket that led past the White Hart up the hill towards the Royal Mile. There was no steam or horse traffic to interrupt his thoughts. Moths and gnats swarmed the globes of flickering gaslight. Fall had started to strip the trees and a cooling wind bustled dry leaves into the gutters. The foggy cold could penetrate even the best wool coat eventually.

All the drunks and the sparrows had gone to bed, but the spirits were still active. Two glowing powder-blue balls the size of melons flew past. They spiraled around each street light as they flew, chasing each other and the moths like children on a playground.

"Steam can be powerful, but it's too heavy for speed unless you're a locomotive," Jimmie said to no one. "And the coal smoke from the steam power plants are killing my city. Electricity and the new reciprocatin' engines will come into use, but they are years, if not decades, away. I need a reliable source of refreshable power today to run lights, transport and manufacturin' machinery. Chemical? Wind-up? No, absurd." He stared into his glass.

The White Hart was closing, but Jimmie knew of an after-hours pub the police permitted to stay open. The street was empty of hansom cabs, so he had to walk. No people were about either.

Great night for a murder, he thought.

His boot heels echoed on the paving stones and his breath condensed into a cloud in the cool night air. The gas street lights barely lit the sidewalks.

Up ahead, he heard a low buzzing noise. Jimmie pulled up his coat collar. Ghost balls had become the nighttime flies of Edinburgh. They clustered around the gas street lights, spooked horses, and hindered most evening transport. Jimmie started to cross the street to escape them, but he stopped when he heard someone squealing in delight. He went up to an old wall made from weather-blackened volcanic blocks.

The wall surrounded an old church cemetery. Among the rows of weatherworn headstones, trees, and small stone statues of angels, a pudgy man in black was chasing ghost balls as they popped out of the ground.

Who is this fool? The man swung a butterfly net like a hand-and-a-half longsword, apparently trying to capture spirits. He cried out when he got one, and then he quickly put it into a large glass container with a sturdy lid.

Jimmie hopped the wall into the cemetery. "Excuse me, sir," he said. "Sir?"

The man stopped. He was winded and more than a bit startled to encounter anyone alive in the graveyard after midnight. "Yes? Can I help you?" His accent placed him well south, not from Edinburgh or the Highlands to the north. His cheeks were rosy from exertion.

"Excuse me for askin', but I'm curious about what you're doin'." Jimmie doffed his bowler and nodded. "I'm Mr. James Wattnott, an engineer and businessman."

"Good evening. I'm Reverend George, Moderator of this old kirk, St. Adrian's, Presbyt'ry of Edinburgh, Lothian Synod, Church of Scotland. I was just capturing a few wee bogles. Lots of them here in this cemetery, you know. The White Ladies walk here, nurtured by the moist soil of Scotland, a Society of Souls out for a stroll under the stars." He grinned with satisfaction over his lyrical words. He looked Jimmie up and down. "Out late, young man?"

"Out walkin' and thinkin.'" Jimmie shivered with the chill of the cemetery.

"It's a frosty October evening. Care for a hot cup of tea and an oat muffin while we talk?" Reverend George raised an eyebrow. "There may be some cider brandy to sweeten the tea."

"Why, thank you, Reverend George, sounds perfect for this cool night. Also, I'm curious what you do with the spirits in the jar."

"Come into my rectory kitchen, young man. It's amazing, if I say so myself."

The tidy church kitchen was cozy, with a cast-iron coal stove, a sturdy but rough oak table, and four ladder-back chairs of different designs. To Jimmie's amazement, the room was well lit with glowing jars of captured ghost balls.

"I've been storing bogles in jars for the last decade." Reverend George broadly gestured to encompass the room. "When the ghostly infestation surged after the Great Potato Famine, I thought it might be a good way to keep their numbers under control, but then I discovered they made excellent lights, especially when several are contained in a jar together. They don't like that and get angry, I suppose. More light for me. I've given up trying to keep their numbers down. Impossible task anyway."

"How long do they last?"

"They generally fade in several months and begin to disappear, so I release them when I notice they are dimming and get new ones. I think they may recharge after a while underground. Perhaps they eat." Reverend George offered a bowl and spoon. "Sugar?"

"Thank you. And the net?" said Jimmie.

"Made with pure silver thread woven into the mesh of the net, with a spring-loaded, gear-driven lid to close it off like a mousetrap. Pure silver will control a bogle, you know. I coat the inside of the jars with a thin silver wash as well. And a secret ingredient." Reverend George held up a small earthen jug. "Milk or brandy, Mr. Wattnott?"

Jimmie leaned forward. "Uh, brandy, yes, thank you. Does the social class of the spirit, uh bogle, make a difference?"

"My church is a poor, workingman's parish, and the souls buried in my yard are mostly the same." The reverend tilted back in his chair to think. "Perhaps common people are better than the rich, when it comes to the strength of the spirit. They've been tested by time, by the troubles in their difficult lives."

"I see. Please, what is that secret ingredient?"

"Well, along with the silver wash, I found that a little dusting of mandrake root powder enhances the color of the light, as well as stabilizing the illumination." The Reverend smiled and sat proudly straight in his chair. "Too much mandrake and they become wildly unstable. The real science is determining how much of the powder to dust."

"Mandrake root? You mean atropine," said Jimmie. "Probably makes them hallucinate."

"I grow it myself, you know, from belladonna seeds I bought in Italy. I dry the root in a small tin over the stove and then crush the root in a marble mortar and pestle." Reverend George held up a thumb and finger. "Just takes a pinch."

"So simple."

"Yes, it is." He leaned forward. "Mind you, you never want to handle the pretty things directly. Even little ones will numb your hand. I can't imagine what a big one would do. Syphon your entire life's energy away perhaps." The reverend's eyes were round and jolly.

"If I come back tomorrow night, can you show me how it works?"

"Delighted."

Later, alone in his personal lab, Jimmie fashioned silver thread into a durable version of Reverend George's butterfly net and made capture containers from large pickle jars with sturdy, sealable lids and a ghostly grey film of silver on the inside. The butterfly net flap closed with strong steel springs and lightweight brass gears. Three bamboo fishing rods bound with copper wire made a long and sturdy grip shaft.

The next night was chilly again and a bit misty, so Jimmie brought fortification for himself and Reverend George in the form of a Scotch dew that blended well with their tea. Collecting was fun, if not exhausting, running through the cemetery with the silver-laced net and popping ghost balls into jars.

The ghost collecting was successful. Jimmie returned to the Velociter factory with four jars containing glowing ghost balls.

"Sir, you look terrible," said Abernethy the next morning. "Your health is beginning to concern me."

"Never felt better. Go out to the factory floor and get me two of those carriage lights we put on the Brougham. Take out the oil lamps and devise a way to seal the glass enclosures," said Jimmie. "And don't make any plans for after midnight."

"Midnight, Mr. W? My only plan was sleeping."

"Not tonight, Abernethy. Tonight, we discover our fortunes."

It was like catching minnows in lakeside shallows. To start, a candle or a dram of whisky made a good lure. The silver net worked perfectly. Jimmie and Abernethy captured several dozen by the end of the evening. In the lab, they determined that one ghost to a lantern made a passable area light for streets and walkways, while two or more spirits in one lantern with a little shot of atropine from the chemist's made strong hansom cab headlights.

By the next day, the Lothian Velociter Company was marketing the brass and crystal lanterns to cabs, doormen, and carriage drivers, and even the police showed renewed interest. By the end of the following week, they were demonstrating ghost-powered street lights to the Edinburgh city council.

Lighting the streets with low maintenance lamps that also helped to alleviate the ghost problem? Pure genius. Three days later, Jimmie had a patent and prepaid orders for 250.

Jimmie and Abernethy experimented. The lab was filled with new scientific instruments, courtesy of the recent rise in profits, and the storage room was filled with captured spirits. They tried three different mixtures of atropine and even made their own raw mandrake powder. Jimmie's desk was overtaken with blueprints and further patent application forms. His daughter's little statue was moved to a shelf.

"You know, Abernethy, I think we need better quality ghosts. The cemetery ghosts are easy to catch, but they're older and dimmer. I think younger and fresher ghosts will be brighter and will last much longer. I suspect sudden deaths will deliver more energetic ghosts, too."

Abernethy put down his soldering iron. "The only way I can think of getting those energetic ghosts, sir, is to make 'em yourself. With mortal violence."

"Burke and Hare grave robbin', eh? Well, remember what happened to them." Jimmie raised his eyebrows. "They were publicly executed on the Royal Mile. No, I think we need a city-wide spirit collection system of men and vehicles. Some crews will work the cemeteries, of course, but others should be stationed where we would logically expect to find fresh ghosts. We should attend every execution at the prisons. We should arrange to be present at every hospital's critical ward. We should follow the police and firemen to major fires and fatal accidents." Jimmie's eyes unfocused to look deep into the future. "Is there a war goin' on some place?"

"Always is, sir…some place." Abernethy turned back to his work.

"I'm drawin' up designs for a steam-powered ghost collection vehicle to industrialize the large-scale capture and storage of energetic spirits. The collector will have incandescent lures and silver thread-lined tubes connected to rows of silver-misted containment jars. Here in the factory, we'll have racks of proper jars to store the spirits until they are bottled in a product. One to a jar, unless more Gho-Power is needed. Oh, did I mention that? I'm trademarkin' ghost energy as Gho-Power."

"Very catchy, Mr. W."

"I have other ideas, too, but let's work on these for now. I think we may be able to extract electrical power from bottled ghosts as well. The Gho-Dynamo. No batteries and almost no weight. Imagine the uses."

The Royal Infirmary of Edinburgh, known as the RIE, was the first major nonprofit hospital in Scotland. The solid stone edifice and castle turrets sheltered a progressive medical institution. Jimmie gained access to the wards through contributions and good works.

"Good morning, gentlemen. I am Professor Wattnott, inventor and developer of Gho-Power." Jimmie addressed a group of prominent doctors and the Administrator of the RIE in his best university English. They were all stuffed into the Administrator's too-warm office, a frowning flock of expensive tweed, starched whites, and stone faces. "I am pleased the new operating lights I donated to your hospital are working so well."

"Thank you, Professor Wattnott. They work exceedingly well and reliably," said the administrator from behind his large and well-polished desk. "The clusters of lamps backed with the silver plated reflectors give my surgeons unprecedented light over their patients. Is there anything I can do for you in return?"

"Perhaps. Consider this." Jimmie pulled them in. "You treat acute cases in your hospital. From time to time, unfortunately, patients die. It is a fact of life. Their spirits often zoom around the wards, bothering patients and staff, disrupting critical medical duties. I have developed an automatic spirit capture system that, once installed in your wards and operating and treatment rooms, will end the ghost problem forever. The devices use Gho-Power themselves and require no operator."

"Hmmm. Perhaps." The administrator pushed his wire-rims back on his nose, and he turned to look at his doctors. "Fresh ghosts are often very disruptive. Does the collection harm the departed in any way?"

"No, sir, absolutely no harm whatsoever. The body is never touched. You get the body, I get the ghost. It's fairly balanced. And of course, I will be happy to make a generous contribution to the Hospital benefits fund with each one collected."

"Yes, well, let's try an experiment and see how it goes," said the administrator. Several of the doctors had looked bothered by the suggestion, but less so when the contribution was mentioned.

"Excellent." Jimmie clapped his hands together. "Shall we start with the children's and accident wards?"

The RIE collection soon was providing a steady stream of energetic ghosts. Things were going so well that Jimmie was in a thoughtful mood again.

"Abernethy, we need to build locations around Edinburgh, and perhaps Scotland itself, to refresh customers' Gho-Power devices without them havin' to come across the city to this factory. These—let's call them fillin' stations—will be kept stocked with vigorous captured ghosts and devices to rapidly refresh lanterns, runabouts, commercial vehicles, hansom cabs, everythin'. For a fee, of course. We could sell a service program to cover regular maintenance. And we could display the full range of our products for sale at each location." He could see the wall of Gho-Power inventions in his imagination, searchlights, emergency beacons, and perhaps even handheld torches, packaged in colorful boxes with his picture and the Scottish flag on the side.

"Great idea, sir." Abernethy was busy with an experiment to draw electrical power from a Gho-Power container and to perfect the Electro-Leash, a device to remotely control a free-flying ghost. He sat at his workbench in the corner of Jimmie's office, surrounded by tools, prototype devices, and jars of spirits.

"Mr. W, I heard those doctors at the RIE refer to you as Professor."

"Yes. The University of Glasgow, where the eminent James Watt perfected the steam engine years ago, awarded me a Scottish engineering medal. I thought it only appropriate to assume the title, purely for business reasons. Not to worry."

Abernethy raised his eyebrows. "Boss's privilege, I'm sure."

"Let me show you my map of possible fillin' station locations. We might have to talk to the town council about modifyin' traffic patterns to make it work efficiently. Now, let's—"

Shouts rang out from the street in front of the factory. Drums added a non-musical backbeat.

Jimmie got up from his desk to look out his streetside office window. "My God, a group of chantin' women with signs is blockin' the entrance to the factory." Both men hurried out the front door.

Fifteen women in proper dresses of silk and satin, high hats, and button-up boots, were standing in front of the tall garage doors of the Velociter Factory. Some carried signs reading "The Anti-Ghost-Syphoning League," "Hands Off My Mum," and "Leave My Gram In Peace." Their apparent leader stood on a short stool to address the group and curious onlookers. Two women pounded small drums to the beat of the slogans.

"This factory is an abomination," she preached. The crowd yelled in agreement. The assistants beat their drums. "They are stealing your dead children, your dear departed mother, and using them for commercial gain, without regard to your wishes as relatives or to proper Christian morals. Join us in opposition. We will block their factory every day and interfere with their business, and we will lobby the City Government and the Secretary of State himself to outlaw the wicked and scandalous practice of ghost syphoning and exploitation."

The woman on the stool spotted Jimmie. "There he is, the infamous hooligan that started this business, the shame of Scots everywhere, Mr. James Wattnott."

On cue, the group surrounded Jimmie and Abernethy. "Who are you, madam? I shall call the police," said Jimmie.

"I am Mrs. Judene Gutherie, suffragette and temperance activist, and now the leader of the Anti-Ghost-Syphoning League, the women of which stand before you now."

"You cannot interfere with the operation of my legal business."

"We are legally in the public street, Mr. Wattnott. Call the police if you must, you coward. We shall not move."

"Oh God," Jimmie said as they ran back into the factory. "Send a messenger to the Chief Inspector with a complaint. I'm goin' to South Gyle to talk to the Scottish Prison Service about their execution schedule. Use the factory ruffians if you have to, Mr. Abernethy, but I want those infernal women gone by the time I get back."

The Calton Gaol was a stark, fortress-like prison on Calton Hill, not far from Holyrood Palace where the Queen sometimes spent her summers. The grim brick and stone structure confined the physical like the silver-washed jars did the spiritual. Jimmie scheduled an interview and demonstration with the Deputy Prison Governor. It went very well. The Deputy Governor bought several Gho-Power searchlights for the prison walls, and he invited Jimmie to a future execution.

Jimmie was in luck. William Duncan, the violent murderer of three women, two men, and several children, maybe more, and a superb high-energy ghost prospect, was the next scheduled execution at Calton Gaol.

"Grab the sturdiest ghost container we have, Abernethy. We have an opportunity to collect what may be the most energetic ghost in our experience. He is exactly what we need for the electrification experiment."

The execution and the collection were routine, but the containment was not. They struggled to seal the convict's wild and chaotic spirit in the reinforced, thick-walled bell jar.

"Feel how he strains the container. His power is incredible. This may be our airship power source, at last."

"I know he's encased in a heavy glass container with a machined silver lid and Swedish steel reinforcement, but he still scares me, Mr. W. We wouldn't ever want to let him out." Abernethy drove the steam-powered delivery flatbed out of the prison yard. "I'm not certain even our strongest Electro-Leash could handle him. Sir, did you note the color of his ghost ball?"

"Yes. The ball had a distinctly scarlet point at the center."

Abernethy shivered. Blood red. Evidence of his evil works.

"Take a note, Abernethy. Never any atropine near him, not even his jar."

"Yes, sir."

As they drove out the back gate of the prison, a group of women were amassing at the main prison gates.

"Oh blast," said Jimmie. "The State has properly executed a heinous criminal, and look who is here to protest: our beloved Mrs. Gutherie." Mrs. Gutherie was on her stool, loudly preaching to her small army.

"Don't let her see us, sir. If she knew we collected his ghost, she'd be outside the factory door within the hour trying to free him."

"We may have to take care of that woman one of these days."

"I'll keep a container ready, sir."

Duncan's power demanded very careful handling. He was vaulted separately because he drained the power from other bottled Ghosts, and people working near his jar reported severe headaches. Only Jimmie and Abernethy were permitted to work with him, and no atropine was ever administered. Abernethy managed to improve the Electro-Leash control link, while Jimmie brainstormed plans to tap his energy. Business went on, but not always well.

"Our routine collection is goin' smoothly, but we simply need more energetic ghosts for gentlemen's carriages and commercial carry-alls." Jimmie flipped through his account ledgers on his office desk. He scribbled figures on a tablet, but the numbers just wouldn't come out in the black. Only his desk lamp was lit. The room was otherwise in shadows.

"I have orders for extra bright lights I can't fill. I'm losin' money. With

the fillin' stations goin' up, I'm over-extended. The banks aren't happy."
He closed the books with a determined slap. "The spirits with violent or
tragic deaths from the hospitals, asylums, and gaols have been fantastic," said
Jimmie. "That's what we need more of." He lifted his tea cup to his lips, but
put it down immediately; it was cold.

"Uh, sir," said Abernethy. "The Chief Inspector was here today. He was
happy about the lighting systems we sold the Constabulary, but he seemed
especially curious about our collection processes and our agreements with
those institutions."

"Mrs. Gutherie has been campin' in his outer office, I think. She's even
petitioned the Secretary of State and conspired to involve the Church of
Scotland against me. She tried to swear out arrest warrants for both of us
just last week."

"Arrest, sir? My God."

"Yes. For murder, theft, and child molestation." Jimmie leaned back in his
leather chair. "Tell me, have you tested the stronger Gho-Power Electro-
Leash?"

"Yes, sir. The electricity extraction project is going well. We harnessed
two ghost balls from the Royal Infirm'ry and controlled them as they flew
around the factory. It looks like we may have the solution for a mobile light
for the Fire Service."

Wattnott stared at his hands. "Will it control Duncan yet?"

"I—I'm not sure. Scary prospect, that."

"Work with the engineers and see what must be done to boost the controls
and to strengthen the harness so that I can use Duncan safely," said Wattnott.

"For Burke and Hare types of collection, Mr. W? Remember what
happened to them. Up the long ladder and down the short rope."

"I won't ask you to participate. We need extra powerful spirits, and violent
death boosts ghost potential energy. And I must protect my business and all
of your jobs as well. I'll fix my League problem at the same time."

"Yes, sir. Right away, sir."

Wattnott sat in a common commercial steam-carriage, indistinguishable
from many others on the street at nine o'clock in the evening. He had four

glass containers in the hold: one for Mrs. Gutherie, two for any other perfect candidates he came across that night, and a big one with Duncan imprisoned inside. That one was padded, tied down, and secure from any mishap lest he escape. Duncan's container hummed, more felt than heard.

Wattnott was parked up a dark alley outside the Union Hall where the League hosted weekly rallies. This evening's meeting was breaking up. Someone came up to the carriage.

"Abernethy! Good God, man. You frightened the life out of me," said Wattnott.

"I couldn't let you do this alone, sir. Besides, I have more experience controlling Duncan than you do."

"Get in, Angus. She'll be on the street any minute."

Mrs. Gutherie came out with three other women. As they walked down the street, Wattnott's steam-carriage followed. Grit crunched as the wheels bumped over the cobblestones. Abernethy threw coal into the steamer's boiler and adjusted the vapor pressure to make ready for the chase. The carriage's stack belched black smoke. Then he struggled into his leather harness. It carried heavy copper cables to Gho-Power batteries and connectors to a control box for the Electro-Leash that tied Abernethy to Duncan. He signaled Wattnott that everything was ready. Abernethy switched on the control box and opened the safety latches on Duncan's bottle.

Soon, two of the women hailed a passing hansom cab, leaving Mrs. Gutherie and her remaining companion alone on the dark and narrow urban street.

"That's Mrs. Gutherie's assistant. Better take them both," said Wattnott.

As Wattnott drove the carriage past the women, Abernethy opened Duncan's bottle. His brilliant ghost ball exited immediately. A sinuous spark emanated from Abernethy's harness and connected with Duncan's glowing ball. The spark was azure blue with a deep red core, and it maintained constant contact with Duncan. His ghost ball yanked on the harness and almost pulled Abernethy out of the carriage. The ball swooped into the sky and slammed into a nearby Gho-Power streetlamp. The lamp shattered.

Duncan's spirit ball consumed the much smaller ghost ball inside. The women froze.

Abernethy worked the levers on his controls. Duncan struggled to break the Electro-Leash, but couldn't. The ball swooped back and went through each of the women. They screamed and fell dead to the ground.

Wattnott stopped the carriage and leapt from the driver's perch with the silver capture net as Abernethy struggled to maneuver Duncan back into his bottle. As soon as the ladies' spirits emerged from their bodies, Wattnott netted them. He hurried to the carriage and quickly bottled both spirits into separate containers. Abernethy was lying on the floor of the carriage, flushed and breathing heavily. He smiled at Wattnott and gave him a thumbs up. Duncan was safely bottled, too.

"Hold on. We must get out of here quickly," said Wattnott. He jumped back into the driver's perch and hurried his steam-carriage back to the Velociter factory.

The fresh spirits were superb. Their light was cold but intense, and their fade factor was miniscule. Duncan was brighter than ever and getting stronger with every kill. Abernethy experimented with the new spirits and was beginning to tap them for increased electrical power.

With all the activity, the lab was a mess. Jimmie's new separate office had fine leather chairs and a small whiskey bar for clients. His daughter's artwork was in the bottom of a wooden box in the closet. Mrs. Gutherie's bottle was in Wattnott's secret vault, away from public view. Her ghost light was tinged with blue and was very bright. The fury over her murder soon faded to nothing.

Wattnott and Abernethy routinely went out with Duncan to harvest more first-class spirits.

This night, the carriage was parked near a playground waiting for a brief moment alone with suitable targets. "Look, Abernethy, two children with a nurse. Her fear will skyrocket when the children are scared by Duncan, and she'll be ideal for harvestin'," said Wattnott. "I want to try controllin' Duncan this time."

"Be careful, sir. He always manages to eat one or two other spirits when he's out of his bottle, and he's getting much stronger. Never seen any other ghost do that."

They switched positions, and Wattnott put on the harness. The children ran ahead of their nurse; it was time to strike. Duncan roared out of his bottle, and he yanked Wattnott out of the steam-carriage and onto the street. An empty collection bottle and a vial of Russian atropine shattered on the ground. The nurse and the children screamed as Duncan flew through the nurse. She dropped. The children ran down the street screaming. Abernethy ran over to capture her spirit in the net. Duncan looped through the cloud of powdered atropine.

Duncan pulled Wattnott all around the playground. He flew straight up, and the red and blue spark from the Electro-Leash vanished, releasing its control.

"Hide, sir, hide!" yelled Abernethy.

Before Wattnott could rise, Duncan's ghost ball swooped down and hovered over him. "Congratulations, Wattnott," said a voice emanating from the ghost ball, "you've finally reached my degree of depravity. I think I will eat you now."

Duncan's ball flew through Wattnott's chest, and he collapsed back onto the cobblestones. Abernethy rushed forward with the silver capture net.

"What I have for you here, Chief Inspector, is a special version of the Velociter Company's Police Spotlight," said Abernethy, "called the Drum & Justice. The spirit bottle in this lantern contains two very antagonistic male and female spirits, together with highly refined atropine. Their constant battle produces extraordinary light, and the silver reflector projects that light in a well-defined cone that pierces darkness like no other light ever made. I'll have it mounted on your new Electro-Gho-Power Police Velociter, powered by the most potent Gho-Power unit ever produced. We call it the Duncan Wraith Gho-Dynamo. It'll go nearly thirty miles per hour. No horse or steam vehicle in Scotland can outrun it."

"Excellent, Mr. Abernethy. If this is typical of your new product line, this company will see more of the Lothian and Borders Police purchases. You've really improved the business since Mr. Wattnott retired."

"Thank you, sir. A drop of the Glen, Chief Inspector?"

"Absolutely."

About Michael Chandos

Steve is a former space engineer living in the woods in Colorado. He is a member of the Mystery Writers of America, the Short Mystery Fiction Society and the Romance Writers of America/Kiss of Death Chapter. He is published in mystery and SF anthologies in the US and England, and online, under his Michael Chandos pseudonym. He is a Colorado Licensed Private Investigator.

Nihon Daitan'na by T. J. O'Hare

Beautiful women
sing songs in my dreams — houris
from a paradise

The Emperor awoke with this *haiku* in his head. He had composed it in his sleep, and as he drowsed, he ran over it in his mind. It had no season word, so it probably fell short of perfection, but considering it came from below his consciousness, he was quite happy to accept it.

His three-legged crow cawed. This, the Emperor realised, was probably what had awakened him. He sat up in bed. The sun was rising. He turned towards the sun-goddess and bowed low in obeisance to her, with all the respect that was due to his paternal great-grandmother.

He rose and stepped towards his bedroom window. The wind chimes were still. The entire morning was still, like an egg within its shell.

He glanced to the north-east and saw a single speck of cloud—except it was no cloud. It was one of the *kurofune*, the black ships, American aerial corvettes, where Commodore Perry had stationed them about the Kamagawa peninsula.

Perry had come to open up diplomatic and trade arrangements after two hundred years of Japanese isolationism. It was all made clear in the various letters and missives that had bombarded the Chrysanthemum Throne for a year.

The Emperor frowned. This morning was the day he would hold audience with his court as to his response. The shogun was pleading ill-health, so it was up to him to show the way forward.

He spread his hand, and all the censers in the room sprang alight with small sparks of flame. The scents nourished him at an emotional level, and he made his way to his robing chamber. He showered in the Imperishable Mist of Immortality, and dried himself off with a towel, a part of his daily routine. He dressed as befits an Emperor on the brink of making a momentous decision.

He chose not to take breakfast, but met his entourage in the antechamber where they led him to the throne room, known as *Matsu-no-Ma* or The Pine Chamber. His three-legged crow sat on its customary perch.

Here the court was assembled, many in Samurai armour, many robed as Shinto priests, many in Zen garments, and a large contingent of variegated nobles and landowners. There was a single representative from the northernmost island of Hokkaido, a shaman wearing a bearskin cloak.

The presiding priest of the hour performed a short ritual to call upon the spirits, and then the proceedings began.

The Emperor's herald stood up and took centre stage, proclaiming the majesty and history of the Imperial line.

'Find yourselves in the Imperial and immortal presence of your Heavenly Sovereign, Jimmu. Be aware of his ancestry, that he is the great-grandson of Amaterasu, the sun-goddess. He it was who summoned the Divine Wind to destroy the invaders. He it was who—'

The introduction went on for some time. The Emperor knew it by heart. He never grew bored with it, for it reminded him of his station and his duties. Yes, he was Emperor, but others had come to claim the title. They had paid for this temerity by exile into the Realms. Exile the upstarts and usurpers to the Realms, and let them make or re-make their own kingdoms and destinies. He had spies among their ranks, and received regular reports on their progress, or, often, the lack of it.

Depending on how things went today, the Realms might well be a solution to this somewhat irritating American intervention.

The herald finished his speech, and the other members of the court rose to speak in their turn. As expected, all chose to state their needs with regards to the incursion. The talk went on for hours, as the Emperor scanned each face in the gathering and read their hearts and intent. All were stalwartly against the opening of Japan.

The priests called up various *kami*, so that the spirits of the land could also have their say. Two particularly troubling spectres arrived near the end: they named themselves as Nagasaki-*kami* and Hiroshima-*kami*. They had come from the future, and they had fearful news for the people, the land, and the court, if they should choose to open their country to the American ambassade.

Both were phantoms of flame and shadow, and they told of engines of sorcery deployed by a later American aggression that would destroy two Japanese cities each with a single explosive device. The *kami* left behind a cloud of malign despair when the priests dismissed them.

The last to speak was the Ainu shaman. There was a ripple of derision through the assembly, for the Ainu were considered hairy barbarians, but since the Imperial Throne had claimed their island centuries before, they were considered a useful resource.

'Imperial Master,' began the shaman. He was aged, but not weakened with age. 'My islands have been plundered by your courts for centuries. You have raped my valleys for their gold; stolen the salmon from the mouths of my children; reaped our forests for hides and venison. I wish to put to you a severance of our people.'

There was a stir among the assembly, and several samurai put hands upon their swords, but the Emperor raised his hand.

'Thank you, my lone subject from Hokkaido. I have heard your words, and I shall weigh them in the balance.'

Then came the doctors of philosophy, who were, if anything, eager to open their gates to outsiders. They envied the Americans for their steam engines, their Vernium lift generators, and their artefacts of technology; the ability to raise heavier-than-air machines up to the heavens, as witnessed by the four corvettes currently circling the capital at the height of one half *ri*. This was accomplished by Vernium lift generators, named after the greatest Western scientist of the nineteenth century, Jules Verne.

Naturally, there were two schools of philosophical thought. The traditionalists wished to maintain their studies in what the West had come to name as Shinto-tech or *kami*-tech. The forward-thinking factor was keen to integrate their Shinto-tech with Western ideas of locomotion, including the invaluable steam technology and Vernium aerial tech.

The case of India arose, as the Emperor knew it would. Under the British Raj all so-called *chakra*-tech was suppressed in order to keep the natural energies of the subcontinent out of any power play by nationalist parties wishing to overthrow British rule. He had witnessed the effect of Kundalini on the human anatomy firsthand, and was impressed. But the Indian nationalists lacked a power base. Their various kingdoms were too fragmented. They needed a Rajah or a Mullah to unite them against the British. None was forthcoming.

It was midday by the time everyone had spoken. The herald rose and uttered his speech of dismissal before the Emperor returned to his quarters. There a simple meal awaited him.

He ate it alone, in his shrine room, contemplating the faces of the various gods of his people that towered over him. Overhead was the sun-goddess, Amaterasu, with her extended open palm that held the five rice grains that had been grown in the fields of heaven. Planted in the wilderness of the primal earth, they transformed the ground into arable and habitable lands.

Beneath her was her brother, Susanoo no Mikoto, the god of summer and storms. He still held the legendary sword, Grasscutter, in his hands, even though legend said he had gifted it to his sister in reconciliation. History and legend vied with each other as to how many swords there were named Grasscutter.

Reaching up, the Emperor took the sword from the hands of the image and drew it from its scabbard. Even in the dimly lit shrine room, the sword shone like a sliver of the crescent moon.

Silently, soft-footed as a cat, he performed several *kata*-movements, recalling his sword skills. The actions and the rhythms brought him insights, knowledge that he had not been aware of before he worked with the sword.

Divine as he was, and therefore a *kami* himself, the sword was another *kami*, a deity, a divinity, or a spirit. Enclosed as he was at the centre of his palace, he felt a wind press on his face, clasping his robes against his limbs and torso. He recognized this wind: it was the *kamikaze*, or the 'divine wind' that had driven back the fleet of enemies a thousand years before.

He spread his arms, the scabbard in one hand, the blade in the other, and the divine wind carried him out of the palace, up through the central openings.

Overhead, the American corvette was sailing onward, serene in its aerial confidence. The divine wind bore him up, and he felt his own turbulence buffet the hull of the corvette. He sped above its barrel-shaped hull. There was a nacelle of glass and bronze, where the wheelhouse was situated. Riding the *kamikaze* like a wind-horse of his ancestors, he nudged it to land just before the first pane of glass. His robes settled about him, and with the tip of Grasscutter, he tapped on the glass.

Within the wheelhouse, he saw marines scurrying about with loaded carbines. A small group of bodyguards surrounded a man the Emperor judged to be the commodore. A brass windlass was turned from within, and the window pane was opened.

Invoking the *kami* of his tongue and speaking his best English, the Emperor said, 'I would like to come in.'

Commodore Perry broke through his cordon of guards. He, too, wore a sabre at his hip. 'You shall need to disarm, sir, and identify yourself.'

'Commodore Perry, I am disappointed that you do not recognise me. I presumed that your espionage services would have furnished you with my portrait—for how else could you send an assassin to slay me on my hunting trip?'

'You certainly look like the Emperor,' conceded the Commodore, 'but I cannot imagine why you would present yourself to me in my own wheelhouse, without ceremony and the customary diplomatic gestures.'

'I come here because I do not wish your vessels to land on the sacred soil of my islands. I have come to dismiss you from my realm.'

'That would be most unfortunate.'

'For you, true. Not for me. And since you have decided to forgo my honorific, I shall come to the point. You have never met anything or anyone like me before. I am the direct descendant of the sun-goddess. I am divine.'

He turned to stare out the starboard ports of the wheelhouse. 'Observe your craft, named, I believe, *Macedonian*.'

The corvette was of an older vintage than the current vessel. It still showed some of its marine past, with the remnants of masts and spars jutting out from its refurbished hull, along with the paddle-steamer wheels that now carried the Vernium-tech.

A plume of bright yellow flame broke through from its superstructure. The *Macedonian* lurched in mid-air, then began to wheel in a slow and desperate downward spiral.

The Commodore strode to the ports and looked out, his face ashen, bright red spots flaming on his cheeks. 'You, sir, have just slain two hundred men.'

'You, Commodore, slew them when you brought them into my bailiwick. Japan is sacred, and we wish no foreign devils to walk our soil.'

'This is war,' replied the Commodore.

'No, Commodore. This is destruction. You and your vessels may depart. For every hour that passes, another vessel, in no particular order, shall succumb to the *kami* of my land. You have just witnessed a fire *kami*. Perhaps a wind or a water *kami* would be instructive, to let you know that every element of my land is against you.'

'We are only four vessels today,' snarled Perry, 'but the whole of the West is looking on. If not the United States, then you shall parley with the Czar of the Russias, or the British Empire. You cannot—you dare not—hide behind your isolationism forever.'

The Emperor stepped back onto the decking outside the wheelhouse, and the divine wind bore him upwards and on to the site of the collapse of the *Macedonian*.

Fishermen had set sail and were rescuing the crew. Some shots were fired, but once the *Macedonian* settled on the water and begun losing buoyancy, the resistance petered out. Most of the crew were rescued, and the officers were brought aboard the Imperial barge.

Thinking back on his encounter on board the *Susquehanna*, there was one visage that had stood out from the crowd of Western faces. A shaven Polynesian savage, tattooed from head to foot with the designs of his mythology. An odd personage to be in the Commodore's company. For now, the Emperor dismissed it.

Below, from his aerial vantage, the Emperor could view the remaining ships of Perry's squadron. He knew enough of their military culture to read the semaphore signals that were being despatched by means of flags. Perry, on board the *Susquehanna*, was ordering his ironclad ship the *Mississippi* to fire upon the Imperial palace.

The Emperor knew the capabilities of their firepower. The *Susquehanna* was equipped with ten Paixhans guns, the latest in artillery weaponry, capable of firing explosive shells that could demolish a vessel with one shot. The development of this gun alone had meant the end of wooden warships and the rise of the ironclads.

The Emperor grimaced. Perry had not been made a Commodore of the American navy by being easily cowed. He had personally led land forces against the Mexican city of San Juan Bautista, capturing it during the Mexican-American War, having taken port after port.

The Commodore was not a physical coward by any means, but he had no real inkling of what he was up against in this present conflict.

Flying upwards once more on the divine wind, the Emperor hewed at the ailerons of the *Susquehanna* so that, although she was still able to fly, she could not maneuver in order to aim.

The other air-corvettes were sweeping closer in order to start an aerial bombardment. It was a swift hop and a jump for the Emperor to deal with them in the same manner. Although they could no longer maneuver, he was able to thrust them seawards with a gust of the divine wind. The *Plymouth*, being an older order of converted paddle-wheelers, lost its ability to maintain its trim and barrelled through the skies like a child's toy.

It would take several hours for the Americans to regroup and repair their vessels. By then, the Emperor knew that the battle would be over. Or rather, irrelevant.

He returned to the Imperial Palace and presented the sword Grasscutter to the statue of Susanoo no Mikoto. By now, his Imperial household guard had been deployed about the newly built Shrine to the Imperial Regalia of the Three Sacred Treasures. These Treasures had once belonged to the incarnate sun-goddess Amaterasu.

The Regalia was often interpreted as the Mirror, which represented the sun; a Jewel that represented the moon; and the Sword that represented the stars.

The Mirror was named *Yata no Kagami*, 'The Mirror of Light *Ta*,' and was considered to be the means for the gods to discern Wisdom or Truth.

The Emperor Jimmu knew that there were deeper levels of understanding concerning the Mirror. When installed and dedicated properly by the informed priests of the Shinto, it was actually the equivalent of an inter-dimensional astrolabe. Just as a mariner's astrolabe divided the heavens and declared the position of the vessel, this Mirror was able to navigate throughout the Realms.

Along with the Mirror, the priests had brought along the *Yasakani no Magatama*, the Gem of Benevolence. This was the adornment of the Mirror and formed a frame of stylized, fang-like teeth carved out of jade by godly hands about the circular outline of the Mirror. When they were set together in this manner, they became a *kami* of navigation.

The third piece of the Regalia was the sword *Ame-no-Murakumo-no-Tsurugi*, named the Heavenly Sword of Gathering Clouds, which represented valor in the ancient Japanese culture. The Sword was set between the Jewel and the Mirror in such a manner as to empower all three objects with the necessary *mahou*-power.

The person appointed to navigate by means of this magical construct was Shima Yukio, a blind Shinto priest with albinism. He was already in the shrine when the Emperor arrived, dressed in the white robe of a *kannushi*, priest, and *eboshi*, Imperial headgear, which rose from the crown of his head like the dorsal fin of a carp.

He had been appointed directly by the Emperor, who had conceived this plan the previous year, when the American international gunboat diplomacy first began. Shima was in charge of this particular shrine, but it was more than a simple shrine. It was to be the wheelhouse of the new vessel the Emperor had named *Nihon Daitan'na, Bold Japan.*

Japan's lack of a modern navy had given the Western nations the ability to imperil the Japanese mainland and its historical isolationism. The Emperor had decided to go one step further and created his own aerial fortress of *Bold Japan.* No mere marine vessel, no mere aerial vessel equipped with Vernium-lift engines; no, *Bold Japan* was to be the ultimate act of escape.

The Emperor whisked himself aloft, then set himself gently on the open-air section of the shrine. He reached out and set a heavy hand upon Shima's shoulder to let him know that he was there.

'Well, my *kannushi*, it is time for you to open the Oracle and take us out to the Realms. The underworld *kami* have all agreed and shall hasten our departure; the sea *kami* have realigned their hold upon our sacred shores; the wind *kami* have promised to bear *Bold Japan* aloft. Fuji-*kami* has awakened and shall add her underground fires to our potential powers. The signs are all aligned. The Regalia are connected in the way that they were first created to be.'

Before he had finished, Mount Fuji erupted with a single puff of volcanic flame and a plume of pyroclastic cloud.

Yukio Shima gave a loud cry of greeting, 'Welcome, Fujisan, Never-Dying Mountain.'

The cloud remained intact and rose higher and higher, a *kami* unto itself, a veritable newborn goddess. Then, collecting itself into a shimmering curtain of flaming coals and burning gases, it plunged into the sea. It spread itself like a curtain, drawing a rough outline around the islands of Japan, running south to draw in all the islands south of Kyushu, then it turned north and drove a line of fire between Shikoku and the Korean mainland. It shot further north, encompassing the island of Honshu, and then turned east to draw a line between the northernmost tip of Honshu and the island of Hokkaido. Then it turned back south and joined up with its starting point, just outside Yokohama.

The Emperor smiled ruefully. It seemed that the Ainu shaman had been conducting business dealings with the *kami* on his own people's part. Well, he reflected, if that is how it is meant to be, *Bold Japan* would survive without its northernmost territory.

The first earthquake struck the land as the island-mass broke free of the earth's crust. Whirlwinds formed out at sea and thrust their forces within this opening. Lurching like a newly fledged chick attempting its first flight, *Bold Japan* arose from its ancient foundation.

Flames from the magma pot of Mount Fuji licked lava around the ragged subterranean stumps, as if to cauterise them. The sea leaped up along the coastal boundaries, white horses of extraordinary height, weight, and force.

There was no mistaking it now. *Bold Japan* had taken off and was swaying upwards, tracing a path in reverse of that a cherry blossom would take as it falls from its twig. The islands drew closer together and formed one land mass, as the strait waters between them poured down like the rivulets from a bather upon arising from a bath.

New fumaroles opened up across the country, venting steam and sulphurous waters. As if shooting off fireworks, Mount Fuji set off a series of explosive volleys of bomb-sized boulders that exploded in mid-trajectory.

All the debris fell out beyond the curtain of fire, so that none of the population were harmed or in danger.

The Emperor watched the skilful movements of Shima's hands as he sensed the movements of the Regalia, tracking their path through time and space, through *ur*-time and *proto*-space, in order to reach the Realms.

The blue firmament of the world opened overhead and a *vesica piscis*-shaped rent appeared in the heavens. Beyond lay the fiery skies and turbulent vistas of the Realms.

From all around the Emperor, the court began to play: skirling of pipes and blowing of trumpets, shaking tambourines and banging on drums of every type.

Bold Japan rose higher and higher, shifting underfoot, like the deck of a sailing ship on ethereal waves, turning like a wave in the reverse-trajectory of its fall. The higher the island mass rose, the darker the sea appeared beneath them.

The waves were in turmoil as they gushed into the physical gap created by the island's departure. Lava sprayed up from the reservoirs, and sheets of molten gemstones fell down upon the surface of the sea. Tsunamis rushed from every direction and crashed into each other like bulls rampaging, like thunderheads colliding.

Lightning tracked over the waves, walking like praying mantises. The waters swirled in chaotic turmoil, turbulent vortices that threatened to overwhelm the remaining American craft.

And then, the world of their home was left behind. Beneath them, the Realms contained the rent that gave them a diminishing view of their green and blue planet. The island-mass rose higher and higher, and if the rent closed, then it closed in its own mysterious manner.

Here, in the Realms, there were no planets or astronomical heavenly bodies. It was a vast space where similar islands floated, populated with races of unknown origin.

This is a fitting voyage for a warrior-nation, thought the Emperor. The Americans with their gunboat diplomacy had only wanted access to the markets and industries of Japan. A capitalistic adventure, if ever there was one.

Here, the Realms held scope for a truly bold race. *Bold Japan* would be the flagship on which he might further his dreams of imperial conquest.

Down below, clinging to the downed hull of his flagship, Commodore Perry stared up in open-mouthed awe and wonder. He glanced at his savage companion and grimaced. 'I'm sorry for disbelieving you for all these years.'

The Polynesian made no reply, grinning.

Perry turned reluctantly to the captain of his vessel. 'Charge the semaphore,' he ordered.

The captain complied, and a rocket was set off, trailing a line of instructions in semaphore behind it. It flew up for a hundred feet, but that was all it needed.

The USS Submersible *Hiawatha* rose from beneath the waves and opened its hatches, taking on board all the men from the *Susquehanna*.

As Perry looked on, he recognized it was a bitter victory. He had fought for the building of this vessel, driving it through all the political hoops necessary, half hoping it would not be needed on this, its maiden voyage. But all the arcane reports were true. The Japanese had access to other worlds.

He waved to the captain of the *Hiawatha* and saluted as his crew were piped on board the Vernium-powered vessel.

With a noise like a huge gulp, the submersible rose from the waters, a leviathan that had learned how to fly. It shot up, as swift as an arrow, and nestled beneath the underside of the flying island of what had once been the Japanese archipelago.

The Japanese might well have won the day, but there would come a reckoning. His own American manifest destiny would change not only this world of theirs, but also a host of others. The Western frontier had not even been completely opened up as yet, but here was another frontier, one of which they were completely capable of mastering.

About TJ O'Hare

T.J.O'Hare writes short stories, novels, song lyrics, poetry, plays and film scripts.

He co-writes with many musical collaborators: Úna Clarkin, Stephen Dunwoody, John Lindsay, Edelle McMahon, Ronan McSorley, Brigid O'Neill, and Alan Patterson, all of whom can be found on the usual musical distribution sites. His plays have been staged in Ireland and Belgium. He also has a book of poetry, under his own name of Jim Johnston: "Available Light":

https://sites.google.com/a/lapwingpublications.com/lapwing-store/jim-johnston

He is married to Jean and has two grown-up sons. He lives in the North of Ireland.

Monster of the Deep by Thomas Roggenbuck

The small boat bumped up against the starboard side of the steamship, rocking gently in the shallow waves of the ocean water. Wynn fumbled with the striker and attempted to light her oil lantern. Though she clicked the two ends together, no spark was produced. She tried again, but still no luck.

"I don't see anyone on this ship," Henry said, holding his lantern up to better see the upper deck.

"I saw someone swinging a lantern in distress. The least we can do is see if they actually need help." Wynn adjusted a dial to change the angle at which the flint would strike steel and tried again. Still nothing happened. "Do you have your striker?"

Henry dug his striker out of his pocket and gave it to Wynn. In one click, a spark flashed and a little flame flickered inside her lantern.

"Give me yours," Henry said. "I'll see if I can fix it while you check the ship out."

Wynn handed her defective striker over to Henry. He immediately began to tinker with it. She slipped his into her pocket.

The steamship, more of a steam barge really, wasn't anything overly impressive. It resembled a traditional three-mast ship, but relied on three large paddle wheels at the stern, instead of masts and sails, for propulsion. The ship listed starboard, making it easier for them to board from that side. Wynn threw over a hemp rope and hook, catching the edge of the railing after a few tries. Securing the lantern to a loop on her waist, she pulled herself up and tied the rope into a solid knot.

The top deck shimmered with moisture in the moon's light. She unhooked the lantern from her belt and held it at her side while she proceeded around the ship. There were a few signs that a crew had once been there—an empty gin bottle rested against the stairs to the lower decks; disturbed bedsheets in the captain's quarters; cigarette burns scarred every inch of the railing.

The stern of the ship was in rough shape. Whatever had happened had damaged one of the paddle wheels; several of the paddles were sheared in half. Wynn returned to the starboard railing and caught Henry's attention. "I didn't see anything up here, so I'm going to check below decks."

"Okay," he said, glancing up from his work for a moment. "But make it quick. I'm getting cold. There's a fire and warm tea calling me at the lighthouse."

Wynn rolled her eyes and hid a smirk, though a cup of tea would be welcome now. The stairs creaked under her feet as she went below deck. Darkness pressed against her, overpowering the feeble light of her lantern. She swung it around, only catching glimpses of the lower deck before black swallowed it again. She crept forward, trying to see anything out of the ordinary, but she saw nothing.

Wynn turned to head down to the final deck when a flash of light made her stop in her tracks. She looked around, holding her breath, and waited.

"Hello?" Her voice echoed in the empty space.

There was another flash of light almost directly in front of her. Wynn threw her hands in front of her face, eyes stinging from the brightness. Once her vision cleared, she saw more flashes, mostly around the hatch. A low whining started coming from the center of the ship. Perhaps someone was attempting to start the engines. There was another flash, then another, then nothing. The darkness was heavier now, pressing against her. She proceeded back up. Someone had been making those lights. If she didn't see them, Henry should have.

Wynn reached the edge of the railing. "Did you see anyone, Henry?"

"See who?"

"I saw a bunch of flashing lights. Someone had to be swinging lights around up here."

Henry shrugged. "No. I have been working on your striker and almost have it fixed."

"So you didn't see anyone or anything?"

Henry shook his head, keeping his focus on the striker. Wynn sighed and pushed herself onward. She would finish looking through the ship at least. There had been the noise coming from below deck, though she longed to be finished and back at the lighthouse. Wynn recoiled from the thought that she hoped no one was left. She checked the cargo holds and the crew sleeping quarters again.

"Anyone here?" Her call received no answer; onto the last one. In the bottom deck, water dripped from somewhere and the cool air pressed against Wynn's skin. Her light revealed a crack in the side of the steamship, small enough to let water leak in, but not enough to sink the ship.

As she explored the deck, her light showed her more of what she saw above—an old diary soaked in water; a pair of fuel tanks that had remained intact; cargo holds that were untouched or ruined by water. An abandoned ship. Wynn focused on the split in the wall. Something had malfunctioned and damaged the vessel and the paddles, and the ship ran aground along one of the many reefs. Then someone had signalled for help. But then where was the crew?

A shimmer of light caught Wynn's eye. She looked toward it as another flashed. Then another. The whining pitch followed as before, though this time it felt more like a roar. She wanted to hide, to jump off this weird ship and head back to land, but as the lights flashed, she moved closer to the crack in the wall.

The noise didn't sound like an engine down here, at least, not a working one. It also came from behind the wall, and not farther back by the engine and fuel tanks. Wynn crept nearer to the wall, hand outstretched. The lights flashed faster and the noise grew in pitch, weaving a beautiful symphony together. Wynn was mesmerized.

An arm grabbed her from behind and shoved her in a dark, cold place. A door slammed shut. The change in environment cleared Wynn's head. The whining was less intense in this small space, but Wynn covered her ears to block the sound anyway. After a few more moments, silence returned and she looked up to who or what had pulled her away.

A scruffy faced man sat in front of her, his knees almost touching hers, and a large blue seaman's uniform wrapped around his shoulders. The dim lantern light couldn't reveal any more details about the man, but Wynn could see they were in one of the holds. She slumped onto a bag of flour.

The man spoke first, his voice was gruff. "Did Patrick send you down here?"

Wynn shook her head. "You're the first person I've seen since I climbed aboard."

The man deflated, and his eyes grew defeated. "I told him not to go, but he insisted. Swore he could get help. That thing must have gotten him, too."

"What thing?"

"With all the lights and noise. That's how it distracts its prey before slaughtering them."

Wynn stared at him. How long had this man been cooped up in this hold? Sea monsters were only just myths. Perhaps he suffered injuries that made him delusional. "I haven't seen any monster since I arrived, and I definitely did not see one from the lighthouse."

"Then how do you explain the lights and the noise? All the missing crew? I've heard their screams. I'm the last one. And the next."

Wynn felt sorry for his loss regardless of how the crew had perished, but determination took its place. "What's your name?"

"Kal."

"Well, Kal, I'm going to get you out of here. My friend, Henry, is waiting in a boat we've tied to your ship. We'll get on that boat and to land as fast as we can."

He glared at Wynn. "That's what everyone else thought. Get on the lifeboats and get the hell to land. Well, they've all been eaten, and the only way I survived this long is by hiding here. It'll get us as soon as we step out."

"You think I'm going to wait it out here with you?"

"It'll be safer."

Wynn ground her teeth. Getting off the ship was clearly the smarter option. If there really was a monster and it was determined, then Kal would be waiting a long time before he'd get his escape.

"Look, you can stay here where you're cold, wet, and in danger as soon as you step out of here, or you can take a risk and get back to land. We have some great tea and a fireplace at the lighthouse."

Kal clenched his fists. "I'd rather die than forsake the memories of my friends for some luxury."

Wynn's mind went back to the boathouse and the harpoon gun on the wall. She tried to keep the pleading out of her voice. "We can get a gun or two and maybe some more people, then kill this thing, but we have to leave this room and get on that boat."

Kal looked at his hands and grimaced.

"I didn't know any of your crew, and I'm sorry they're gone, but hiding here isn't the answer. You'll run out of food and fresh water eventually. We have a good engine on the boat, so it goes fast. We'll be on land in minutes."

After a moment, Kal nodded. Wynn flashed a weak smile, grabbed the lantern, and opened the cargo hold.

As they stepped out into the darkness, every step thundered. Kal's breathing was fast and loud, no doubt seeing memories of his now gone friends. Wynn forced herself to keep moving. When they clambered onto the top deck, Wynn was relieved to see the moon's light reflected on the damp wood. She hurried toward the edge of the ship where Henry would be waiting in the boat.

Except there wasn't a boat there. Wynn raced up and down the starboard side, swinging the lantern back and forth, trying to spot any movement in the water. A few shattered pieces of wood floated nearby, and the hook and rope dangled uselessly. Wynn pulled the rope up and only half of it remained, ripped and bloodied. A hand clung desperately to it.

Kal's words came back to her. *With all the noise and lights. That's how it distracts its prey, before slaughtering them.* He had been right about a monster; she had been below deck when the lights first appeared. Henry had been an easy target. Wynn blinked back tears and dropped the rope.

Kal joined her at the railing, peering into the darkness. "Where's this boat?"

"Gone." It was the only word she could say.

"Did your friend leave?"

She could only stare at the spot where the boat had been. Where Henry had been.

Kal growled. "You said there was going to be a boat and there's none here. What are we going to do now?"

"I don't know."

Kal clenched his fists. "So, you dragged me up here only to find out your method of escape is gone? You pulled me out of safety to stand in the open for the monster to eat? Your friend was eaten by that creature, and you, too, are going to stand here?"

"My friend is gone. I need a moment."

"I've heard my friends' screams for the last day and it's possible I'm next, and you want a moment?"

Wynn faced him. "It's called respect. Now back off."

Kal huffed and stomped away. "Should have known you didn't have a backup plan."

"Why don't you swim then? Make it easier on me."

"I thought you wanted a moment."

A blaze of light cut Wynn off before she could reply. Kal's footsteps stopped. Faintly, the whining began, until the sound vibrated the boards under their feet. The ship rocked as something slammed against the side and nearly sent Wynn tumbling overboard. Kal caught her coat and pulled her back.

"Come on," he shouted, scrambling for the stairs. Wynn hurried after him. The flashes of light were rapid and disorientating. The whining reached an incredible pitch and was twice as loud below deck. Wynn's teeth were on edge, and she covered her ears in a poor attempt to block the noise.

Before she could ask what they were doing next, something crashed against the deck, cracking several of the boards. Water droplets splashed onto their heads as they flailed.

Wynn scrambled toward the stairs to the lowest deck. If she could get down there, perhaps she would be safe. Or maybe the monster would be exposed, and she could kill it. The thought brought her to a stop. Kill it with what?

The world pitched starboard as the monster rammed the steamship. Wynn threw her hand against the wall and heard Kal stumble. He managed to recover and hurried over to her.

"Down below," she said.

"Are you crazy?" he shouted back. "It'll crush us down there."

"Better than up here." Wynn didn't wait to hear his reply. She raced down the stairs. Kal was right behind her.

On the lowest deck, the water now reached her knees as she waded through. Wynn swung her lantern around, spying the fuel tanks she saw earlier.

She pointed to them. "What is in those?"

Kal followed her finger. "Paraffin. Keep that lantern away from it. Very explosive and dangerous."

Wynn nodded. "We need to set them off, preferably as the monster strikes."

"Did you not hear me? It's explosive. Put that flame near that stuff, and you'll be cooked."

"If you haven't noticed, there is a mythical sea monster trying to eat us. I'm willing to take a risk."

"We can't even carry a tank up one deck, let alone two!"

"At this rate, we won't have to." Wynn took one step forward as the monster rammed against the ship, shaking it violently and breaking more wood along the port side. Water gushed through the gap. Wynn struggled to keep her balance, but the force of the blow was too much, and she splashed into the water. The lantern went out, plunging the room into darkness. Her plan to light the paraffin was ruined.

Something tightened on her arm and she tried to pull away. "It's me. Keep moving." Kal's rough voice snapped her mind into focus, and she crawled to the tanks. The smell of paraffin was overwhelming. Wynn's eyes watered, and she coughed.

In a flicker of the creature's light, she saw Kal's face. He didn't look as confident as he had sounded just moments ago. Any color had drained from his face, and sweat lined his brow. He stared wide-eyed at Wynn. A pang of guilt hit her. She had promised him safety, but now they were going to die.

Another flash of the monster's light flickered between the broken boards. Wynn's breath caught. It was trapping them. They had run right into a corner like idiots and now had no way out.

The boards shattered, and the lights flooded the bottom deck.

"Get this thing open," she shouted at Kal. Though his face was screwed up in pain, he nodded and moved to the side of the tank. The lights spun around an unknown center. They were mesmerizing. Wynn wanted to stand and watch them when a large tentacle, as thick as her arm, smashed through the layers of wood next to her head. She yelped and jumped back.

Wynn pressed herself against the far wall as it smashed down again and again. A section of wood next to her head exploded inward, and another long, slimy tentacle forced its way in. She shrieked and curled away as the monster kept tearing the wall away piece by piece.

"Almost ready," Kal shouted, barely audible above all the noise.

Wynn's stomach twisted. She still had no way of lighting the paraffin. This was going to end soon and terribly if she didn't think of something. Wynn shoved her hands into her pockets, desperate for anything, and felt the cold touch of a striker. She pulled it out and stared at it in dumb amazement, forgetting the maelstrom around her. She ripped a chunk of fabric off her coat, prayed it was enough, and joined Kal.

"Open it," Wynn yelled as loud as she could. Kal twisted the wheel and paraffin poured out, mixing with the water.

A whole section of the wall flew away, revealing a maw nearly as wide as the steamship was long and circular rows of sharp, white teeth. Tongues twisted in the air between the teeth, beckoning for them to jump in. There were too many waving tentacles, each one emitting light at the tip. The creature's flesh was the color of blood and drawn tight across bone. Wynn shuddered.

The attack left the port side raised a few feet in the air, leaving the paraffin tank dangling dangerously above the creature. The tank only needed to be shoved out a little farther.

Wynn and Kal pushed against it, feet sliding on the paraffin-covered floor. It moved an inch. The lights now surrounded the pair, and the circular pattern tightened, its brightness blinding.

They gave another push, and the tank moved another inch. Paraffin now began to pour into the water below. The whining intensified until it vibrated the tank against Wynn's back. Her ears throbbed painfully. Tentacles were swinging wildly, smashing boards and the water's surface. One grazed Wynn's cheek; another caught Kal's leg, and he toppled to the floor.

"Kal!" Wynn reached to help him up, but as soon as she did, the tank slid inward again. Her feet slid on the slick floor, useless in her attempt to stop it. Eventually it stopped, but it was too far in the belly of the ship and in too much water for her and Kal to push out again. The other tank remained untouched.

She hurried to Kal's side and pushed some loose boards off him. "Come on, Kal. We can do this." He didn't move, and Wynn shook him harder. He had to wake up; she couldn't move the other tank by herself. If he didn't wake up, she wouldn't have time to formulate another plan. The monster's attacks were growing more and more vicious, the crying and screeching were almost unbearable, and the lights flashing so fiercely her head ached.

"Kal!" Wynn hit him, tears in her eyes. He wasn't going to move. The crew of this ship had died, Henry had died, and now they were going to perish. No one would ever know why. Another tentacle smashed through the side wall of the ship, sending splinters of wood splashing into the water below. She gave him one last shake.

He groaned and rolled onto his side. Relief flooded through her. Though Kal's leg bent oddly, he stood with her help.

They opened and pushed the second tank. With the near constant light, Wynn could see a dangerously large hole in the larboard side of the ship. Any longer and they could be swept out of the ship and directly into the monster's mouth. Wynn shivered at the thought and pushed harder. She hardly noticed the noise anymore or the pain from it. She funneled it into her determination to push the tank out.

With one last shove, the tank fell. Paraffin poured out and over the monster's exposed flesh. Wynn pulled the striker out of her pocket. She lit the strip of cloth and dropped it. It fell agonizingly slow and almost flickered out. Then, as if the gates of hell opened before her, a wall of flame shot up, engulfing the monster and the edge of the ship. Wynn turned her face away in time, but the heat from the blast was still enough to burn her skin.

The monster shrieked and flailed, water and wood flying everywhere. Then it vanished out to deeper water.

Kal staggered to her and clasped her arm. They looked at each other for a moment, bloodied, beaten, but alive. Kal's leg was swollen and angled wrong and Wynn's ears felt as if she had lit them on fire. A cold blanket of silence wrapped itself around them while small fires danced on the edge of the wood, providing little light. Wynn had no idea how they were getting back to shore, all the lifeboats were destroyed, but they had to. The explosion only frightened the monster, so it would return, and when it did, Wynn knew the fate that would meet them.

About Thomas Roggenbuck

Thomas Roggenbuck graduated from Lawrence Tech University with a degree in Audio Engineering. He currently lives and works on his family's dairy farm, enjoying reading and writing science fiction and fantasy in his spare time. You can find him on Twitter @SrThomasThunder.

Coburn

The more she struggled, the more trapped she felt, her limbs tangling with the cords that enshrouded her body. She reached for her companion, his body hot and slick with sweat and pressed against hers, but the cords got in the way. His own struggling separated them more than it brought them together.

Mere yards away, faces leered. Chief among them was one horrid face, his hard eyes conveying not mirth, but disappointment and contempt. Her heart sank, bile rose in her mouth, and she stopped struggling.

Aylen tried to follow Lord Furies's steward closely. The trim man had long legs and set a brisk pace, but the halls through which they passed were distracting in their opulence, more so than the house where Aylen had grown up. It was difficult not to gape.

First, there was the Great Clock that towered above the entryway, easily six stories tall. The front hall was, in fact, the base of the clock, and Aylen could make out the massive gears turning with exact precision high overhead. Clocks were a great favorite in the house, as every hall and room passed had one, and no two were alike.

Then there were the elevated tracks, only a foot or so wide, that ran along the walls and occasionally crisscrossed overhead. They would be just within Aylen's reach if he lifted his hand, which he almost did. Face flushed, he managed to refrain from following through. Now and again, little train cars would come trundling along the tracks and disappear into tunnels built into the walls. He wanted to ask the steward about them, but didn't want to appear ignorant.

Aylen could almost pinch himself to ensure that he was not, in fact, dreaming. To serve in the house of Aldebrand, Lord Furies, the King's favorite inventor, was beyond the young man's wildest dreams. He would start at the very bottom, probably shoveling coal, but he was eager to do any task, however minute, that was required of him. And one day (he dared hope), he would assist Lord Furies directly and learn the man's secrets.

Finally, the steward stopped before two grand oak doors. Aylen smiled at the shapes of gears and seashells carved into the wood. Fitting for an inventor whose estate was by the sea.

Though the steward had not knocked, a voice came from beyond the door. "Enter."

The door on the right popped open of its own accord, no doubt from some mechanism hidden in its frame. The steward pushed it all the way in and held it open for Aylen to proceed as bidden. Aylen tried to tamp down his excitement, but it was difficult after all the wonders he had seen, including the trick with the door.

A gaunt, bearded man with wild, iron-gray hair and pale, mottled skin hunched behind a heavy oak desk. He was garbed simply in brown suede pants and a white shirt, sleeves rolled up to his elbows. His left eye held a loupe as he peered at a small contraption in his hand into which he was fitting tiny gears. Aylen held his breath, afraid to make the slightest sound lest he disturb the delicate process.

The steward evidently held no compunction as he announced, "Aylen, the new apprentice from the Capital."

"Yes, yes," muttered the lord. "Young man, sit there. Steward, you may go."

By "there," Aylen assumed he meant the chair before the desk, and he perched anxiously on its edge.

Some minutes passed before Lord Furies put aside the contraption on his desk, set down his tool, and let the loupe drop into his hand before placing it on the desk. He sat back in his chair and regarded Aylen with soft brown eyes that had heavy wrinkles stemming from their corners.

"So." His voice was deep and on the raspy side. "Your name is Aylen."

"Yes, Lord Furies."

Lord Furies waved a hand. "Please, none of this 'Lord Furies' business. Call me Master Aldebrand. I have held that title longer than I have 'Lord Furies.'"

"Yes, Master Aldebrand," Aylen corrected.

Aldebrand nodded. "Better. I understand you come to us from Lord Martius. Not a son, though, but a ward. Is that correct?"

"Yes, Master Aldebrand."

Aldebrand smiled a little and shook his head softly. "Please, a simple 'yes' or 'yes, sir' will do. And relax, young man, I am not going to hurt you. You are here to learn, and I am pleased to teach you."

Aylen's heart fluttered. "Yes, sir."

Aldebrand stood. "Come, walk with me. I will show you the forge, and we will talk along the way."

Aylen nearly knocked over his chair as he got to his feet, which Aldebrand was kind enough to overlook. "Yes, sir. Thank you, sir."

Aldebrand softly shook his head again. "I am told you were a foundling?"

"Yes. Lady Martius found me when I was a baby and took me in."

"How very kind of her."

"I think so."

Aldebrand gave him a small smile, and Aylen thought he saw a twinkle in the elder man's eye. "I have always been fond of Lord and Lady Martius."

"Lord Martius is a great admirer of your work."

Aldebrand nodded. "Yes, I know. How very good of him."

They made idle chit chat for much of their walk to the forge located some distance behind the large house. Aldebrand asked Aylen about his life with Lord and Lady Martius (it was a good one), what sparked the interest in what the Master called gadgetry (he'd always enjoyed taking things apart to see how they worked), and so on. He pointed out sites along the way, as well. There was the large estate kitchen, the dining hall and dormitory for the apprentices, the beach where they liked to cool down after a hot shift in the forge, the workshop, and the gardens which were, Aldebrand confided, "the purview of Lady Furies."

Aylen had heard about Lady Furies while he was in the Capital. She was said to be seductively beautiful and much younger than her husband. Many at court had fought for her hand after her coming out, and her father had been pressured by the crown to marry her off quickly to put an end to it. At the King's suggestion, Lord Furies had made an offer of marriage. Of course, this was a boon to her and her family, and she had accepted.

While he harbored no hope of ever meeting her, Aylen was admittedly curious about the wife of his idol, who couldn't be too much older than himself. He wondered if she ever came near the forge.

They could smell the forge well before approaching the massive building. Aylen smiled at the taste of coal dust and metal on the back of his tongue. So lost in his own pleasant thoughts was he that he almost missed Aldebrand stopping dead in the path ahead of them. Aylen peered at his Master's face, which wore a slight scowl. Following his gaze, Aylen's eyes landed on a slight figure dressed in workman's pants and shirt, but no apron.

"Sweet," Aldebrand grumbled. "What brings you here?"

"Idle curiosity," answered Sweet, raising her hands in a shrug. She had green eyes and straight, black hair cut to her pointed chin. Her olive skin was scrubbed clean, as were her clothes, Aylen noted, making her seem very out of place. Forges were filthy.

"Curiosity?" Aldebrand's eyebrows lifted. "What here could raise that, I wonder?"

Sweet's gaze shifted to Aylen.

"Ah, I see. Well, satisfy yourself later. We have business."

Aldebrand stepped past Sweet, who fell into step beside Aylen.

"I'm Sweet. What's your name?"

The apprentice cast a nervous look at his master's back, then murmured, "Aylen."

"Aylen," she repeated slowly, as if tasting the word. "That's a lovely name. I think you're rather lovely, as well."

Aldebrand threw a hard look over his shoulder. Sweet ducked her head and danced to the side.

"I guess I'll see you later, Aylen," she said. "Enjoy the forge."

Eden gazed out from her private balcony. From up here, she could see across her garden, over the wall, and out to the sea beyond. There were no ships on the water, but two dirigibles puttered in opposite directions. One looked to be an airbus, probably carrying excited tourists to one thrilling adventure or another. Eden tried not to think about it.

Two of her three companions lounged beneath the old pomegranate tree. Light-skinned Asphodel lay in the shade, her back propped against a cushion. She was braiding her extravagantly long honey-blond hair, twice as dark as Eden's, into a thick rope. Her doe-like eyes were fixed on her lover, Rosalind, whose dark brown skin glistened ever so slightly with perspiration in the heat of the summer sun. Tendrils of the red silk scarf that Rosalind used to tie her cloud of black curls back from her face waved gently in the slight breeze. She played her flute as much for Asphodel's enjoyment as Eden's, who had reluctantly been drawn from the darkness of her bedchamber to listen.

The day was half over, and this was Eden's first sight of it. She had woken late with no energy to go down to the dining room. She'd rung for food to be brought to her rooms where Asphodel, Rosalind, and Sweet had gathered around and shared breakfast with her. Eden had listened quietly while the other women chatted, offering small smiles when addressed. Then, one by one, the three had departed, first Sweet, then Asphodel, then Rosalind.

First, Eden tried reading a book of poetry, but her mind couldn't focus. Then, she started writing a letter to her mother, but found she had little to say. It was just one of those days, she supposed, and so she reclined on the settee, hands folded in her lap until the sweet sounds of the flute had found their way to her.

She was thinking that she should probably go down and join her friends when Sweet breezed into the room, exclaiming, "You're still here!" Whether this pleased or dismayed her was difficult to tell from her tone.

"Yes." Eden smiled weakly. "And where have you been?"

"Out. Exploring. You know, the usual." She shrugged, then her face split into a bright grin. "Except not all usual. Shall we go down into the garden?"

Eden could tell Sweet was bursting to share a story, and she wanted all four of them together before she told it. Sweet relished an audience.

When they entered the garden, Rosalind stopped playing. "I was wondering when you would join us," she said, tucking her flute into the bag that hung from her waistband.

Asphodel rose and opened up a sunshade for Eden to sit beneath (for her skin was milky white and burned easily in this land so far from where she'd been born). Rosalind arranged cushions on the ground for them all to recline against. Sweet preferred to kneel, her back straight and tall, practically vibrating with excitement.

"All right," Eden said once she was settled, Asphodel on one side of her, Rosalind on the other. "What do you have to say?"

Sweet inclined her head, then grinned. "There's a new apprentice! Just arrived today."

Rosalind snorted. "Is that all?"

Sweet's enthusiasm wilted only slightly. "Not all. He's from the Capital. A ward of Lord and Lady Martius, but not a son. Lady Martius found him as a baby while out walking. The poor thing! All alone, just imagine! And she was so taken by the child that she took him home with her and raised him with the love of a mother and all the privileges of a lord." Sweet finished her embellished tale with a sigh.

"A foundling taken in by the Lord and Lady?" asked Asphodel. She exchanged a glance with sedate Rosalind. "I suppose that is a little romantic. And now he's here as an apprentice to Lord Furies?"

"That is what I said." Sweet relaxed in the grass now that her news was told.

"Well," said Rosalind. "That's hardly a privilege of a lord's son. If he really had the privilege of a lord's son, he'd be at court, not in a forge."

Sweet stuck her tongue out at her. Rosalind chuckled.

Eden spoke for the first time, and they all looked at her. "What is his name?"

"Aylen."

She smiled softly. "That's lovely."

"That's exactly what I said!" Sweet waggled her eyebrows at her friends. "He's not bad to look at either. Thick black hair, skin like buffed leather."

Asphodel chuckled and Rosalind rolled her eyes, but Eden looked pensive. "Young?" she asked.

Sweet nodded. "Young and strong. Like a bull."

"And he's from the Capital?"

"Yes. And the Martius estate, of course."

Asphodel peered curiously at Eden. "Are you thinking you'd like to meet him?"

Eden gave a slight shrug. "He's someone new."

Asphodel and Rosalind shared a wary look. Eden ignored it.

Sweet offered, "I'm meeting him later. Lord Furies chased me away before. What do you want me to learn about him?"

Rosalind arched a brow. "If Lord Furies chased you away, how did you find out his foundling story?"

Sweet gave an innocent shrug. "Words travel on the wind."

"You're such a gossip," sighed Asphodel, shaking her head.

"I'm a communicator," Sweet corrected. "I keep us all informed."

After a tour of the forge, Aylen had been put right to work shoveling coal "to build up his muscles" his new supervisor had joked. By the time the whistle blew at the end of his shift, he was completely filthy. He followed the men to a room with long water basins where they all did a quick scrub of face and hands before pouring out the door and into the dining hall. Aylen was ravenous, and he was allowed to eat and drink as much as he liked. Master Aldebrand was generous.

"Who's going down to the beach?" a man to Aylen's right asked the table. "Nothing like a good swim to top off the day!"

"Or for cleaning out the ears," answered a man to his left, who emphasized his point by vigorously digging into his ear with a still coal-encrusted fingernail.

"I'll join you," said Aylen, happy to jump in and get to know his fellows, who seemed like a friendly lot.

When the men got to the beach, a familiar figure was perched on a rock awaiting their arrival.

"Sweet!" several of the men cried.

"Have you come for a swim?" asked one, his voice insinuative.

She tossed her head. "You know I don't swim, you lugs."

"Came to watch then," said another, causing uproarious laughter.

Sweet gave an exaggerated wink that elicited more roars.

The men stripped off their clothes and rushed into the water. Aylen was shocked. Just who was this Sweet person who dressed like an apprentice, yet never did any work, and wasn't bothered by a small army of naked men frolicking around her? Nor, come to that, were they bothered by her. He supposed he could ignore her as well, though he felt compelled to turn his back while he removed his shirt.

"Aylen," Sweet called in a sing-song voice.

He looked over his shoulder at her, brows raised.

"Yes, you," she said. "I don't think there's another Aylen on the entire estate."

With his chest now bare, he could not bring himself to face her. "What can I do for you?"

Sweet hopped off the rock and approached, hands clasped behind her back. "Are you shy?"

"Shy? No...."

"Turn around then. It's weird talking to your back." He reluctantly obliged, though he folded his arms across his chest, and Sweet tapped a finger against her chin. "I think you are shy."

"And I think you're... Forward."

Her face split into a wide grin as she clapped her hands together. "I suppose I am. Did you enjoy the forge?"

She had a quick way of talking, jumping from sentence to sentence like a hummingbird flitting about a flower.

When Aylen didn't answer her, she cocked her head and asked, "Do you think you'll like it here?"

This, he was quick to answer. "Of course!"

"Why's that?"

"It's been my dream to serve as an apprentice to Lord Furies! I mean, Master Aldebrand."

Sweet nodded thoughtfully. "You have no ambition to surpass him?"

Aylen blinked. "I'm sorry?"

She waved a hand. "Never mind! No one ever answers that question."

He watched as she hopped lightly up onto another rock, then over to another, and another.

"I suppose you're here to go sea bathing," she said. "Better get to it."

"Ah, er, yes."

Aylen did not feel comfortable removing his pants with her right there, so he went into the sea half-dressed.

Hector, one of the men who'd shoveled coal with him earlier, swam over to join him. Jerking his chin at Sweet, he said, "See you've been noticed. That was quick."

"I'm sorry?"

"Sweet. She's one of Lady Furies's entourage. Gets into everybody's business."

"Lady Furies?"

"No, Sweet! Lady Furies keeps to herself mostly these days."

A man Aylen didn't recognize drifted over to join the conversation. "Can't hardly blame her," he said cryptically. "Considering what happened."

Aylen took the bait. "What happened?"

"It's sad, really." Hector shook his head.

"What is?" Aylen persisted. He wasn't generally one for gossip, but clearly these men were going somewhere with this.

"Couple years ago," said Hector, "there was a young prince visiting the Lord and Lady. He romanced Lady Furies right under Master Aldebrand's nose!"

"The cheek!" cried the other man.

"Aye," agreed Hector. "Our Lady is young, you know, and I suppose she was inexperienced with men. That blasted prince seduced Lady Furies! And they were caught. Together." Hector gave Aylen a suggestive nudge.

Aylen raised his brows in surprise. "Together? Surely not… Um…"

The other man laughed while Hector elaborated. "Oh, aye, *together*. They met up one night during a party; sneaked off to the adjoining garden. And that's where the trap was sprung."

"Trap?" Aylen queried.

"Aye, trap. A real, literal trap of Master Aldebrand's own making, net and all."

The other man continued, "He wanted to catch them together, you see, for everyone to witness. To humiliate them. Everyone in attendance came out to laugh at the ensnared lovers."

Aylen was well and truly shocked. It was one thing to uncover your wife's infidelity, and quite another to expose it to the world. He couldn't help but ask, "What happened next?"

Hector answered. "They were let loose. The prince was sent away, of course, off to seduce another man's wife no doubt. Lady Furies ran off to her rooms and hid for weeks with only her entourage for company. Ladies always have it harder than the men, don't they?"

The other man seemed to have grown bored now that the story was told and swam away. Hector treaded water, gazing up at the darkening sky.

"Is that really true?" asked Aylen. He found it difficult to believe an important lord like his new master would stoop to such a mean trick.

"It is, I'm afraid," replied Hector. "As I said, Lady Furies keeps much to herself, though you might see her and her entourage out walking sometimes, always at a distance. There aren't many parties held at the estate anymore either."

"What about Master Aldebrand?"

"He still dotes on her. Makes her all kinds of jewelry and things. Maybe he means to make amends for the way he treated her. They were always an odd couple, though. I suppose that's the age difference. He's easily old enough to be her father."

Aylen thought over this story, walking slowly as they all headed to the dormitory that night. He imagined the lovers trapped like fish in a net, the other nobles standing around tittering. They must have seen her as a foolish girl, first married off at the King's insistence to avoid scandals, then to be caught in the middle of one. Knowing how the nobility liked to gossip, Aylen felt sorry for her. Had she loved the prince? Had he loved her? Or had loneliness brought them together?

Aylen well understood loneliness. He had been raised in the house of a lord. Lady Martius had adored him, but he was not the son of a Lord. Thus he was party to the noble life of his benefactors, but not truly part of it.

Time passed quickly for Aylen, and by the end of his first week, he had become privy to the strange ways of the Furies estate. The little trains he had seen when he first arrived were used for transporting small goods and communications. There were tracks all over the house and grounds, and they were especially useful in communicating between the house and the forge.

The clocks all over the estate kept precise time with each other. Aylen hadn't the foggiest notion how Aldebrand was able to keep them all in sync, but that was why he was the apprentice and Aldebrand the Master. Time was very important to Aldebrand, it turned out. Inefficiency was not tolerated, should it ever manage to crop up, which was unlikely. From day one, Aylen was cautioned not to let himself run behind, or *he* would be left behind like a broken cog on the workshop floor. Aylen didn't mind; he enjoyed being a part of something bigger than himself.

He did not, however, make the friends he had hoped for. But he was still new. There was still time, he told himself. He just needed to find his place. That was sure to help.

At the request of her husband, Eden went down to the dining room for dinner. She was seated just as the great clock tower struck the hour, and a flurry of footmen, led by the butler, brought in the first course. Aldebrand began eating as soon as he was served, his cutlery clicking with the precision of a clock. Eden did her best to keep up.

After a few moments, Aldebrand said, "You look lovely, my dear. How has your day been?"

Eden raised a brow. So, he was in a chatty mood, no pressing deadlines weighing on his mind. "Dull," she answered.

"Dull? How could that possibly be? Have you already run out of toys?"

Toys, Eden thought with a sigh, as if she were a child. That was what he thought of her, she supposed. He made her toys—music boxes, wind-up dolls that danced, little boats that propelled themselves through the water, and dozens of other trinkets—all of which had their limited amusements.

Sometimes when they were first wed, he'd crafted intricate jewelry that had appropriately dazzled her. Now, though the pieces were still astonishing and perfectly showed off the famed skill of Master Aldebrand, Eden had grown tired of them. Her jewelry collection surpassed the Queen's, Eden well knew, which fed her vanity. Yet with no more house guests, no more parties, no more trips to the Capital, for whom would she wear such treasures? Asphodel, Rosalind, and Sweet had seen them all a hundred times, even worn them.

"Perhaps," said Eden, "I need another kind of diversion. Of the social variety?" She asked this without much hope, but she refused to acquiesce to her husband's preference for a solitary life.

Aldebrand stared down at his plate as he chewed his food. He was pretending to ignore her, she thought, pursing her lips. Eden stabbed at her plate with her fork and dragged the tines until they screeched. Aldebrand continued to chew methodically.

As Hector predicted, Aylen did see Lady Furies and her entourage out walking. There were four women all together. He recognized Sweet in her strange garb, but any one of the others could have been Lady Furies. They were all speckless and elegant; even Sweet had a fluid grace.

There were female apprentices and crafters, Aylen had worked with a few of them, but they were few and mostly kept together outside of the forge and workrooms. He liked his fellow workers, men and women, yet they were worlds apart from the nobility in dress and manner.

Sometimes, when talking with them outside of their jobs, Aylen felt he couldn't relate. He hadn't been raised by hard-working parents. While not idle, Lord and Lady Martius had no professions. Aylen had wanted for nothing, had everything handed to him, even his position at the forge, though he didn't like to acknowledge it. Despite all of this, Aylen was still not a noble. He was a foundling. Nothing could change that.

One day, when Aylen was taking a solitary promenade to clear his lungs and stretch his legs, Sweet appeared as suddenly as if she'd flown down from the sky.

"We meet again!" He jumped when she spoke, and she giggled. "Sorry. I saw you walking, and I thought I would join you. That is, if it's all right with you, of course."

Somehow, Aylen felt he had no choice. Not that she was unwelcome company. He still didn't know what to make of her or why she'd singled him out.

"It's all right," he said.

There must have been something in his voice, because she answered, "You don't trust me."

"I don't know you."

"That is true. Let's become friends, then!" Sweet looped her arm through his, and he stumbled. He apologized and adjusted his stride. "We should walk in one of the gardens," Sweet went on heedlessly. "Have you been? I think they're lovely. Do you like flowers?"

Aylen had to take a moment to form a coherent response. "I haven't. They do look very nice from what I have seen. From when Master Aldebrand pointed them out to me, I mean."

"And do you like flowers?" she asked again.

Aylen blinked. "Yes. I suppose I do. Lady Martius always had cut flowers in the house."

"Ah!" Sweet placed the back of her free hand against her forehead. "Cut flowers! Such a tragedy. I will never understand why people insist on cutting flowers and keeping them trapped in vases only to allow them to whither and die. Is it for their own amusement, do you think? Do they even realize?"

Furrowing his brow, Aylen did his best to answer. "No. I think people like to look at them. They're very pretty. And they really brighten up a house when it's cold or gloomy outside."

Sweet arched a brow. "Aha, so the flowers are for decoration. How predictable."

Aylen had quite lost her meaning, and neither of them said another word as Sweet steered them toward the south wing of the house, which faced the sea. This was not, he soon realized, the way to the garden he was expecting, the large one he could see from the forge.

"Where are we going?" he asked.

"To the garden!" she answered. "You've forgotten already?"

His face warmed. Of course, she had said there was more than one.

They soon arrived at a stone wall that stood a few heads taller than Aylen and was attached to the house, like a natural extension of the ground floor, only with no roof. The top limbs of some trees waved as they approached, dancing in the breeze. Sweet turned when they reached the wall, and they circled around the outside, entering the house through a door on the opposite side, which made Aylen nervous.

They continued down a hall, through another door, down another hall, then through another door that Sweet unlocked with a key. She tugged on Aylen's arm when he hesitated to follow her through.

"Come on!"

"Where are we?"

"Not important. It's how we access the garden."

The foyer they entered was round and on the small side compared to the rest of the house. A stairway circled the outside, and another door stood opposite the one through which they had entered. This is where Sweet led him next, and she held the door open, insisting he go first. It led back outside, into the walled garden. Why had she brought him here?

"Sweet, is that you?" someone called.

"It's me!" Sweet hollered back. "And with a friend!"

She took Aylen's hand and pulled him behind her as she hurried toward the source of the voice. More voices joined it, all feminine.

"Oh! A friend!" said a woman with tan skin and blond hair plaited into two long braids down her back.

"Indeed." This speaker had dark brown skin and hair and observed Aylen with a more critical eye.

The third woman, pale, with vanilla blond hair twisted on the top of her head, said nothing. Sweet brought Aylen before the trio, clearly intending to present him to them.

"What is your name?" she finally asked. Her voice was polished with an edge of command.

"Aylen," he answered.

The woman inclined her head slightly, acknowledging him. "I am pleased to meet you."

"You should make him bow," the first woman said.

Aylen looked at her in surprise. The second woman swatted playfully at the first and chided, "Asphodel."

"This," said Sweet to Aylen, using her hand to indicate the third woman, "is Lady Furies."

"Oh!" Aylen did bow then, though Sweet quickly pulled him upright again. This seemed to amuse Lady Furies, who smiled ever so softly.

"It's quite all right," she said. "We do not stand on ceremony here."

A horrifying thought dawned on Aylen. "Is this your private garden?"

She inclined her head again. "It is. Welcome."

Aylen didn't know what to say. He wanted to know why Sweet had brought him here, but it seemed gauche to make such a demand in front of Lady Furies.

"Aren't you going to say that you're pleased to meet her?" demanded the one called Asphodel.

Aylen opened and closed his mouth a few times before stammering out that it was, of course, a pleasure to meet her. Sweet slapped him on the shoulder to shut him up.

"Don't mind Asphodel. She's a tease."

The remaining unnamed woman stepped forward and gave a slight curtsy. "My name is Rosalind. Sweet has told us quite a bit about you, Aylen."

Aylen looked at Sweet in surprise. "But she doesn't know anything about me!"

Lady Furies's soft pink lips broadened into just shy of a real smile. "I think you will find that our Sweet knows a great many things about a great many things. Come, sit by me."

Asphodel and Rosalind moved to make room for him, and Sweet plunked down opposite. Seeing no other option, Aylen sat and tried to relax.

Lady Furies reached beside her and pulled out a dish of fruit. "Would you like some, Aylen?" When he tried to refuse, she insisted and he relented, taking a dried fig. "Do you like figs?" she asked.

"Yes. Lady Martius had them grown in the greenhouse."

"I don't believe we know Lady Martius, do we, Asphodel?"

"No, my lady."

Lady Furies returned her gaze to Aylen. "Tell me about Lord and Lady Martius."

Naturally, Aylen obliged her. Lady Furies asked question after question about where Aylen had grown up at the Martius estate, what took him to the Capital, how he found life there. She would have kept on questioning him if Sweet hadn't eventually stood and announced that it was probably past time that she should be returning Aylen to the forge. Aylen bolted up. He was a complete idiot! How could he have let this distract him? The ladies smiled at him, including Lady Furies. Aylen gulped. She was arrestingly beautiful, fine wisps of blond hair caressing her soft cheeks.

Sweet tugged at his arm. "Come on, let's go! I'll take you all the way to the forge. They can't do anything about you being late if I'm with you."

The blood drained from Aylen's face. "Late?"

Aylen's supervisor for that day was clearly not pleased when Sweet delivered him nearly an hour after he'd left to the forge. She had insisted on accompanying him all the way, "Or you'll be in real trouble." And, indeed, while the supervisor was stone-faced and tight-shouldered, he said nothing about the tardiness, only sent Aylen to shovel coal. Sweet gave him a wink before they parted, as if to say, "I told you."

While he worked, Aylen wondered about this light chastisement. Did Sweet, as one of Lady Furies's companions, have free reign? She certainly behaved as though she did. Was it common for her to steal people from the forge for Lady Furies's amusement? That would explain why she—he—they had gotten away with it.

Hector plunked down by Aylen at dinner with the words, "So you're back at coal shoveling? Haven't you been here too long for that?"

Aylen cleared his throat, which was coated in dust in addition to embarrassment. "I'm still new. And I'll take any task. I'm here to learn."

Hector belted out a laugh. "Only thing you learn from shoveling coal is to avoid doing the thing that got you on shoveling coal. So what was it? Something delicious, I hope."

Aylen took a long swallow of water, then mumbled into his cup. "Sweet wanted to show me the gardens."

"Eh? Sweet?" Hector looked disappointed. "Well, that is its own kind of trouble. Hard to say no to her, seeing as she's part of the entourage. Hard to know when she's acting for herself and when she's doing Lady Furies's bidding, know what I mean?"

Aylen did not know what he meant. He did wonder, though, if Sweet might have sought him out at Lady Furies's request. Which seemed odd.

The ladies had said Sweet had told them about him. Aylen thought back to the questions that Lady Furies had asked him, all about himself, yes, but also the places he had lived. She must have been curious, though she had once lived in the Capital herself, and must still have friends there to keep her up to date. And she must visit with her husband, musn't she?

He wondered about her and her entourage, as everyone called them, sitting together but apart from everyone at the far end of such a great house in a walled garden. He had wondered if Lady Furies was lonely. Perhaps this was his answer.

Eden was alone in the shade of the pomegranate tree while Asphodel and Rosalind went to refill the fruit tray and wine pitcher. The exchange with Aylen replayed in her mind. Perhaps she was being melodramatic when she asked herself when the last time was they had entertained someone new in their garden.

Eden lay back on a pillow, stretching her legs and arms out in the grass. Once Aldebrand had visited her regularly, but he was too busy with his "special projects" these days to bother. No, that wasn't entirely right. His visits had stopped after The Incident, as it had since been delicately termed by her companions.

Hurting Aldebrand had not been Eden's intention. Their marriage had been coerced on both her and Aldebrand's sides, but the elder man was not unkind to her. He had done everything he could think of to make her comfortable in her new home, his home. She was given governance of the gardens, the running of the household, the obligatory parties and entertainments that a lord was expected to offer his fellow lords. She was Lady Furies and allowed, nay, expected to reign as such.

But Eden didn't want to be Lady Furies, had never wanted it. She did her best, but her heart just wasn't in it. It was silly, of course, to harbor any hopes of a rescue. She was married! End of story. And then he came.

Ignacio, with his warm brown skin and dark eyes that burned like coals, had overwhelmed her. Passion went into everything he did, from sport on the field to sport in bed. Eden had not intended to let her interactions with him go beyond innocent flirting, had not dreamed of taking him into her bed. But it happened—gloriously—and she would never regret it. Ignacio fulfilled needs she hadn't even known she'd had, and the brief weeks she'd spent with him were spent in paradise.

They had grown too bold in their trysts, so naturally they'd been found out. It was a big house, but eyes still saw and tongues wagged. Eden knew they never should have met in the garden, yet she had felt invulnerable. Stupid. More than her heart had been shattered in that net, her pride was mortally wounded. If Aldebrand had not forgiven Eden for her indiscretion, she equally had not forgiven him.

Aldebrand was not entirely to blame for her misery, even though he punished her daily by depriving her of the life she had once known, treating her like a mere model for his creations. No, more than Aldebrand, Ignacio had betrayed Eden. When discovered and challenged by Lord Furies, Ignacio had run. No apologies. No farewells. By dawn the next day, her prince had vanished. Her friends trickled away, giggling behind their hands, never to return.

As Eden was reliving that moment, the wound ever-fresh in her heart, Sweet reappeared. Eden reached out a hand, and Sweet lay on the ground next to her, curled against her side, head resting on Eden's shoulder.

"Wasn't he lovely?" asked Sweet.

"He was," Eden agreed. "Thank you for bringing him."

"He isn't a prince, but he has courtly manners, and he knows our kind of people."

Eden let out a harsh laugh. "Our kind?"

Sweet stroked her face softly. "You know. The people in our circles. The nobility."

"I know, Sweet, but I am not sure we belong among them, not anymore." She sighed.

Sweet propped herself up on her elbow and looked down at her mistress.

"I know Lord Furies doesn't have any interest, but must the parties really stop? You are still Lady Furies."

"And he is Lord."

Sweet pushed herself to a sitting position. "I'll talk to him." Her tone was decisive and made Eden laugh. "You don't think he'll listen to me? I can make him listen. Who can say no to me?"

Eden patted her hand, smiling indulgently. "Yes, talk to him for me. In the meantime…."

"In the meantime, we shall entertain our company in the garden."

Eden grinned.

Sweet chose her moments well. She didn't want to draw too much attention to Aylen, so she occasionally targeted other men and women of the estate and forge in hopes of throwing off the scent. Though none were invited to her lady's private garden, she did occasionally bring them to enjoy a short walk or sit with the entourage while they were out and about the grounds or at the beach.

They were all adept at excusing themselves at the appropriate moments to return to their work without their absences being disruptive. It was a pity Aylen was not, but he was still green. Or perhaps, Sweet secretly hoped, he was too taken by Eden to care. For Sweet was a true romantic deep down, and she hated to see her lady so despondent.

When she saw Aylen leave the dining hall alone one night, she took the opportunity to sidle up to him. It had been over a week since his visit, and she wanted to know what he thought of the excursion.

"I hope you didn't get into too much trouble." She knew he hadn't, but she wanted him to know that she cared.

Aylen jumped. "Sorry, I didn't hear you approach."

Sweet grinned. "People tell me I'm like a cat. Slinking along with ease, without a whisper."

He nodded, answering wryly, "Yes, I understand that comparison. What can I do for you tonight?"

"I thought you might enjoy another excursion." He only raised a brow, so she continued. "You know there are flowers that bloom best as the light dies. Come, I'll show you."

She couldn't read his expression, and her heart sank as she thought he might say no. Then Aylen answered, "I'd like that very much."

Her grin grew. "Lovely!"

She looped her arm through his and led him, skipping, back through the house and into Lady Furies's private garden. She hadn't lied when she spoke of the night-blooming flowers in the garden. There were several lilies, moon flowers, and more planted. Aylen seemed to understand, though, that the flowers were not the real reason he was there.

Sweet silently clapped her hands together as if in prayer when Aylen left her side and approached Eden, who stood admiring the evening primroses. Asphodel and Rosalind moved to flank Sweet.

"So, he's back," said Rosalind.

"You knew she would bring him again," answered Asphodel. "We all did." She sighed and shook her head.

Sweet looked at Asphodel in surprise. "You disapprove?"

"It isn't that, Sweet dear." Asphodel pushed a lock of Sweet's hair behind her ear.

Rosalind picked up her lover's trail. "We worry, that's all. What would happen if they're seen together?"

Sweet sniffed. "Well, there certainly won't be another net, if that's what you're implying. Everyone's learned *that* lesson. But, my dears, we can't go on this way."

"What do you intend to do about it?" asked Rosalind.

"I'm going to talk to Lord Furies."

Her friends gasped. "No!" cried Asphodel as Rosalind was saying, "You can't!"

"I don't see why not. He can't be happy with the way things are."

"He's happy with his workshop," answered Rosalind.

"And the army who works for him," added Asphodel. "He isn't lonely."

Sweet allowed a shrug. "Even so. You watch."

"Oh," said Asphodel. "We're watching."

Rosalind nodded. "Count on it."

When he left her, Aylen found himself haunted by Lady Furies—no, Eden. She had asked him to call her Eden. It was difficult to think of his boss's wife by her given name, so he tried to put her in the same light as the ladies he had met while living under the roof of Lord Martius. There were several ladies with whom Aylen was on a given name basis. Either they had grown up together or been introduced in the proper circles and become, for lack of a better word, friends. Eden had told him she wanted them to be friends, though they had only met twice. Very much wanting to be her friend, Aylen had agreed, and not because he thought it might further his career. In fact, he feared quite the opposite.

He could not ignore her, though. And he liked that he could talk freely with her about the feasts and festivals of the Capital without worrying if he sounded haughty. Eden was the kind of woman Aylen was accustomed to socializing with, that he had been raised by Lord and (more so) Lady Martius to please. And he did wish to please her. To tease out a smile now and again was a triumph.

As he walked back to the dormitory that night, Aylen wondered if he might make a gift for her. But what gift could he create that rivaled anything her famous husband had already given her? He would have to think about it.

After more teasing from Asphodel and Rosalind, Sweet did go see Lord Furies. It wasn't often that Sweet ventured into his labyrinthine part of the house. She enjoyed the little trains that rolled along above her by the ceilings, like good dogs sent out on a mission by their minders. She followed one for a time until it disappeared into a wall above a locked door. It was probably a miracle that she was able to find Lord Furies's study door at all, but find it she did, and she gave a good loud knock.

"It's me!" she called, gazing into the little glass lens that she knew allowed Lord Furies to see whoever knocked at his door. She had no idea how it worked, but she had seen the screen behind his desk that provided a black and white moving picture of the room's threshold, and this glass was part of what made that picture.

The large door opened, and she slipped inside. Lord Furies was behind his desk, pawing through a small pile of gears.

"My lord," she began, but he cut her off with a gesture.

"No time for pleasantries. What is it you want?"

Sweet reset her composure and squared her shoulders. "I am here for the benefit of my lady."

Aldebrand waved his hand impatiently.

"I request a party."

He looked up at her, one bushy brow raised.

"Yes, I said a party. For my lady to preside over. For amusement."

"Amusement." He sounded like the word left a bad taste in his mouth. "Why?"

Swallowing her impatience, Sweet forced a smile. "To alleviate boredom. Ease the ennui. Soothe the malaise."

Aldebrand gave her a withering stare. "Malaise? Is my lady ill?"

"As good as, my lord."

"Hmph!" He returned to his work. But as he hadn't dismissed her, Sweet stood her ground. After a moment, he raised his head again. "What is it?"

"You have not answered me, my lord."

Aldebrand heaved a sigh as he sat heavily back in his chair. "You want a party. The King wants a submersible. To which do you think I will give my priorities?"

"But you need pay no attention to us!" Sweet was quick to answer. "It will be no different than usual…."

She shut up when she saw she had upset him. Aldebrand rose to his feet, pulling himself up to his full height, more than a head above Sweet.

"Enough of this nonsense."

Sweet backed a half-step away. "It isn't nonsense. Which you'll see, mark my words. My lord."

Spinning on her heels, Sweet left the room.

Aylen became a regular fixture of the garden, sometimes sharing lunch with Eden, a meal she was never summoned for by her husband. She told him about the flowers, why she had chosen them, under which circumstances they grew best. In turn, he shared with her what he remembered of the flowers Lady Martius had grown in her greenhouse.

"I should like to see them," Eden said with a sigh more than once.

"When next you visit the Capitol, I'd be happy to write you a letter of introduction," Aylen offered once, but the sorrow in Eden's gaze stopped him from making it again.

Since Aylen was an apprentice, Eden also showed him the clockwork gifts Aldebrand had made for her over the years. The delight they brought him helped her remember when they had been new and wonderful to her, as well. Aldebrand's first gift had been a tiny carousel with miniature painted horses that went up and down, around and around as the music chimed, and she had been awed by it. No other suitor had brought her such a unique gift, let alone one he had crafted himself.

"I would love to take this apart and see how it was assembled," said Aylen about the wind-up dancing doll.

"You are welcome to," answered Eden.

Aylen looked aghast. "I could never!"

Eden shrugged her thin shoulders. She was so thin these days, and more than a little tired, even with her new friend. "I do not believe Master

Aldebrand would notice. He never comes here." Eden saw the pained look this brought to Aylen's eyes. She hadn't been seeking pity, only stating a fact.

"Still," he said, setting down the doll to watch it dance again.

Eden idly played with her earring as she, too, watched the toy. She had begun to wear jewelry again, and her companions were styling her hair into more intricate twists and braids.

"Did Master Aldebrand make those?" Aylen asked, his eyes on the earring twisted between Eden's thumb and forefinger.

"Yes. Did you know he was a jeweler once upon a time?"

Aylen nodded. Of course he knew, she thought. Her husband's talents were world renowned.

"I should get back to the forge," Aylen finally said and rose to leave.

Eden impulsively took his hand to stop him, simultaneously realizing her foolishness and deciding not to let go. "Will you return this evening?"

"If you wish me to, I can."

"I do wish you to. Please. We can watch the sunset perhaps."

"I would love to."

Aylen brought her hand to his lips and kissed it.

An hour later, a butler rang at the door to Eden's apartment. Rosalind answered and accepted the proffered note. Asphodel saw it in her hand and asked, "From Lord Furies?"

"Looks like it."

"Another invitation to dinner no doubt."

Rosalind's lips tightened. "No doubt."

They went together to deliver the note to their lady, who sat beneath the pomegranate tree. Eden merely glanced at the contents before passing it back.

"No," she answered.

Her companions shared a concerned look. "No?" Rosalind asked.

"No," Eden repeated.

Asphodel ventured, "My lady…."

Eden raised her brows at her. "I said no. Not tonight. I have other plans. Rosalind, will you play for me? I am in the mood for music."

Rosalind forced a smile and pulled out her flute. "Of course."

Asphodel twisted her hands in her skirt and bit her lip, then she said, "I'll inform my lord."

Eden thanked her.

"What a lovely idea, my lady!" Sweet beamed at Eden and began to light the candles that the two of them had sprinkled around the garden.

"Thank you," answered Eden.

Was it her imagination, or did Sweet detect delight in her mistress's voice? When Eden had come to her and told her of the invitation she had given to Aylen to join her that evening to watch the sunset, Sweet had been overjoyed and more than willing to help set the proper mood.

While Asphodel and Rosalind were off together, Eden and Sweet had set out cushions and blankets on the balcony that overlooked the garden to make it more comfortable. It was the only spot that overlooked the sea, so it was the natural place from which to watch the sunset. Sweet had also pilfered a jug of wine, bread, cheese, and dried fruit from the stores.

Eden cast a glance at the entrance to the garden. "He should be here any moment."

Sweet thought Eden looked nervous, and she smiled. "Should I make myself scarce?"

"No, no, I would prefer that you let him in."

Sweet nodded. "You go to the balcony then. I'll keep a lookout."

Eden agreed and went to arrange herself. Rosalind intercepted Sweet in the foyer.

"Do you really think this is a good idea?" she whispered.

Sweet opened her eyes wide. "Whatever do you mean?"

"Sweet, please."

From her tone, Sweet guessed that Rosalind was not sharing in the mood. Asphodel was probably in agreement, but was nowhere to be seen. "You worry too much."

"And you too little. Have you considered the consequences if this evening backfires?"

Sweet gave an exasperated sigh. "How ridiculous. She's happy, can't you see that?"

Rosalind was quiet a moment, then answered simply, "If you need us, we'll be in our room."

"Yes, yes." Sweet made shooing motions with her hands, which was met with a stern look. Rosalind departed, however, without another word.

When Aylen arrived, Sweet led him quickly to Eden on the balcony. When he had settled himself, Eden dismissed her, and she retreated from the room, perching on the railing of the staircase so she could see both the closed door to the apartment below and her mistress through the open door to Eden's private chambers.

Sweet couldn't hear what they spoke about, but the brilliant smile on Eden's face told her everything she needed to know. Her own heart felt light. Asphodel and Rosalind had each other; they didn't understand what it was to be alone. Or worse, to be discarded as Sweet felt Aldebrand had abandoned Eden.

The light slowly faded from the room as the sun slipped below the horizon. Eden and Aylen rose from the balcony. As they passed Sweet on the stairs, Eden said to her, "We're going to walk in the garden."

Sweet gave a short bow. "Of course."

She trailed after them, sticking to the shadows and out of the way. The candlelight, the moonlight, the starlight…. How romantic. Her heart fluttered when Eden took Aylen's hand and led him to the pomegranate tree. The pair talked, smiled, laughed, and Sweet was over the moon, clutching her hands to her chest. And then, the magical moment she had been dreaming of. Eden stared into Aylen's eyes, and there was no more need for words.

Aylen moved closer. He hesitated. He bent his head.

Eden bent hers to meet him.

Sweet's fingernails dug into her palms. Just a little more….

"What is going on here?"

The booming demand sent Sweet crashing back to earth. Shaking off the shock, she looked first to Eden, who stood with her fists clenched at her sides, chin in the air. Sweet then turned her eyes to the doorway that led into the garden from the foyer where the worst possible outcome for this romance stood. Sweet felt both terrified and enraged at the same time.

Aldebrand stood tall and very still, his shadowed eyes staring straight at Eden. Shaking, Sweet moved to place herself in between Eden and Aldebrand. The latter's eyes immediately flicked to her.

"Ah, Sweet." His voice was hard. "You told me to mark your words, and so I did. I came here to satisfy myself of my wife's welfare when she refused to join me for dinner. And so, I suppose, I have."

"And how do you find her?" Sweet asked.

"It was a party you wanted. It seems you have had it. I hope it was enjoyable."

Aldebrand turned to go, which lit a fire under Eden, who rushed across the yard. "Is that all you can say?"

He stopped and turned his face to her. "What should I say?"

Eden didn't seem to know how to answer. Husband and wife regarded each other in silence for a moment, then Aldebrand inclined his head and departed. Eden stared after him.

Sweet turned her attention to Aylen, still standing beneath the pomegranate tree, white as a ghost, and marveled that he hadn't passed out. To Eden, Sweet murmured, "Perhaps we should call it a night."

"Perhaps." Eden sounded defeated. She still didn't move.

Sweet went to Aylen and gently took his arm. "I'm sorry. Shall I escort you to the dormitory?"

He looked at her as if he didn't really see her. His mouth opened and closed a few times, but words failed to emerge.

"Yes, I think I shall. Come on."

As she led him through the foyer, Asphodel and Rosalind emerged from their room. Without a word to Sweet, they went to tend to Eden.

At the dormitory, Sweet spotted Aylen's friend Hector and passed the still shocked Aylen into his care. Hector's face was questioning, but he didn't ask anything of Sweet or Aylen.

When Sweet returned to Eden's apartment, she found the door to Eden's rooms locked. She retired to her own room, exhausted.

Eden did not refuse Aldebrand when he summoned her to his study two days later. For once he was not fiddling with something. Eden wondered sardonically if she should be flattered that she had his full attention. She arranged herself in the chair opposite him, spreading her skirts, shifting in the seat to find the most comfortable position, and delighting in making her husband wait. Finally she nodded her head and allowed him to speak.

"I hope you are well."

He did not sound insincere. She could play this game, whatever it was.

"Yes. You?"

"I spoke to the young man."

"And sent him away, I suppose."

"I did not." She could not hide her surprise. He continued. "He thinks that you are lonely."

Eden stifled a laugh. "Does he?"

"Sweet believes you are sick with boredom."

This time Eden did laugh, short, and a little harsh.

After a moment, Aldebrand said, "I think I have made a mistake."

Eden sat taller and leaned forward. "Really?"

"I should not have locked you away. Clearly it has done no good."

She rolled her eyes and sat back again.

"I mean it literally, I have caused only harm. I apologize."

"Apology not accepted."

Aldebrand nodded. "That is fair. I have made you so many gifts to try to please you, to make up for what you lost by coming here and marrying me. I had quite run out of ideas until yesterday. That young man provided them this time. He is clever, I think. That is why I keep him on. He suggested something I believe you will agree to. A trip. To the Capital."

"For how long?"

"As long as you wish. For the rest of your life if that is what you truly want." He bowed his head. "Though I hope you will consent to return and share dinner with an old fool every now and again."

Hope stirred in Eden's breast. "I think I can agree to that."

Aldebrand's lips twitched into a small smile.

The apartment felt empty. Only a few trunks each of clothes and other necessities for all four women had been packed up and sent ahead to the estate's airfield—Eden intended a shopping spree as soon as they arrived—and the windows wouldn't be shuttered until they had gone, but the atmosphere was different. Eden could taste it.

There was one more thing to do before departing. Eden waited alone beneath the pomegranate tree for Sweet to bring him. Though when he arrived, he entered the garden alone.

"Aylen." Eden flushed with joy and raised her hand to him. He took it and kissed it before sitting beside her. "I wasn't sure you would come."

"I could never deny you."

Her brows drew together. "Don't say that!"

He grinned. "I finally thought of a gift for you."

She laughed a little. "I thought I'd had enough of gifts until now. What have you brought me?"

He shook his head, still smiling. "It isn't a thing exactly. I've written to Lady Martius. When you arrive in the Capital, expect an invitation to tour her greenhouse."

Eden's eyes grew big. She clasped Aylen's hand. "Really?"

He nodded. "I wanted you to have a friend."

Blinking back tears, Eden managed to answer, "You are my friend."

"I hope so." He chuckled. "Though I think we will be distant friends for a time. Master Aldebrand was quite clear."

"I'm so happy he's allowed you to stay."

"As am I! To spoil my dream so soon...." He shook his head, then met her eyes. "But I don't regret a thing."

"Neither do I."

They sat in silence for a few moments, then Aylen rose and wished her safe travels. Eden took another walk through her garden after he'd left, bidding it goodbye. When she went into the foyer, Asphodel, Rosalind, and Sweet were all waiting.

"Ready?" asked Sweet.

Eden took her friend's proffered hand. "Absolutely."

About Crysta K. Coburn

Crysta K. Coburn has been writing award-winning stories for most of her life. Her first short story was published at the age of sixteen after winning runner-up in a local writing contest. She earned her bachelor's degree in creative writing from Western Michigan University in 2005. She is a journalist, fiction writer, poet, editor, podcast co-host, and one-time rock lyricist.

Treason in the Sky by Jacy Sellers

Finn tinkered with the training plane's clogged thermal line, managing to dislodge a green, glassy rock. She extracted it with tweezers, then let the peanut-sized rock fall to the old hangar's dusty concrete floor next to her feet. In an effort to prove her savvy machinist skills, she planned to get this single-engine plane airborne today.

Her primary job fixing broken war machines wasn't her lifelong dream, but it was her assigned life, just as it was for every orphan from the Tower. Either way, she hoped to get noticed enough through hard work to move into an engineering role.

"Attention!" the static voice of Commander Heaton called from the overhead speaker. "All soldiers must line up for the next raid selection."

Finn pinched the rubber fuel line closed, then tossed her reddish-brown braid over her shoulder. She knelt below the plane's tank and snaked the line into a small bucket to drain the residual oil. Soldiers darted in from every direction to form a line in front of her. As a worker untrained in combat, she wasn't allowed to be a part of the war recruitment. All fifty soldiers, robust men and women, wore faded tan jumpsuits adorned with artillery belts and laced boots. A patch with a one red star and three horizontal blue stripes, symbolizing the ten-year-old nation of Valor, adhered to their left shoulder sleeve. Finn wore the same patch on her grease-stained jumpsuit. Named for the small brave population, Valor emerged after America fell to Germany in the Second World War.

On the opposite side of the hangar, double metal doors slid apart from the clean room detox chamber. Finn watched with admiration as a group of crisp black uniforms marched in with a mission for young blood at the Dominion Training Camp. Finn took notice of the muscular woman in a decorated, corseted uniform and tall silver boots. A colonel had never come to their training camp before. The tension in the degraded hangar built as the soldiers straightened their backs and puffed out their chests. Armed with a handgun on her waist, she wore silver spiked goggles with black lenses and the brightest red lipstick Finn had ever seen. Finn never wore color on her pale lips. Make-up was a rare possession by the influential upper class, those fortunate with political power and money.

"Colonel Forge," Commander Heaton stuttered. "We didn't expect to have you today. If I had known, we—"

The Colonel shot up a leather-gloved hand, and Heaton snapped his mouth shut. Finn swallowed hard. She'd never witnessed a woman throw authority around like it was free will.

"I'm not here for your pleasantries, Commander. I heard you have the most skilled soldiers, and I'm here to see for myself."

"Yes, Colonel." Heaton juggled a clipboard and pushed his assault rifle over his shoulder. "We have trained the finest pilots from youth. They have nothing else to live for besides flying and fighting."

Finn herself had joined the Dominion Training Camp five years after it opened in the deserted valley of a state once called Colorado. She was twelve and brought in from the Crimson Tower Orphanage on the northeastern side of Valor. The rest came from the National Children's Home on the western side. Both were institutions for children who lost their families in war.

"I need five." Colonel Forge spoke as though she ordered meat from the butcher as she motioned to one of her uniformed soldiers. A square-jawed man in black positioned himself behind her, pen at the ready.

The Colonel clasped her hands in front of her and strode to the lineup. Square Jaw followed behind. The soldiers all held their breath as she walked by. She studied each of them in turn, scoffing or sighing as she pursed her lips.

Finn crouched lower as the woman neared the end of the lineup. The oil had filled the bucket faster than she anticipated. As Finn tried to reach for another bucket, she knocked the first one. Oil oozed across the floor and pooled around boots, including the Colonel's heels. Heaton's feet came into Finn's line of view as she redoubled her efforts to stop the rubber line from leaking further.

"I'm so sorry, Colonel. This is one of our machinists." Heaton gestured to Finn, sparing a glare over his shoulder. "She's usually not in here during the recruitment."

He stepped into the puddle of oil and grabbed her upper arm. "Back to the dorms. Now."

As Heaton jerked her up, Finn swiped the now oil-covered green glassy rock from the floor. She was already moving and pocketed the rock when the Colonel said, "Hold on. How good is she at fixing planes?"

Finn stopped, her facial muscles tightening, expecting Heaton to lie in order to keep her. In this time of war, machinists were valuable.

"The best I've ever had. She works even when she's not required to," Heaton said, lips curving into a smile.

The Colonel studied her long enough for sweat to bead on Finn's temples. "I will take her, too."

Murmurs trickled through the hangar. Finn's heart swelled as if she'd been hand-picked for a rare collection. An opportunity to be a part of the greater good for her country invigorated her loyalty.

"Everyone. Five minutes to gather your personal belongings," the Colonel announced.

After Finn and the other recruits grabbed their sacks from the attached dormitory, they returned to the hangar. Finn's sack may have been smaller than the rest, but it had to be the heaviest. She carried a broken music box filled with several pieces of the same green glassy rocks, an assortment she'd accumulated while working at Dominion because she was attracted to the color.

Heaton waited for them. "They're at the landing pad. Thank you for your service. We are Valor." He saluted, and the five recruits returned the gesture as they marched past him through double doors. Finn gave Heaton a tight hug. "Make the world good again," he whispered. She refused to let him see her wet eyes as she left him behind.

Inside the sterile room between the hangar and the outside environment, they each put on goggles and air masks.

"Ready?" asked a curly haired male recruit at the exterior door.

Finn tightened her goggles to avoid any burning gas fumes, then shot up her hand with the others. He slammed his palm against a red button, and the doors to the valley's smoky wasteland peeled open. Exterior spotlights illuminated the remains of a treeless, crumbled city grayed-out by ash and edged with a barbed wire fence. Ghostly fingers of smog streaked across sections of the moonless sky. Scattered concrete chunks, the desolate shells of two-story buildings, and dusty shadows. Turning left towards the landing pad behind the others, Finn marched around the larger pieces of stone, searching for any last minute pieces of green glass.

A subtle whooshing sound echoed. Finn's eyes widened as a massive aluminum airship hovered hundreds of feet above the camp, dwarfing the landing pad. The reconstructed, multi-level cruise ship with shiny white wings topped with steam-enhanced propellers resembled a floating city.

"Whoa." Finn admired the bottom panels bolted together like a metal quilt.

The Colonel appeared next to her. "It's rather lovely, isn't it?"

Finn closed her mouth. Sweat pooled under her arms in the presence of the powerful woman. She liked it very much, especially since she dreamed of working in the air after witnessing the freedom of flight from her camp. Finn hated being grounded for years.

"It's powered by steam and they call it Zelpun. I'm only borrowing it," Colonel Forge said casually and climbed up a ladder into a transport pod.

The pristine white and gold ship rose up from the middle of the grime of the collapsed nation. A soldier helped Finn into the same pod. They were stacked vertically like a Ferris wheel, something she faintly remembered from a storybook in a candy-striped room.

"Buckle up!" the soldier said.

Finn almost didn't find a seat, but managed to strap herself in before the pod catapulted into the air. In seconds, they landed on a platform on the back of the ship. With shaking legs, Finn tumbled out of the pod. They entered the ship through a riveted archway.

"Welcome to your new home." Colonel Forge turned to her soldiers. "Take them to processing."

"Come," commanded one robot in a digital, male voice, raising its claw gripper to guide the line of five recruits plus Finn.

On a single wheel, the robot sped ahead, leading them into white metal corridor with a curved ceiling and bright LEDs. Finn lagged at the end of the line with the second robot on her heels.

"Do you have names?" Finn asked, her machinist's brain dancing in circles at the prospect of meeting a real robot.

Her eyes trailed up and down the sleek metal casing, infatuated with how the robot was built. Humans were saved for more important war-related tasks such as combat, while robots were constructed to be assistants for the higher ranked officers in war. The task on this ship for robots was apparently to process recruits. The philosophy was set forth by President Burgundy of Valor, a man filled with visions of intercontinental domination. His philosophy left a sour taste in Finn's mouth. Why should people be treated as if they were so disposable?

"I am called EP-2, and that is EP-1," the robot squeaked from its square monitor face.

"What's E.P.?"

"Electronic Processor."

The line followed EP-1 up a short ramp and into a round cream-colored room surrounded by ten black doors.

EP-1 motioned to a rolling storage container. "Place your items in here and each pick a door."

They placed their sacks into the container, then each faced a door, which opened automatically. Finn peered into a square, white chamber, much like a shower stall. As soon as she stepped inside, the door closed behind her.

"Dispose of your clothes in the chute," chirped a robotic voice from above.

Finn spotted a square embedded into a wall with a pull, but hesitated in removing anything.

"You have twenty seconds. Nineteen. Eighteen...."

Why the hell was it counting down? What happened when it got to zero?

With a sigh, she peeled off her grubby Dominion Camp jumpsuit. As the last number vibrated through the speakers, water sprayed out of the top of the chamber, raining down on her naked body.

"I had one sock left!" she called out in annoyance.

Finn's muscles relaxed under the warm water. It had been days since her last solo shower. The water ended, followed by blasts of warm air to dry off her hair and body. A compartment under the shower head popped open to a stack of folded laundry. Grateful for fresh clothes, Finn dressed in cargo pants, black boots, and black button-down shirt. After she braided her hair into a rope, she stepped out of the chamber. EP-1 led the other recruits to their assignments while EP-2 led Finn to an oval room with a rubber floor.

A few soldiers ran laps around the outskirts of a track, while one lifted weights in the middle. EP-2 stopped behind a medium-built man wearing a black T-shirt with "Lawrence" printed in white across his square shoulders. His right arm was human, and his left had the exposed wires and mechanics of bionics. He turned to peer at Finn with copper-flecked eyes as she stood with her arms tight by her sides. A whistle hung around his thick neck, and he wore trainers, not the military-issued boots.

"Lieutenant Lawrence. This is Julia Finn, reporting for duty," EP-2 said before spinning away.

Lawrence furrowed his brow. "Oh great," he grumbled, pulling out a thin tablet from his back pocket using his human arm. "Why do they always give the strays to me?" The words were muttered under his breath, but loud enough for Finn and a scruffy soldier in training clothes to hear.

"Because you know how to whip them into shape," the soldier declared with a gap-toothed grin.

Lawrence glared at the bearded man who gave a quick salute and followed up with, "Sir." As he jogged off to run laps, the name "Rascal" flashed at Finn from the back of his shirt.

Finn dropped her head to hide her flushed cheeks. She wanted to ask if his other arm included the integrated lasers as designed by President Burgundy. A rumor had floated into her camp within the last six months about the president's announcement in transforming humans into cyborgs. She'd never seen an arm like that in real life before. He flipped through the tablet's information. "Finn. Finn. Finn." He jammed his finger against the screen. "I don't see you listed in the ranks."

She sighed. "It's probably because I'm not a soldier. I'm a machinist."

Lawrence stared hard at the tablet's screen, scrolled with his index finger, then raised his eyebrows. "There you are. We call them mechanics here. It doesn't matter."

He shoved the tablet into his pocket. "Everyone trains daily. We want to make sure you're in top physical shape to defend yourself, if necessary." He blew his ear-piercing whistle. "You've got ten laps, Finn."

He spun on his heel and returned to watching the rest of the soldiers. Lawrence didn't pay her any more attention, so she jogged into the laps. The half-dozen other soldiers, both men and women in their early twenties, ignored the shorter and younger girl.

By the end of ten laps, Finn struggled to catch her breath and dizziness swarmed her brain. Lawrence waited for her at the finish with a sleek metal canister. "Drink."

Finn gulped the cool water eagerly, letting some of it dribble down her chin.

"We fly 80 percent of the time," Lawrence said. "You'll get dehydrated. Keep the bottle and refill it as needed."

"Thank you." Finn wiped her mouth, grateful the dizziness subsided.

Lawrence studied his tablet. "You're to meet with Ketron next. He's the head mechanic downstairs in the Hold."

As Lawrence ushered Finn out of the room, a new group of soldiers entered for what must be the next round of training. Clearly, the room was too small to fit more than twenty at a time.

"How many people are on this airship…Zelpun?" Finn asked.

"We call it Zel. There are a hundred soldiers, five mechanics, and twenty leaders, including Colonel Forge. And you."

"Did she recruit you, too?"

"In a way." Lawrence picked up the pace, and Finn struggled to keep up with his long-legged strides.

He banged open a door at the end of the corridor and they went down three flights of stairs. Finn followed him into a brightly lit maintenance shop with high ceilings. Four fight jets lined one wall, while one bomber sat in the middle of the room, wires and parts spilling out like a ripped carcass.

A heavy-set guy in cargo pants stood on a ladder, tightening screws into the bomber's weapon bay doors. Two other guys tinkered with engines on nearby tables.

Lawrence cleared his throat. "Ketron."

Ketron turned slightly, slipped the screwdriver into his work pants, and descended the ladder. Lawrence planted his feet in front of Ketron, who was wider and taller than Lawrence. Grease spotted his apron, and soot was smeared across his stony face.

"This is Julia Finn. She only worked in a basic Air Corps training camp, but she's skilled with the weaponry boards and mechanical engineering."

Finn forced a tiny smile, eager to get started on anything. Her fingers itched to explore the bomber's guts.

"Interesting for a young one such as yourself." Ketron glowered and gave her the once over with his narrowed eyes. "Are you some sort of prodigy, or did you know someone high in the ranks?"

Finn's mind flashed to an engine on a table, where a timer threatened her productivity. Fix the engine or get lashed. She blinked away the memory.

"We'll have to test your skills, Finny." Ketron wiped his hands on an already greasy rag.

"It's Finn."

Lawrence turned to Finn with a frown. "You'll report to Ketron. He oversees all mechanical operations of our war machines." He lowered his voice and slipped something into her hand. "Stay alert."

The odd warning startled Finn, but she kept a straight face and slid the hard object into her back pocket. Lawrence lingered as if he didn't want to leave her with Ketron and his mechanics.

"Don't worry, Law," Ketron barked, throwing an arm around Finn's shoulder. She stiffened. "You know we take good care of the new recruits."

Lawrence lurched. "If you lay a hand—"

"Whoa. Whoa." Ketron stepped away. "Now. This unit isn't about hazing…anymore. Colonel shut that down, remember?" He swiveled his head around to his men, who encroached on the conversation. "We swore we wouldn't be dunking heads in cold water or stealing meals or anything of the sort with the newbies. Right?"

The mechanics nodded in agreement to their leader. Lawrence grimaced and took one last look at Finn before leaving, his eyes creased with worry. Finn's courage fragmented just slightly.

Ketron cocked a crooked smile at Lawrence's back and hollered, "All right! Get to work. These machines aren't going to fix themselves." He turned to Finn. "And Finny. I need you to fix the fuel gauge on that Owl-X. It's showing empty when I know it's full."

Finn grit her teeth, but made no objection as he led her toward a giant black plane in the corner. She'd only heard about hybrids from Commander Heaton, but no one she knew had ever actually seen one. They were legends, run by the elite.

"I… I…can't. I've never worked on a hybrid plane before."

"It's a *gauge*." He scowled. "If you can't handle that, then I'm sending you to waste duty. You want to deal with other people's shit?"

Finn wanted this prick to eat shit. Instead, she straightened up and scurried to the Owl, an extraordinary bomber named after the stealthiest bird of prey. She walked under the black wing, reaching up to trace her fingertips along the body's sleek chrome. Tingles swept over her skin at the majestic beauty. According to the stories, the Owl was the perfect spy plane, with its wide and flattened design, able to reach an incredible 3,000 mph, about four times the speed of sound.

She climbed a narrow ladder and stepped onto a metal grid floor inside the low-ceilinged fuselage. Five harnessed seats lined either side, while supply trunks claimed the middle. She made her way to the front. When she heard a muffled cough behind her, she whipped around, seeing nothing except for the sealed cargo door. She crept back a few feet, half-expecting to find someone hiding behind a trunk, but didn't see anything besides the interior grid frame of the plane.

When Finn entered the plane's silver-trimmed cockpit at the front, it stole her breath. Three cushy, black pilot chairs with armrest controls faced the tinted windshield panels, which stretched the entire length of the state-of-the-art space. The digital display board included various holographic displays, including the new synthetic rendering radar, which painted a picture of the ground below.

Finn fingered the knobs, buttons, and the gears before focusing on the fuel gauge in the middle. Nothing seemed broken. She narrowed down the troubleshooting to a faulty floating indicator, so she made her way outside the plane to uncap the tank.

Blackness as dead as the night consumed the tank's inside. She needed tools and walked to the cabinet across the room, close to where other mechanics tinkered at a workbench. Finn hoped to find an X-ray gun, so she could examine the tank for any malfunctions. As she bent down to the bottom shelf, she heard whispers on the other side of the cabinet.

"There's too many new recruits on board," said a high-pitched voice.

Finn froze in place, staying crouched at the cabinet, her hands wrapped around the wooden handle of a tool.

"We can't wait anymore," said a gruff tone. "Ketron wants us to initiate the plan tonight."

She had no idea what they were talking about, but their whispers sounded like treachery against Valor. A heated sensation of anger crawled up her neck and into her face. Finn slowly leaned around the cabinet and spied two mechanics at a workbench, half facing her direction. A scarred man with Crabb on his name patch leaned down. Beside him loomed another man with tattoos of spiders and creatures similar to gothic wallpaper. His shirt was missing the name patch.

"Tonight? Dammit," said Crabb, the one with whiny voice. "We should have grabbed Lawrence when we had the chance. He hardly comes down here."

"It would've been too obvious. Don't worry, he'll get what's coming to him." The other man snickered.

Finn's hand twitched at the remark. She caught a splinter from the hammer and lost her grip. The hammer clunked onto the floor. She winced and plucked out the tiny slice of wood from her palm.

"Did you hear something?" asked Crabb.

"You're paranoid. Everyone here already knows—" The tattooed man stopped.

Finn moved behind the cabinet and squeezed her eyes shut, hoping they didn't see her.

"Hello there!"

Crap.

Finn opened her eyes to find both men gawking at her.

"Just grabbing some supplies." She stood, gripping the hammer in one hand and throwing a tool belt over her shoulder.

"What did you hear, darling?" The tattooed man leered. Finn wanted to punch him in the throat for the term of endearment.

"What did you say?" Finn asked in a loud voice, nearly shouting. "I grew up around machines most of my life. I might be losing my hearing."

"Doubtful with the technology they have today." Crabb punched a fist into his other hand a couple of times.

"You know," the tattooed man said. "Ketron said we shouldn't haze the *guys*. But he didn't mention the *girls*."

Crabb snorted and ran his hands through his slick hair before reaching a giant hand toward Finn. She ducked away and swung the hammer, knocking him square in the jaw. Blood sprayed out, and he fell to the floor, grabbing his face.

"You bitch!" the tattoo man yelled. He shoved her shoulders, slamming her body flat against the metal floor. The hammer fell out of her hand, and his forearm pinned her neck. She coughed and choked, trying to shout but failing to make any audible words. Blackness cloaked her eyes. She expected to greet death in war, not aboard an airship named Zelpun.

An ear-piercing siren jolted Finn awake, and she was greeted by the overwhelming smell of sour milk. There was a sudden shift in gravity, and she rolled until her body collided with a hard surface. Rough fabric scratched against her cheeks and arms. Another tilt, and she rolled in the opposite direction, landing in a suspiciously squishy pile reeking of rotten cabbage.

The sounds and the movement stopped, then everything remained still. Finn only saw a blurry criss-cross pattern. Her body had been forced to curl into a ball, contained within a tight fabric. She extended her arms as far as she could, but rough burlap limited her reach. Next, she tried her legs, but those were trapped, too. Beeping blared through speakers above as the floor rattled beneath her. There was a pop of an ignition, followed by a trace of gas infiltrating her nose. A warmth rose from the floor up through the fabric. Sweat beaded on her forehead.

"Thirty seconds before incineration," said a robotic voice. *"Beep! Beep! Beep!"*

Her heart rose into her throat as she realized where she was.

They dumped me down a freaking trash chute.

The heat intensified, wafting burnt garbage into her nostrils. She pushed against the fabric, clawing, struggling to rip it without any success. An overwhelming tightness seized her chest. Lights flashed through the woven fabric to accompany the repetitive beeps, and her head pounded. Something dug into her through her back pocket. She maneuvered her right arm and pulled out a pocket knife.

Thank you, Lawrence!

She flipped open the blade and sliced the fabric, exposing her eyes to a cramped, metal space. A trace of the stench of burnt flesh invaded her nose, and she gagged. Wriggling out, she pulled herself out of the burlap, letting her feet sink into the wet bags. She could only kneel under the short ceiling. Of course those assholes threw her out like garbage. She shuffled bags and discovered a rectangular panel in front of her. It had to lead somewhere that wasn't the incinerator, and it looked wide enough for her to squeeze through.

"Twenty seconds," the robotic voice said.

The heat burned her knees and the soles of her new boots as the floor rattled. She pawed at the panel. No handles. No hinges. No luck.

"Ten seconds," the robotic voice said.

Finn fought a wave of panic just as the panel shifted, then slid away. Two gloved hands popped through and grabbed Finn's upper arms. The grip tightened as the floor sprung open beneath her, intensifying the scorching heat. Bags of trash dropped into rising orange flames. Finn's legs dangled for a few terrifying seconds until the arms yanked her out. She landed on the regular tiled floor of the ship, and luckily, only the bottoms of her pants were saturated with garbage juice.

"Colonel Forge!" Finn exclaimed.

"Shh! Forget the formalities," she whispered. "Call me Ginny." She pushed her goggles onto her forehead. Her braided raven hair melted into her black lace corset. She wore matching black slacks and carried a semi-automatic belted across her torso in addition to her silver handgun. She still displayed bright red lipstick, as if it were her signature.

"You don't have time for a shower." She shoved a plain black shirt and pants at Finn. They stood alone in the middle of a dimly lit tunnel, and Finn didn't worry about modesty as she peeled off the uniform.

"How did you know—"

"Surveillance. I'm sorry I couldn't make it here sooner."

Anger sparked in Finn's chest. "What the hell is happening? Those mechanics—"

"Are traitors." The voice came from farther down the tunnel. Lawrence appeared, backing in from the shadows, clutching an assault rifle. "I knew they'd try something."

Finn threw her arms up. "You knew? So you left me there with them?" she hissed.

"I didn't know *when*." Lawrence adjusted his rifle and kept moving down the tunnel and away from the trash chute. Ginny followed him, her hand over her handgun.

Finn remained planted behind them. "I could have been burned alive by the incinerator!"

Ginny halted and turned to her. "But you didn't, and he didn't want to raise eyebrows by not following procedures."

"What the hell is happening?" Finn choked out. "Why would you bring in new recruits if there's a freaking mutiny happening?"

"Calm down," Ginny hissed. "It's complicated, but we have to go, and then we'll explain everything."

Another siren wailed. It repeated louder and louder.

The Zelpun tilted, and Finn stumbled. Her eyes darted between Ginny's stare and Lawrence's half-smile. They seemed too relaxed while her racing heartbeat encouraged her to bolt. She had to get out of there and soon. Ginny motioned for Finn to follow them, but Finn pivoted in the opposite direction.

"Wait!" Ginny called after her. "We're on your side!"

Finn didn't stop until she found a doorway to the stairwell. Unsure of her destination, she decided to go up four flights and exited onto the Executive Level.

As soon as she emerged into the softly lit corridor, two bodies in the same solid black as herself lay slumped against a gold-painted wall. Finn gasped. A streak of blood trailed down the wall above them, and more blood pooled on the blue floor around their heads, each with a single bullet hole. Their mouths gaped open, eyes wide.

Finn held a hand over her mouth, swallowing back bile. She bounded away, passing a few closed doors, and slowing to peek around a corner. Two men dressed in uniforms guarded double doors. A sign on the right was labeled Captain's Quarters. She recognized Rascal from the training room. He'd acted friendly before, and Finn needed answers. She straightened her posture and walked with confidence.

"Rascal, I just saw—" The men both aimed their rifles at her, and her confidence evaporated.

She threw her hands up in surrender. "Whoa! I'm on your side."

"What are you doing here? I thought they disposed of you like the rest of the newly recruited trash," Rascal sneered.

Finn lost her breath. She had smelled burnt flesh in the trash chute. Is that what happened to the other recruits from Dominion? Her eyes welled up. "I survived…because…I'm on your side. We are…Valor." She could barely choke the words out as her pride faded.

"Only traitors against the president and Valor wear *black*," said Rascal, his voice harsh. "Newton. The indicator."

He grabbed Finn's raised hand and turned it over. Newton, a man with a deep scowl, hovered a wand device over the underside of Finn's wrist. A white swirl with spikes on the edges appeared. Finn's mouth dropped; she had a mysterious, invisible tattoo painted into her skin. She'd seen that symbol before, but where? A stone wall. A cold, dark room. A single metal chair. A spotlight. Fragmented images, then the memory escaped her as a ringing pierced her ears.

The uniformed men glared at the marking.

"Where'd that come from?" Finn stuttered.

"You *are* one of them." Newton returned the indicator to his pocket and leveled his gun at her chest. "Crabb should've checked you earlier. It's a good thing you didn't burn up in that incinerator."

The two men appeared unaffected by the ringing. Finn shook her head, her braid swinging side to side. "Why is that?"

Rather than answering, Rascal seized Finn's hands and cuffed them. The ringing subsided.

"You don't have to do this!" she cried. "We are Valor!"

Newton tapped a device on his wrist and spoke into it. "We got one."

In seconds, the doors they guarded whooshed open, and Finn caught a glimpse of the luxurious quarters. Lavenders, greens, and yellows sprinkled through floral patterned walls and plush couches. The sounds of light jazz music. Ketron appeared, wearing a heavily decorated black uniform of striped badges and star medals, representative of the highest ranking in Valor. This was not the mechanic Finn reported to just hours ago. The doors shut, and the lovely world of color and music disappeared.

"I wondered why they let you join us on this ship," he sneered. "You seemed too old for the trials, but I guess you were selected for your pretty face." Ketron dragged his rough finger across her cheek, and she flinched. "Rascal, be careful. We wouldn't want to set her off. Take her to the bullpen, but isolate her for now."

The rumor around camp was that a bullpen was an enclosure for sexual gratification for the men in the field. She trembled. She'd die a traitor before she let them turn her into some sex toy.

Ketron left her with Newton, Rascal, and their nasty smirks. Finn had almost no idea what Ketron was talking about, but she didn't want to find out. She stepped back, squatting into an awkward defensive position. A rush of adrenaline flooded her veins, and Finn forced herself to stabilize her weight on her left leg. She kicked her right foot to target Newton's groin. He squealed and held himself. Next, she swung her rope braid and whipped Rascal across his glowering face.

"You bitch!"

"Not the first time I heard that today," she snarled.

At that moment, she wished she'd had more combat training. But even as she prepared to duck from Rascal's swinging fists, Newton clocked her knees, and she fell forward.

Two gunshots, and the bodies of the two men fell next to her. Someone grabbed Finn's arm and dragged her away from the pooling blood.

"If you want to live, you've got to trust us," whispered Lawrence. His human arm pulled Finn to her feet, and his cyborg arm freed her from the cuffs.

She wavered as the ringing returned, but Lawrence steadied her.

"This is no time to be dead weight unless you plan to stay that way." Ginny pursed her red lips, hands ready on her semi-automatic.

She gestured at Lawrence as if they shared a secret telepathic language.

He led the way around the corner, also carrying his weapon at the ready. With no other choice, Finn followed, slithering along the walls until they reached the two bodies she'd found before.

Ginny sighed, kneeled, and with two fingers, closed their eyelids. Over the wailing sirens, a voice came through the loudspeaker.

"Attention. Traitors walk this ship. Find and exterminate them. We are Valor."

Finn felt her heart breaking with the phrase. It meant nothing to her now. Boots pounded the floor, the sound growing nearer.

"We've got to get off the ship." Lawrence opened the door to the stairwell.

Under sirens and blinking red lights, they flew down stairs until they arrived at the holding bay, where Finn had been last before her incident. Lawrence peeked around the doorframe, then motioned for Finn and Ginny to follow. They made their way to the Owl.

An ear-piercing shot rang out, and Ginny yelped, gripping her arm to stem the tide of blood. They scurried into the Owl and sealed the door shut as figures with guns charged through the doorway behind them. The sirens silenced within the soundproof walls of the giant plane.

"I'm fine," Ginny growled, clutching her arm. "I'm getting this bird out of here. Lawrence, get the kids strapped in."

Ginny disappeared into the cockpit, and Finn followed her, taking the seat behind her. Pings bounced against the exterior metal hull, ricocheting like beads of hail.

"Everyone thinks we're traitors." Ginny inspected her wound. "Dammit. There's no exit. Finn, find me pliers. I need this bullet out."

"Are you serious?"

Ginny furrowed her brow and cranked the engine on. Chrome rattled to life, then settled into whispered hums.

Finn went to searching among the compartments affixed within the cockpit's interior. In seconds, she found a toolbox with needle-nose pliers. She tried to hand them to Ginny, who batted Finn's hand away with her gloved hand.

"I can't reach it. They got me from behind."

Finn shuddered. "You want me to—?"

"Yes. After we're in the air. Buckle up."

Shots pattered against the bulletproof windshield and the exterior. Ginny crashed into other planes, crushing them as if aluminum cans in a vice, steering toward an opening hatch door. The hatch lowered, sucking untied parts out into the blackness. A surge forward, and the Owl flew off the airship with a couple fighter jets right behind.

"I'm taking this to full throttle!" Ginny spoke into a radio.

The Owl shuddered and flashed through the air, leaving behind the fighters and Zelpun. Finn felt her body float until Ginny clicked a few switches and punched some buttons, settling into auto-pilot.

"The bullet, Finn. Finn?"

Finn was entranced by the Owl's ability to sail into the sky. She'd never flown before, and even though her stomach rolled, the weightless feeling gave her pure joy. She jumped when Ginny touched her shoulder, bringing her back.

"Sorry," she murmured.

Swallowing hard, she angled the pliers, pushing the tool into Ginny's torn flesh. Finn twisted and clamped the hard bullet, then slowly pulled it out. Ginny never moved, but she held out her gloved hand for Finn to deposit the bullet. Finn wiped off the pliers and returned them to the tool box. She found a first-aid kit and took out some bandages and disinfectant.

Nothing reached them now, and the Owl climbed until they settled at forty-thousand feet. The flight was as smooth as if they weren't even flying.

Finn wrapped Ginny's arm gently and said, "Tell me everything. Why am I here? And why do they think we're traitors?"

Ginny sighed, toying with a purple ribbon beneath her glove. "Everyone on the Zelpun is against our plans to rescue more kids like you."

Finn cocked her head. "You're rescuing...children?" Her mind raced to the recruits, who may have died in vain in the midst of everything going down on the airship. "If that's *really* what you're doing, where are the rest of them?"

Ginny stood and exited into the fuselage while Lawrence took her place at the controls.

Finn followed her. She rubbed her temples. The ringing returned, and she tried to rid herself of the confusion.

Sitting in the harnessed seats, the five recruits from Dominion had their own conversations. Finn's mouth dropped. Beside them were four younger kids, boys and girls. They all wore the solid black outfits.

"Every time we recruited soldiers from a camp, I rescued a kid." Ginny rubbed the top of one kid's head.

"Rescued? But why?" Finn flopped into a seat.

"The President expects us to win the war against Germany at whatever cost." Ginny sighed deeply. "That cost includes child soldiers. The other leaders on Zelpun didn't agree with my philanthropy. So, we took things into our own hands."

Ginny shook her head and spoke as if to herself. "I should have seen it coming. Our soldiers expect battles against Germany, not saving kids. We caused this treason." She motioned for them to buckle up.

"So what's the big deal? Aren't we supposed to help our own people?" Finn asked.

Ginny got up. "Do you remember your parents?"

Finn shook her head. "I don't recall much before my life at the camp. Except maybe a red and white-striped room."

"You're from the Tower, too?" asked a kid with dimples.

"Yeah, but I…don't remember much." Finn bit her lip. "Does the Tower have anything to do with trials?"

Ginny nodded. "Many of you lived at the Crimson Tower, classified as a military training facility we believe to be called the Obsidian Institute. All of it is off the grid." Ginny patted a few kids on the shoulders. "We're heading to a safe haven now, so you can be debriefed and reunited with your families."

The children cheered, though several leaned heavily into their seats, yawning. Finn caught herself closing her eyes, unsure of the last time she'd slept. She flitted them open and found Ginny gazing at a tiny sepia photo of what looked to be a young blonde girl.

"Who's that?"

Ginny slipped the photo into her pants pocket. "Somebody I lost years ago. I like to look at it as a reminder of why I'm doing this. Now get some rest. We've got a little time."

Finn's eyes grew heavy, and the hum of the engine lulled her to darkness. Her body flowed out of her control in the bubble of a dream. She peeked to find blurs and figures shifting around her. Unfocused, with clogged ears, her limbs moved automatically.

Turbulence and screaming jolted her awake again. Only, instead of being in her seat, she was pinned beneath Lawrence. Pressed against the metal floor, his bionic hand clamped around her neck. She couldn't breathe.

"What... the... hell?" Finn sputtered.

Lawrence let up on his pressure. "Finn? Finn? Are you all right?"

"Have you lost your mind?" She swatted his metal arm away and sat up.

"You don't remember? You...tried to kill us all."

Finn froze. The four kids sobbed in the back of the plane. The recruit with the curly hair was propped up on the floor with a freshly bandaged leg. Others hovered nearby, avoiding eye contact. Ginny towered in front protectively, a gun aimed at Finn, her other hand thumbing a small black device.

She handed it to Lawrence. He whispered, "Your chip wasn't removed in processing as we thought. Those useless robots."

"What? I'm sorry! I'm sorry!" Finn cried.

Lawrence touched his human index finger to her lips. "Shh." His hazel eyes glittered.

He pressed the box against the back of Finn's neck. A suction forced her skin to pucker. Finn yelped as something burst out of her flesh. Lawrence opened his cyborg hand to show Finn a tiny black square coated in her blood. Finn grew dizzy. He clamped his hand until the square crunched, then he released his fingers and dust blew away. Lawrence cleaned up the area and placed a bandage across the back of her neck.

"Glad that's destroyed," Ginny said, holstering her gun. "All is well now. Please return to your seats and strap in."

Movement blurred through the space as they all followed suit. Finn mouthed a sincere *I'm sorry* to every one of the others, and they each nodded their acceptance.

The plane jostled. A frown crept across Ginny's red-stained lips, and she put the chip-removing device in her pocket. "Lawrence, how are we on fuel? We should almost be there."

"Not sure. It's been on empty the entire time we've been in the air. Let me get us off autopilot." Lawrence stood.

"Fuel?" Finn shuddered. "There's something you should know about that. Ketron assigned me to fix that gauge, but I never had the chance before I was knocked unconscious."

The plane tilted. "We're going to crash!" a little girl shrieked, causing the other kids to cry out.

"No. We're fine," said Ginny. "There's a secondary line for the steam engine. Let me switch it over."

They went to the cockpit. Lawrence eased the plane off autopilot, and Ginny flipped the switch for the secondary energy source. A whoosh of air swallowed the sputtering from the lack of fuel. Everything stabilized and they took seats in the pilot chairs. A hint of pale yellow light shimmered off a line of bleak clouds. The beginnings of a sunrise morphed brighter into various shades from purple to blue to yellow. For a few glorious seconds, Finn forgot they were at war.

"See. Darkness doesn't always win," Lawrence said noticing Finn's gaze.

"Why me? Why these kids?" She couldn't take her eyes off the sunlight beaming across the horizon.

"I hate anyone having to go through war, especially the younger generations," he said. "They started life in a bad place. As small children, you were stolen away from your parents...by clandestine German agents. After embedding a command chip, the children are put into trials and trained at the Tower."

"Trained for what?" Finn tore her eyes away from the rays of soft light.

"Tower soldiers are assassins for Valor," Ginny said in a low tone. "But with the chip, Germany takes control over them within our country. They must have activated your chip. I'm so sorry."

Finn hugged her knees. "It's not your fault. In fact, it's because of both of you I'm not an assassin. Besides, you're trying to stop this, right?"

Ginny took a seat with them in the cockpit. She flipped on the music, and a low jazz of trumpets played.

"After we drop off the kids, are we going to rescue more like me?"

Ginny took Finn's hand and squeezed it. "Like us." She allowed her lips to curl at the ends. "No more programmed assassins."

"You were one, too? How did you know?"

"It wasn't until I started training with Lawrence. He tried to stop me from killing other Valor soldiers and figured out how to remove my chip, but not before I took off his arm."

Finn gasped.

"I don't miss it," Lawrence chuckled, raising an empty soda can and crushing it with ease. "This new arm is much better."

"After that, I remembered that there were more from the Crimson Tower. I felt we needed to save them, too. I enlisted in the Air Corps, trained, and ranked my way up. By the time I had my own ship and soldiers, I used it as a way to rescue kids as I found them."

"Too bad the others didn't see it the same way," Lawrence said. "They think we're with the German agents."

"So, why are you still doing what you're doing?" Finn asked.

"The world is a bad place," Ginny pulled out the small photo again. "And I'm ready for a revolution."

About Jacy Sellers

Jacy Sellers writes mysteries, thrillers, and fantasy. Her debut, a young adult fantasy, "A Feather's Force" is available on Amazon. She's a member of Sisters in Crime. When she's not writing, you can find her studying ghost stories and exploring thrift stores. Jacy is represented by Jana Hanson of the Metamorphosis Literary Agency. Follow her on Twitter @JacySellers.

Catchin' Gargoyles by Tim Kidwell

The four of us—Goss, Bryan, Wil, and I—met up at Ol' Wiss's for a beer and something to eat. The something to eat was always secondary to the beer. Though tonight, for whatever reason, Wil wanted something with more kick. And to oblige, we started with whiskey. We stood at a table in the back, away from the chill blowing in through the front door. The tavern creaked and whistled as the wind clawed at its wood siding and rattled the leaded glass windows in their ancient casements. An iron potbelly stove nearby made the air shimmer, its fiery grate staring like the yellow eye of a bayou beast I'd once seen in Louisiana.

"Another," Wil breathed, holding high his glass so Fiona, the only serving girl working, could see before slamming its rim down on the table.

"That's five," Bryan said and steered Fiona away with a small shake of his head. She took his hint with a cheerful nod and altered course.

"Let's get some food in you before we drink the night away, shall we?" said Goss.

Save for us and a tall man—taller than any I remembered seeing—seated at the bar, the place was deserted. Ol' Wiss put a lopsided ceramic mug in front of the man, its contents smoking. The stranger slapped a gold three-dollar piece on the bar. Ol' Wiss stared at the coin a moment, then asked, "You want something to eat, too?"

The man shook his head. "Just the drink." He wore a long leather coat, gone yellow with age and worn smooth and black at the elbows and collar. A long, scruffy mane stuck out from beneath a slouch hat so beaten it almost had no shape at all. Perhaps most interesting was the prosthetic leg he made no qualms about hiding. It wasn't one of the fancy new permanent nervewire types you see on those who can afford such luxuries. No, his was a simple but elegant piece of curved stainless, springy and light, and extending from his knee to where an articulated foot met the floor. A cuff and straps held it securely to the man's thigh. Among the many straps, the bracing housed a line of thin knives, a small pistol, and canvas pouches held shut with brass snaps. What else he might have hidden in his coat, I couldn't say.

"What're you staring at?" Wil asked, slewing his head around at the stranger. He took a long stare at the man at the bar and rolled his attention back to me. "Like what you're seeing?" The drink narrowed his eyes, and his words were already mush in his mouth.

"A bit too lofty for my tastes," I chuckled.

"Fiona," Goss called out. She spun from wiping an already spotless table. Her teeth showed from between her full, pink lips. One of her front teeth was chipped, just the corner. It made her smile devilish. "We'll take some stew and bread if you have it."

"We'll have plenty for you tonight," Fiona answered and strolled through the kitchen door. Not a minute later, she emerged carrying four bowls trailing hot fog shouldered on a wide platter, a board of bread, and a dollop of butter pierced by a short, wide knife in a bowl.

Wil pushed his empty glass toward Fiona. "I'll have a beer—"

"Oh, no you won't," I cut across him. "It's a cup of coffee or nothing for him until he puts the stew away."

"You sure you want to do that?" The man at the bar leaned heavily on his elbow and took a long pull of his toddy. We all blinked mutely. "I mean, you can. And I'm not saying you shouldn't."

"Seems you're using a lot of words to say nothing," Wil replied with enough belligerence that it might as well have come with dueling pistols.

Ol' Wiss watched from behind the bar, absently rubbing his whiskered chin with his thumb, face carefully neutral.

"Are you saying our food don't live up to your tastes?" This from Fiona, who bobbed her head to clear her black bangs away from her eyes. "If so, there are plenty of other holes for you to dive into."

"Fiona!" Ol' Wiss snapped, his friendly face suddenly sharp as flint.

"No," the tall man said with a shrug. "Right she is, and no offense taken." He walked over to our table and stared all the way down at us and then Fiona. He exuded a pressure that made us all shift a step as he joined our intimate group without invitation. Gingerly, he slid Wil's bowl of stew toward the center of the table with the back of his hand, which was covered by a sweep of coarse black hair. "And I didn't mean any offense to you or your establishment," he rumbled to Fiona.

Fiona returned his stare without a hint of fear or apology. She rolled her eyes and swung around the bar, shaking her head and muttering beneath her breath. "If you don't mean to offend, then don't say something offensive." She took up residence next to Ol' Wiss.

"Friend, I think you angered her," Goss said.

"Plainly," followed Bryan.

"Twasn't my intent. But I do have somewhat to tell, if you'll listen."

"Is it a story we've heard before?" Wil exhaled as he dragged his bowl of stew close and raised a spoon full of rich broth and generous chunks of meat to his lips. He blew carefully, tasted tentatively, then slurped it in greedily.

The man grunted. "I hope not, for it just happened to me recently."

You might have heard of me: Querulous Creed. No? Doesn't matter. You remember the last battle at Winchester back in summer of 1864? I see you do. The blast. The damn pit that opened up out there. Well, as you know, one of the side effects of that little to-do has been gargoyles.

Now, I don't know if you've ever been up close with one, but gargoyles ain't much bigger than your common rat. A bit smaller than a raccoon or opossum. And they're little more than a nuisance, if I'm honest. Cunning bastards, but not what I'd call *intelligent*. What makes 'em a challenge is their hands. Just like ours, five fingers and all. And wings. They ain't quick like bats, but they can mount the air as well as a pigeon might.

As you might guess, I make my living killing the little bastards. Gargoyles, that is. Not pigeons. Though, I'll catch rats, too. But gargoyles, well, since '64, they've infested Washington, Philadelphia, Baltimore. I even heard they've got 'em as far south as Long Bay and north in Albany. They do love the dark. And they hide. But they ain't like rats, completely unthinking. You get two or three together, and I swear they can plan. They have a way of talkin'. And I can see you don't believe me, but they do. Gargoyles'll work in concert to relieve you of anything they think might be food or just woos their eye. I had one make off with a box of matches from inside my coat pocket. Cackled the whole time, too. As if it'd discovered the secret to…well, to something. But while it was jiggin', I popped him in the heart with my li'l pistol, and that put an end to his celebrations. Arrogant sneak.

By the by, going on six weeks ago, I receive a telegram from a gentleman. Nothing specific in the message, just he wants to buy my services, and a location and time to meet to discuss the arrangement. I think, what am I doing getting a telegram? Most folks who need my skills know where to come down to find me. I have an office and a boy who keeps the books, makes appointments, and the rest. Mervin. He does all the stuff I don't got time for. Or the wits, but I don't tell him that part. Never have I received a telegram.

I agree to the time and place. Nice park. Not too far from here. The one with the gazebo and has that black gate in the wall that borders it on the south. Across from St. Lucia? Yeah, that's the one. I eradicated a nest of gargoyles from that church last year. Bunch of flyers those were. Mean bastards. Had the primary drake take a scoop outta the pad of my hand right there. Healed, but I can still count his teeth from the scar.

This man I meet at the park. He's very well to do. Not an airship baron or nothing, but more money than you lot or I will scrape together in all the hours of our lives combined. He isn't more than this high, including his top hat, which is where most his height came from. That and his heeled boots with silver buckles and long toes. I remember thinking at the time he'd get along better if he tucked his legs up under his chin and rolled. Instead, he waddles on two stumpy legs, not bending at all at the knee from what I could tell. Just rocking back and forth and inching forward. Have to hide my astonishment. He has a couple of strongs with him, all steel jaws and raw knuckles. You know the type. I mean, I'm no shrimp, but these guys drown puppies and think it's a game.

The man shakes my hand with his cold flipper and asks me, "How's business?"

"Brisker than last year this time," says I. "But not so busy I couldn't do with another customer or three." We shared a laugh at that.

He says, "What do you do with the gargoyles when you've killed them?"

I thought that an odd question. No one had ever asked. So, I tell him, and now you'll know, too. All gargoyle bodies are salted, then incinerated. There's no city code, but it's commonly accepted that you stand a chance of a gargoyle clumping itself back together from the ashes if you don't salt 'em first. Before you go rolling your eyes, I ain't never seen it happen, and I'm not certain it's true. But—*But*. The trade says it's a danger, and I'm always happy being safe rather than sorry.

He nods his round head with its top hat and says he'd like to take over disposing of my gargoyles. I'm flummoxed to silence. Don't know what to think or make of him or his offer.

"Most don't know it," he says, seeing my obvious confusion, "but gargoyles are an excellent, just excellent fuel resource." I beg his pardon and tell him he's gotten his facts wrong. Someone has steered him foul. Gargoyle bodies burn no easier than you or I. In fact, you have to get the flame hotter to reduce the carcass to fine powder, bone and all.

He rolls his head over to the side. I think his top hat is gonna slide right off his head onto the ground. I don't know if by enchantment or pins and glue, but it stays put.

"You misunderstand me," he says.

That's all. Now, between you and me, the only thing I ever saw a gargoyle release was smoke. You wouldn't want to breathe it, as it's thick, green and yellow, and greasy. Gets in your clothes and hair and makes you itch. You're stuck smelling it for days. But who am I to disagree. I mean, it weren't me who thought the plans for the gaslights, so maybe he knows something I don't.

"All right," says I. "But even if you got all the gargoyles in the city, I don't think there'd be enough for a constant source of fuel. Not like coal or whales."

His eyes go all round and dark like a bird's. Gives me a chill on the back of my arms.

"No," he says. "Still, I'll pay for expenses and transport. Whatever you charge for each job, charge me the same. I want copies of receipts, of course."

"Of course," I say, and before I know it, I shake his hand, and he and his men make for the black iron gate on the south end of the park. I follow a few paces behind. They reach the gate and the round, little rich man turns around and says, "And Mr. Creed, I want the gargoyles alive."

"What?" I ask, but he must not hear me, because he and his men were gone.

While Querulous had been talking, the rest of us had set to our meals. While Wil ate his with a dog's selfish intensity, Goss and Bryan went at a slower pace. Goss pulled free a chunk of bread and buttered it for Bryan before preparing his own. They stood close to each other, shoulders touching. I like to eat all the potatoes, carrots, and meat out of the stew, saving the thick gravy to sop up with the bread. It had been a long day, and nothing, be it talk of hunting, killing, or disposing of gargoyles was going to dampen my appetite.

The hairy giant before us adjusted his stance, gave his prosthetic leg a shake, and ordered another of what turned out to be rum and boiling water.

"Seems like a good deal for you," Bryan said after swallowing a mouthful of stew and licking a dribble from his lips. "Able to get paid twice for every job." He picked a sliver of beef from between his teeth and sucked it off his finger. "Would you like to hire some help?"

We all laughed. All of us except Creed. His eyes shone through the dark thicket that masked most of his face.

"That's another strange thing," he said. "Next morning, I come down from my rooms to open the shop and one of the gentleman's bone breakers is waiting outside the door."

We all quieted. Even Wil hesitated in his wolfish consumption. Fiona set Creed's steaming mug on the table and left, but stayed close enough to catch his story. Seems her irritation had turned to curiosity as she wiped down the same table for the sixth time. Creed blew on his drink and took a tentative sip.

"Oh, that's good," he whispered, wiping the moisture from the brambles along his upper lip with a swipe of his hand.

"What did he want?" Wil demanded. "The gent's strongy?"

"Well, to work with me," Creed said, cocking his head and raising his eyebrows. Then he scowled. "Or more like, manage me."

Seems I missed that part of our conversations. The strong jerks his thumb over his shoulder at one of them new P&H steam wagons. Back end all boxed in with doors off the rear.

"For the haul," he says. And as if he owns the place, he invites himself in for a sit. "What's on the schedule?"

Now, I know you lads work, but I don't punch a clock, you see. I've an internal chronometer. I do things my way and in my time. Not that I like being late. If I say I'll be somewhere by a certain time, I'll be there, even if this leg has to do the walking alone. But it rubs me raw straight away. Half of me wants to tell him and his boss to forget it. The other half, the greedy half, is already counting the money. And all of me expects they won't be too happy if I backed out of our agreement so soon after making it.

The best time to hunt gargoyles, if you're looking for easier catching, is during the day. Gargoyles hate daylight. Hurts their eyes and gives them the quea-zees. So, they nest up during the day. Find the nest, kill yourself a bunch of 'em at one clip. Catchin' gargoyles alive in ones or twos, that is as easy as kiss my hand. A beginner's game. Capture a whole terror, that's when things get tough. Trapping a terror of gargoyles without killing them in the process? That I'd never done before.

This man, Straker, he follows me into the back of the shop where I work and refine the secrets of my trade. The only other who'd been back there besides me was Mervin, and he weren't in yet. Needless to say, I'm a wee bit nervous about Straker being with me, but I tell him he isn't to touch nothing.

As luck had it, the old St. James Cathedral had hired me to roust out a terror that'd taken to stealin' the consecrated loaves and drinking all the blessed wine. Father Dundee—who I am sure as my eye is winking never touched a drop unless it was sacred—the father, while explaining his predicament, clutched a hymnal so quick he nearly tore it in two. Also, it seems that a smell had started to seep down from where the gargoyles were nesting. A sure sign the infestation was mature.

I tell Straker about the job.

"Huh," he says. "I know the place."

Good for you, I think, but he says, "We used to go to service there every Sunday."

This Straker is full of surprises. I didn't make him for a pious man, but people come in all shapes. Regardless, I tell him to stay out of the way and get to work. I had some ideas about how to reduce the charge on some of the galvanic capacitors for the equipment. So it would knock the bastards out, you see. Not boil their insides.

St. James is a big job. Lots of area to cover, and no way to do it all in a single day. I decide we would begin with the loft. That is going to be the hardest challenge, so I want to get it over. And seeing as there is a steam wagon at my disposal, why not use it?

Gargoyles love a church loft. Easy in and out. Inaccessible if you can't fly or climb like a squirrel. Plenty of shadows to hide in during the day. All to the good. Also, priests hate the idea of tearing off the slate to make a hole in the roof big enough for a man to fit through. Oh, and how skimpy the collection plate when it comes to easing a man's work. All prayers and hard words about "no weight too burdensome for the back who bears it" or some such.

Father Dundee is a skeptic from the top of his shorn head to the hem of his hassock.

"No big show," he says. "Don't want to frighten the parishioners," he says.

"Having gargoyles flying in the rafters during mass ain't frightening them already?" I ask him. His mouth opens and closes two or three times, but he had no words. Eventually, he closes it and waits to show us the way up. I hate being managed. And I'm already feeling a little of that with Straker.

My plan is a simple one: Ease into the loft. Ignite a couple of light bars and use them to drive the bulk of the gargoyles into a tarball—that's what we call a knot of them, cuz they clump together, and it looks like a ball of squirming tar. Then deploy a couple of modified shock nets to get them to quiet down. Then it's all about rounding up the stragglers, finding any eggs, and moving on. Father Dundee thought there may be five or six gargoyles living there. I put the number closer to a dozen, just because estimates are always low and there's a whiff of rotting eggs about the place, a sure sign of a long-term infestation.

I don't think Straker understood what he was in for. Gargoyles ain't huge, but they're big enough. And mean. I learned that early on and had special leather vests and leggings made. Gloves so thick you can dip your hands in melted steel and not think a second about it. Face masks with charcoal filters in case the bastards combust. And then the thick black goggles to protect your eyes from the light bars. Frightens the muck outta gargoyles, but they'll melt your eyes for looking at them. By the time we have everything on, we look like a couple of medieval knights ready for a joust.

Father Dundee shows us to a cramped staircase that turns and turns until at the top is a narrow door no taller than my shoulder.

"That's the entrance," he says. And then he's back to the stairs and outta sight quicker than a two-step jig.

Straker and I listen at the door. We hear them, the gargoyles on the other side, gabbing and grumbling like they do. You'd almost think they had the makings of a mind in those ugly little noggins. But that's just your humanity trying to make 'em something they ain't. Learned folk call it 'morphism or some such.

The gabble is dim, telling me they're a bit away from the door, which makes sense.

"We go in," I whisper to Straker, and he, for all his cold-blooded demeanor, looks as wobbly as a two-legged chair in a windstorm. Man with meat mallets for fists and no doubt knew how to throw 'em to best effect only stood firm on account of his pride. Without me there, he'd have outrun a horse getting away.

I whisper to Straker, "We go in. Just an electric torch. Stay calm and do what I tell you." He just nods, his eyes all round and watery, brimming with the overwhelming urge to desert. But I ain't about to let Straker bolt for the streets. I open the door and push him through before he thinks to escape.

The gabbling went quiet. I duck in behind Straker, close the door, and flick on my electric torch. Straker is already coughing from the stench, poor man. Gargoyles are nasty smelling. Burns your eyes and nose and throat. Boiling bull piss would be less offensive, if you'll pardon my characterization.

There's a catwalk down the center of the loft. Not very wide. Beams crisscross at dizzying angles, joining to support the roof overhead and hold up the ceiling beneath our feet. Nothing but lath and plaster there, so one wrong step and a cherub gets a foot through his little holy face.

I shine my torch along the catwalk, and its surface is coated with gargoyle muck at least three inches thick. But it doesn't end there. There's a whole landscape of hills and valleys, miniature terrain with narrow paths for the bastards, all of gargoyle muck. Straker bends over and is sick. He has the sense to keep quiet. Once he finishes, I nod for him to lead on.

We shuffle maybe a dozen steps, the boards slick beneath our feet. I slowly edge the light along the rafters over our heads. Narrow eyes gleam orange and red in the torchlight. Some gargoyles cling upside down to the beams, their wings wrapped tight around them like little leather cloaks. Others nest in shallow bowls they fashioned from trash and refuse and dried muck. They line the inside of the loft neat as you'd like, as if they'd been set on offer on a store shelf. Far more than the dozen or so I expected.

"Stay here," I whisper to Straker, my lips right to his ear. "Get that light bar ready. I'll head down to the other end. I'll flash the torch three times. Then we light 'em up." I feel Straker shaking. The man is rattled, his bones all but clacking. "Be ready," I says. "And don't forget your goggles."

Then I go on my way, boots squishing and squelching the whole time. I'm fairly immune to the effects of muck stink, but even my nose is flowing. I'm wiping it on the back of my gloves, but pretty soon, I'm just smearing it all through my beard. Almighty! What a stench! At the same time, li'l bastards are glaring down at me. One sits up out of a little gully in the gray-green slime, and he has a half-eaten rat clenched in his jaws. He just keeps gnawing at the rat's innards as I pass, more curious I guess than angry. From what I could count, we were looking at thirty easy. How St. James is still standing was beyond my reckoning. And one hurried move. One loud noise. They all would descend on me. And I'd have been as dead as that rat, thick leathers or no.

But I get to the far end and turn around. Aiming the torch at him, I can just make out Straker. He's standing over what would be the holiest of holies—the place where the altar and other worshipful items are. I'm at the other end, over where the sinners file in. Just so you understand what's about to happen.

All this time, I'm lugging the shock nets over one shoulder, the launcher over the other, and the lightbar in my hands. Not to mention the capacitors for it all. Quiet like, I load the launcher and make sure all the connections are snug. Then I hoist the bar and kick out the tripod. Shining the torch at Straker, it appears to me he's gotten his up and is waiting on my signal.

Goggles down, I click the torch. One. Two.

Before I get to three, Straker screams.

Not a shout. Not yelling a warning. He screams. Like he's on fire. I can't see anything on account of my goggles, but the sudden noise startles the terror. The air goes thick with muck and claws and wings and tails. The whole lot of 'em screeching. I'm hit by half a dozen at least from all sides. Chewing and raking me.

"Light it up!" That's what I holler and jam down the compression switch on my light bar. Night turns to day. A light bar without goggles is like ten white suns. The roiling cloud of gargoyles in the loft drop into the muck. And their screeches get louder, only they're frightened now, not angry. You can hear the change, a lot like a person.

But Straker doesn't turn his light bar on. No. He has seven or eight ripping at his legs and arms. One gargoyle latches onto the back of the man's head and hangs on just by its teeth while whipping him in the face with the pair of goggles I'd given him. Straker lashes all over like a snake with its rear end spiked to a board, one hand over his eyes, trying to block out the light, and the other valiantly failing to dislodge his attackers. All this is bad. Worse is my light is driving the bulk of the terror toward him and the stairs leading down into the church.

Thinking quick, I shoulder the launcher, aim at the forming tarball, and a baby gargoyle fish hooks me. Shoves its dirty claws into my mouth, sets both feet right here on my shoulder, and heaves for all its worthless might. Still have scars inside my cheek from the bastard. Of course, I pull the trigger, and the net goes crackling and sizzling through the air. But my aim was a little high. I catch about a third of the terror in the span, but as the weights close, they snag Straker, too. He goes rigid as a fish mounted on a wall and topples over, smashing through the lath and plaster, and falls into the church below.

I'm too far away to do anything but watch the poor fella disappear to his death through the hole, dragging the net of gargoyles with him and a storm of falling gargoyle muck to boot.

Wil slapped the table with his palm. "That's what happened at St. James!" We all stared at him, surprised at this outburst. He gazed back at us, incredulous. "Didn't you hear about it?" he asked with a somewhat superior note. "I read it in a paper a while back. I remember thinking the details a bit lacking. The church had been damaged in a storm or accident and needed repairs. A lot of repairs. They cancelled services until the next year."

"Imagine you reading," Bryan said. We laughed and Creed looked at us over the rim of his near-empty mug.

"One question," I said.

Creed set down the mug and raised the tangle of eyebrows that met above his nose.

"What does any of this have to do with us eating the stew?" I inquired.

He laughed and laughed. "Nothing," he answered, finally. "What? Were you expecting me to tell you that the rich man who wasn't quite an airship baron ran a secret cannery where he was passing off gargoyle meat for beef? Or that the first gargoyles they found after the blast at Winchester in '64 were Union soldiers, transformed and altered by the hell machine they fired up that day?" He shook his head, but there was something about the humor of his half-hidden smile that wasn't reflected in his brown eyes. "Nah. I wasn't gonna tell you that." He touched the brim of his nearly shapeless slouch hat and headed for the door. He hesitated before pulling it open and disappearing into the gray rain and biting wind. "No. I wasn't gonna tell you that *tonight*."

With those words, Creed walked out. We sat quietly for a time, listening to the storm howl and thrash, staring at our empty bowls and the remains of our meal. When Ol' Wiss finally spoke, it was as if he jolted us from a dream.

"Don't worry, boys. Ain't nothing canned in my stew."

About Tim Kidwell

Tim Kidwell has been telling stories for as long as he can remember. He's been the editor-in-chief of a technology magazine, developed tabletop board and role-playing games, and has had the luck to see three short stories published, including one co-written with best-selling author Margaret Weis. He and his wife live in southeastern Wisconsin with their two children, a Siberian husky named Aisling, and a cat called Nekko Fireball.

The Last Sleep by Sarah Van Goethem

Another child was dead, and I'd been summoned.

I hitched my leather camera bag further up on my shoulder and surveyed the Lewis house. The sunlight that fell over the ice-laden turret and steep roof was a mockery; this wasn't a day for mild breezes and cheerful colors. No, it should be like the night before, with the wind howling through the darkness and shadows the shade of coal.

I fingered the protective black ribbon around my wrist, to prevent the deaths from spreading further, and listened to the rushing river splash along the banks behind the house. I shuddered, thinking of the small Lewis boy. It was a wonder the river automatons had retrieved him at all.

Three healthy Lewis children, now all dead. It was unbearable, too many losses.

My little brother, Larkin, was sick, and I couldn't bare the thought of losing him. I couldn't imagine how Harriet Lewis would deal with losing all three of her children.

I followed the path cleared through the slushy grey snow up to the wide porch. The floorboards groaned under my weight as I climbed the steps, and I hesitated at the double front doors. I'd taken dozens of post-mortem photos, it rarely affected me any longer. And yet, I didn't want to go in. I didn't want to see the little boy—the same age as Larkin, only four years old.

I forced myself to knock just below the wreath of laurel and yew adorned in black ribbons. The knob was bound in black crepe and tied with a solemn white ribbon. White, for a child. For purity, innocence.

Adelaide, the human maid, ushered me inside and took my coat. I pulled off my worn boots and set them on the front mat. The entry hall was dark and silent; the collection of French wall clocks were all stopped a little past ten—the time Cassius had passed away. Only two hours ago.

No time had been wasted in calling me.

"Master Cassius is already laid out in the parlour, Miss Morgan." Adelaide twisted her starched apron in her hands, agitated. "Of course, you would know that…."

I nodded. "Is there anyone in there, now?"

"No, Miss. Mistress Lewis has gone to ready herself, and Master Lewis left an hour ago to make arrangements. He's beside himself, Miss Morgan—"She clamped a firm hand over her mouth and smothered a cry, but just as quickly drew it away. "—I've never seen him so. His only son." She made the sign of the cross. "This house is marked for death."

"It's not only this house, I assure you, Addy." I laid a hand on her arm, letting formality slide. It was only her and me, after all.

"I know, Miss." She scrubbed her hands against her eyes, as if she could somehow un-see the morning's events. "He was always talking about the water sprites, he was. I should've paid more attention."

Servants were not expected to mourn junior members of a household, though Adelaide doubled as his nanny and had likely spent more time with the boy than his parents had. Her guilt was tangible.

"You can't blame yourself for a child's whims, Addy."

In the parlour, the grandfather clock tolled.

Adelaide's eyes grew wider with each of the subsequent tolls. "We forgot to stop that one."

On any other day it would now be calling time, the hours designated to receive and entertain. I wondered if the news had spread yet, or if callers may come, unknowing, greeted only be the wreath of tragedy and drawn drapes.

"I'll show myself to the parlour," I said. "Did Master Lewis specify…?"

Adelaide knew what I meant. Did he want his son seated, a more life-like pose for the photo? She straightened, gathering herself. "Nothing dramatic. There is no one left to pose him with, Miss." She bit her lip. "Unless…."

"Yes?"

She lowered her voice. "Well, there are the dolls." She shook her head before I could respond, dismissing the idea. "Master Lewis said asleep would be fine, but he wanted flowers—a bouquet for Master Cassius to hold."

"I imagine the flowers will be coming from The Clockwork Conservatory?" Really, I was more interested in *who* brought them.

"Yes." There was a movement from the top of the stairs, the sound of a skirt swishing and the patter of footsteps. Adelaide resumed her social position, eyes downcast. "The flowers should arrive soon, Miss Morgan."

Adelaide hurried off to the kitchen, and I slipped into the parlour. The drapes had been left open in this room only, just long enough for the photograph I would take, and sunlight slanted through the stained-glass window in prisms of colors. There was a large sheet draped over the piano, and the mirror over the fireplace was covered in crepe. I'd never seen the mirror; it was always covered for death when I came, but I imagined it was large and ornate, golden.

I was trying to work up the courage to look upon the still boy laid out in the corner. I settled into a plush, blue wing chair, weary. I wasn't ready yet. I'd been up most of the night with Larkin, and my body buzzed with fatigue.

I wouldn't take a picture of Larkin if he died. I'd taken a handful of him alive, healthy, and well. I would only want to see those.

The first photograph I'd taken in this house had been of a deceased Mabel Lewis. She'd been seven, and we'd sat her in one of these very chairs with her sister and brother on either side. When younger Myrtle had passed not six months later, Cassius had sat on the settee with his remaining sister alone, holding her lifeless hand. She'd looked as though she'd fallen asleep, her head lolled to the side.

Now, no one would sit beside Cassius. His Last Sleep photograph would be his alone.

I focused on a fern nestled on a stand near the side window and watched the colors that danced around the fronds in the light. They were so intense, so much more vivid than even the rich colors of the oriental rug at my feet. Larkin used to have colors like that surrounding him, but they'd all faded with the tuberculosis.

I pulled my homemade camera from my bag. I needed to get this over with, then I could go home to Larkin. When Father had passed away, and I'd taken over his business, I'd lugged his old folding plate camera around for only a fortnight before I'd taken to designing something much simpler. I'd re-used an old Waterbury brass lens, but built a much smaller mahogany frame, adding multiple smaller lenses inside and another one outside to act as a viewfinder. I'd also taken to using rolled film rather than plates. The result had astounded me. I knew of no one else who took photographs as clear as mine. Now, if only I could figure out how to add color to them without hand-tinting.

I raised my camera and looked around the room through the viewfinder. The fire crackled in brilliant, warm shades, punctuated by the cool tones emanating from the plants. I wished again that I could capture them and somehow share the vast array of colors with the world.

There was a knock at the door. The flowers had arrived, along with the boy who always brought them. My pulse quickened.

I turned my attention to Cassius to occupy myself.

Through the camera lens, I saw a color around Cassius's body—*shonna*. Pale blue, Larkin would've said. But I'd known it wasn't only a shade of blue, so I'd given a slew of other hues their own names. I lowered my camera to my lap. The color was still there, flecked with bursts of white and silver sparks.

But Cassius was dead. How odd.

Corpses didn't have auras, not after the spirit was released.

I didn't have time to inspect further before Alo arrived carrying multiple bouquets of white roses. I knew the tall, Native boy well by now. He was usually found delivering flowers to all the same places I was called to take photos. He smelled like citrus.

"Tillie." He laid the flowers atop an oak table, tipped his hat at me, and then raised his eyebrows toward the doorway. "Mrs. Whitlock, this is the young photographer I've spoken of—Miss Matilda Morgan."

I spun around.

It was the first time I'd ever seen Lottie Whitlock; up until now she'd been only a whisper on lips, a legend of a lady who'd taken an airship to the Canadian wilderness years ago and come back with a couple of Native children. Alo was the only one I knew, though there was talk of another. I'd never had the nerve to ask Alo about it. Some people had speculated if Lottie Whitlock was even still alive. Rumour had it she'd passed away from consumption.

The tall, thin woman appraised me, and I did the same of her. She wore her black hair in two thick, braided buns on the sides of her head and a corset of a deep wine color. A patterned wool blanket of matching warm hues lay across her shoulder, and a pair of goggles hung around her neck.

I curtsied. "Pleased to make your acquaintance, Mrs. Whitlock."

"Alo tells me your photographs are superb." She came forward, eyeing the camera in my hand.

I blushed, forcing myself not to look at Alo. I brought the camera forward for her to see, but not close enough to touch. "Yes. I made it myself. I'm working on how to add color to my photos next."

She tilted her head slightly. "Is that right?" Her eyes narrowed, and out of the corner of my eye, I thought I saw Alo flinch. "Do you fancy yourself an inventor then, dear?"

"I suppose."

"An artist? A designer?"

Her tone was condescending, and I lifted my chin. Already, I was not overly fond of Mrs. Lottie Whitlock. "All, I suppose."

She looked past me to stare at Cassius. "Perhaps your talents are being wasted on the dead."

I squared my shoulders. "I'm afraid circumstances dictate that I must work for pay, Mrs. Whitlock. Also, giving people and their loved ones a parting gift is hardly wasted time." I shouldn't have continued, but I couldn't seem to stop myself. "I daresay, it's more productive than tending a conservatory."

She didn't react; her attention was on Cassius. She lifted the goggles from around her neck and set them over her eyes.

Mrs. Whitlock approached Cassius and leaned over his chest, listening.

Then, she shrugged her blanket off and dug into a small leather pouch at her waist, produced something, and brought it to Cassius's nose.

A cold chill swept over me. "What are you doing?"

"Yes, indeed, what *are* you doing to my deceased son?"

I turned to the doorway again and froze.

Mistress Lewis had somehow slithered into the room behind us, unheard, despite her layers of black bombazine and crepe. At her side were two little girl automans, exact replicas of the daughters she'd lost.

Bile rose in my throat and I reached out, latching onto the first thing I could—Alo. I'd never been able to see Alo's aura, but as I touched him now, colors flowed from me to him. Mrs. Whitlock gaped, momentarily startled by the look-alike dolls, too. "Mistress Lewis, I…." She turned back to Cassius. "I have reason to believe…" Again, she didn't finish her sentence, but simply rested a hand on the boy's chest.

Mistress Lewis tapped her foot. "This is all very improper, Mrs. Whitlock—"

"Wait!" I inhaled sharply, letting go of Alo to point at the space above Cassius's right foot where silver sparks were flying.

Mrs. Whitlock turned her goggled eyes to follow my finger and sure enough, Cassius's foot moved.

"My boy! You saved him," Mistress Lewis croaked, fainting to the floor between her dolls.

I could think of only one thing to do. I snapped a photo of Cassius and all the beautiful colors that hovered around him as he opened his eyes.

I sat with Larkin that evening while Mama rested. He mostly slept, skin and bones nestled beneath the covers, his laboured breathing worse than ever before. Gas lamps shone through the window, and in their glow I could see the colors around him, all washed grey.

He was running out of time.

I wiped a cool cloth over his head and whispered, "I saw a boy come back from the dead today, Lark." My voice cracked, and I paused before going on. "He was just like you." That was a lie; Cassius hadn't been like Larkin. He'd still had color, even when he'd been dead.

But somehow, Mrs. Whitlock had brought him back into the land of the living.

"I took his picture, right when he came back to us."

Larkin's lashes fluttered, and he looked up at me, glassy-eyed. "Tillie?"

"Yes?" I smoothed his feathery hair off his forehead, knowing nothing would ever feel as soft in my life again as Larkin's hair and skin. "The boy didn't die?" He coughed, but it was weak.

I raised his head and gave him a sip of water. "No, he didn't."

Larkin smiled as he lay back again. "That's grand."

"You should go back to sleep, get your rest." I tucked the blankets in around him, but a small hot hand gripped mine.

"Promise you won't be too sad when I go."

"Lark—no."

"Promise." His eyes held mine, pleading.

My throat was so tight the words barely came. "I promise."

Another lie. I was full of them.

"Will you go make that photo?" he asked. "And show me? Before those angels take me?" Larkin's eyes flicked to an empty space over my shoulder.

I shivered. "Yes."

I rose to leave. I wouldn't lie again; I would go develop the photo of Cassius, and I would bring it to Larkin.

The darkroom was parked in our backyard, an old covered wagon that Father had refurbished. He'd originally used it for wet collodion photography, but I'd repurposed it along with the camera, and it was now loaded with trays, tongs, chemicals, and photography paper.

At first, I'd done it all by hand, but that had eaten hours out of my day. It had taken a few months, but I'd designed a steam-operated sliding plate that did all the work for me. I now had only to take the film from my camera, manually enlarge it to my taste, and then drop the exposed paper into the tray of developer. After that, my manufactured assembly line would do the rest.

I turned the knobs on the outside of the boiler, waiting for it to warm. It usually didn't take long; the tubes I'd run underground to absorb the Earth's heat often kept a fairly even temperature. Soon, my darkroom would be warm and cozy, like a cocoon bathed in red light.

When the steam engine whistled, I turned the main knob down, and went inside. After measuring out the chemicals, I took the roll of negatives from my camera and found the one of Cassius. I slipped it in the enlarger and fiddled with the position and the sharpness of the outline of the body until I was satisfied. Often, I'd run a test strip, but today I was too impatient.

I wished I could stop time now, not wait until Larkin passed. The stopping of clocks shouldn't be reserved for death, it should be for the wonderful parts of life, the parts we wanted to last.

I carefully avoided truly looking at the photograph, looking into Cassius's life-filled eyes or studying the light that I knew was around his body, though it never showed. Photographs were miraculous, yet so limiting.

Perhaps someday I could show everyone all the colors, all the ones I saw.

I dropped the photograph into the first tray and started the timer. While the mechanical arms worked, rocking the exposed paper in the solution and then moving it to the stop bath, I surveyed my wall of photos. I had almost everyone I loved captured here: Mama, Papa, Larkin, my baby sister Phoebe, who'd only lived a day, Grandfather Jack, and even our human maid, Isabella. There was a photo of myself, too, that Father had taken before he passed, and this was the only one where I was glad there was no color; my improper, flaming orange hair didn't show.

We had a few automans, too, but I'd never taken their photos. I shuddered, thinking of the dolls Mistress Lewis had commissioned, replicas of her deceased daughters.

As if you could replace someone.

I took down a photo of Larkin I'd taken in the garden and wished I had one of Alo. I'd offered once, but he'd refused. He thought the act of taking a photo would steal the soul. Maybe that's why he didn't object to me taking post-mortem photos; the soul was already gone.

I remembered what Mrs. Whitlock had said. *Alo tells me your photographs are superb.*

Alo had spoken fondly of me. I smiled in the dark, feeling as if my cheeks were as red as the light overhead. I didn't need a picture of Alo; I had him etched in my mind.

The timer dinged, and I went to retrieve my finished photo. I stepped outside into the cold to view it under the white light of the moon. The contrast was nearly perfect.

But as I looked closer, remembering the pale blue light and the silver sparks around Cassius, I thought of Mrs. Whitlock. The woman who was now known for bringing the dead back to life. And if she could revive Cassius, maybe she could save Larkin, too.

I compared the photos of the two boys, then shoved them in my skirt pocket and set off to find Mrs. Lottie Whitlock.

Snow was falling again as I neared the Whitlock estate, and I hitched up my skirts. Propriety had left me long ago, buried with Father. People had complained at first that a young girl was out and about, unchaperoned, taking post-mortem photos, but as time went on, and my skill grew, the complaints died to mere whispers and despising looks. Most of these came from the women, who I'd come to realize were either threatened by or jealous of me.

The iron gate was frozen solid, layered in ice. I climbed up and threw myself over. My top skirt, a blue delaine, caught and ripped. The piece of woolen fabric twinkled in the moonlight, impaled by a spike, and I thought of the name I had given the color—*chessa.*

I left it there and plodded on. The house was eerily dark and quiet, lit only by a single lamp in a window upstairs. I wondered if that was where Alo slept.

I made my way to the front porch. Before I could knock, though, I heard the faint ticking of a distant clock and followed the sound. I knew where I was headed, before I could see it—The Clockwork Conservatory.

I rounded the house, but instead of a glass building in the rear of the yard, I found a forest of birch trees. The bark shone in bands of *stilo* (white to most people), and in the distance a multi-colored halo of light floated in the sky.

The colors compelled me forward. Instinctively, I knew that's where I would find Mrs. Whitlock. I found an opening in the foliage and followed the gravel path.

Somewhere in the middle, I hit a fork in the path and paused. Overhead, the branches of an old tree rubbed together and groaned. Around me, twigs snapped and bushes rustled. I focused on the dark interior, and colors emerged in tiny wisps, then disappeared. I'd never seen anything like it.

I tried to follow the lightning fast flashes of color with my eyes, but it was nearly impossible.

I chose the right fork and started down the path, but a figure bolted from the trees, slamming me to the ground. Someone was on top of me, crushing my lungs. As I struggled to breathe, a bright light blinded me, and a voice said, "Wait."

Alo.

"It's me," I croaked, "Tillie."

The weight pulled off me, and I coughed, catching my breath.

"What on Earth are you doing here?"

After another deep breath, I found my voice. "Not trying to get killed, I assure you." The light still shone into my face, and I raised a hand to cover my eyes. "Do you mind?"

"Right. Sorry." Alo aimed the light at the ground instead, and I gave my eyes time to adjust to the darkness again. In the trees, swirls of colors continued rotating like the paper pinwheels I used to make Larkin. "Simi, this is Tillie."

I turned to the Native girl who had pinned me to the ground. She had a shawl of the same design as Mrs. Whitlock had worn draped around her. Two thick French braids ran down the sides of her head, and she, like Alo, wore a pair of goggles. She pushed them up on her forehead and narrowed her eyes at me. "The girl who takes dead folk's pictures?"

"Er...yes," Alo said.

Her bitter tone made me wonder if I was still flattered that Alo spoke of me to others. I stood. "That's me. Matilda Morgan, pleased to make your acquaintance." I really wasn't, but I knew I should say so.

Simi only snorted. "Let's bring her to Mrs. Whitlock. She'll be wanting to see her."

"No." Alo's answer was fast, and both Simi and I looked at him.

"Why would she want to see me?" I asked Simi, but then realized it didn't matter. "I want to see her, too. Please take me to her."

Alo beckoned me aside. Between us, a strange color I liked to call *lemmick,* emerged. Alo was oblivious to it. "It's best if you go," he said, his voice so quiet I doubted Simi could hear.

"I *need* to see her," I said. "It's important. My brother is dying." I choked on the last word.

"I'm so sorry, Tillie. But please, go back." Alo touched my arm, and a rainbow of colors enveloped us.

Simi whistled. "I see how it is."

Alo's eyes shot daggers at her. "How *what* is?"

She'd donned her goggles again, and tapped them. Alo slowly slid his own over his eyes. Then, he turned back to me and gently laid his hand where it had been before. The rainbow appeared again, pulsing from me over to him, but this time Alo exhaled loudly, and I realized why—with the goggles, he could see the colors, too.

He could see what was between us.

"Well, well, look who's come to visit." Mrs. Whitlock emerged from the trees, wearing her own goggles and a smirk. "The tetrachromat."

Alo wouldn't look me in the eye as I was led to the conservatory, which was that much worse since he now knew my feelings for him. I felt naked having him see the rosy colors I had for him.

I pushed the thought away; I couldn't worry about my own embarrassment right now. Larkin needed me.

"The Clockwork Conservatory," Mrs. Whitlock announced proudly as we emerged into a clearing.

The giant domed building had walls and a ceiling made of a thick shiny glass, except for the giant brass clock that took up the middle of a wooden dividing wall. It ticked obnoxiously, reminding me that Larkin's time was running out.

As I looked closer, I saw that clear tubes ran up the edges of the building, forming the framework and spouting out the vast array of colors that spattered the sky above.

Simi was smug, hands on her hips. "It's a little like the aurora borealis."

"Can't say as I've ever seen it," I admitted.

"There are many things most people haven't seen." Mrs. Whitlock tugged open a heavy door, and a gust of balmy air blew over me. "After you, Miss Morgan."

I wavered, unsure if I was a guest or a hostage. Mrs. Whitlock had a curious light in her eyes, and Alo was staring at his boots.

Something didn't feel right, but I went in anyway. I had no choice. This was my only chance to save Larkin.

More colors than I could ever name flooded the inside, and I stood in awe. I admired the violets and red hibiscus, the lilies and orchids. There were yellow roses and pearly peach begonias. *Sata, luca, remish.* Colors I'd only seen once or twice in my life, and that no one else had ever heard of, were everywhere.

Sunny buttercups, marigolds, petunias, and pots of geraniums gave off glowing hues. Baskets with licorice vine, periwinkle, and water hyssop hung from large iron poles, and long rows of purple and magenta sweet peas painted the space like an artist's brush strokes.

The whole conservatory was every color I wished my photographs could capture. All the colors that people were, but never knew.

A thrill shot up my spine, and I spun around to face Mrs. Whitlock. "This is incredible."

She nodded. "You see more than the average colors, do you not?"

I saw no point in lying. "Yes. Is that what you meant? Does that make me a *tetrachromat?*"

"Yes, normal people see around one million colors with the naked eye. People like you see ten million." Mrs. Whitlock adjusted her blanket shawl. "Oddly enough, it is the same mutation that causes color blindness."

I frowned. "My father was colorblind."

"Would that bother you, Miss Morgan, a world without color?" Mrs. Whitlock smirked again, and I gritted my teeth, willing myself not to say anything I would regret. I needed her help, after all.

"I suppose," I answered. "And with your goggles, you can see the colors."

"Yes, and much more."

"What else?"

Instead of answering, Mrs. Whitlock started down an obscured stone path that cut through the sweet peas. "Come along, Miss Morgan, we haven't got all night." To Simi and Alo, she said, "Please close up."

"Yes, Missus." Simi went to tend to a lever on the wall, but Alo remained.

He was quiet, but his eyes said it all: he didn't want me to follow Mrs. Whitlock.

"Leave," he said, so softly I was sure I imagined it.

"Miss Morgan?" Mrs. Whitlock tapped her foot.

"Coming." I hurried after Mrs. Whitlock, feeling Alo's gaze on my back.

The aromas of the flowers were overpowering, heady scents of vanilla and jasmine, mint and lavender, and even a tangy citrus that reminded me of Alo. The tubes I'd seen outside connected to planter boxes and ran through the soil. Bright colors tinted the mixture in the clear tubes, creating rows of snakelike rainbows across the floor.

"What are you doing with the flowers?" I matched my footsteps to Mrs. Whitlock. I followed the tubes with my eyes, looking up through the glass to watch the color clouds mix with the stars. "Are you harvesting their colors?" The idea both fascinated and repulsed me.

Mrs. Whitlock eyed me with pride. "That is precisely what I'm doing. You are a quick one."

I ignored her barbed compliment. "What are you doing with the colors, besides letting them drift into the sky?"

Mrs. Whitlock let out a throaty laugh. "That's only a remnant of the gases. The leftovers."

"If that's only leftovers, then the main course must be something else."

She raised a brow. "You would know, since you've experienced it your whole life."

I stopped. "Have you infused the colors into the lenses of the goggles, then, to allow yourself to see what I do?"

"Indeed." Mrs. Whitlock never broke her stride, and I rushed to catch up so I wouldn't miss a word. "The results were more than I'd hoped for, however." She cocked her head over her shoulder at me. "There's really so much in this world that humans don't see. It's amazing what you can do with color."

"I don't understand."

She swept her hand through the air, taking in the conservatory. "You wouldn't. You've taken the colors for granted and missed the rest. As with seeing the auras around people, you know things about them they may not even be aware of, correct?"

"I suppose." I thought of my love colors for Alo and Larkin's illness. I crossed my arms, ready to swing the conversation to where I needed it to be. "But now you can, too—with your goggles. You saw the colors with Cassius."

She smiled. "Yes."

"And then you brought him back to life." The whole reason I was here.

"No."

"Yes, you did. I *saw* it."

Mrs. Whitlock shook her head. "No, you believed what you wanted to. As did Mistress Lewis."

"Cassius was dead," I insisted. "Now he is *alive*."

Mrs. Whitlock sighed. "He was *never dead*." She grabbed me by the shoulders. "*You* know this, Miss Morgan. Oddly enough, it was likely the icy water itself that saved him. The cold slowed his heart, but he was never dead. You saw his colors before I arrived, did you not?

The truth settled over me in a flash of white. She didn't save Cassius, and she couldn't save Larkin. Poor Larkin, whose own colors were only a dull greyish-brown now. I'd seen it infiltrating his aura before he'd become physically ill.

I pulled the photos from my pocket and presented them to Mrs. Whitlock, with the one of Larkin on top. "So, you can't save my brother?"

Her shoulders deflated, and any smugness I'd sensed earlier vanished. "Is that why you're here?"

"I was hoping." Mrs. Whitlock took the photos from me and settled onto a wrought iron bench beside some red dahlias. "Why did *you* think I was here?"

She was studying the photographs, but laid them in her lap and looked up, sheepish. "Well, I…I've had a few folks trying to steal my colors."

"Steal? How do you steal colors?" I glanced at the floor, at the tubes snaking past my feet, filled with reddish dye from the dahlias. "Where are you storing these colors? What would someone steal them for?"

Mrs. Whitlock raised the photographs again, and I knew the answer.

I'd even told her what it was I wanted. I'd been wishing for it for a long time—to have colors for my photographs. Not just any colors, but the colors I could see. Was it possible?

As if she could read my thoughts, Mrs. Whitlock said, "Well, why don't we see if it would work." She got up and went to a door at the end of the path, unlocked it with an ornate key from around her neck, and led me inside another vaulted room. In the middle sat rows of clear vats, all filled with colors. Each vat had a tube that ran to a central tank. Mrs. Whitlock went over and held up the photo of Cassius. "Do you mind if I try something?"

I could barely breathe. "Not at all."

She slid the photo onto a brass plate not unlike the one I had in my darkroom, and the photo disappeared momentarily. I listened to the clock tick while we waited.

"Why the clock?" I asked, twisting my hands together.

"It times the filtering. The clock stops when the colors have run out."

There was a click, and the photo was returned to the plate. Mrs. Whitlock retrieved it, and let out a low whistle.

I pushed forward to see, and my breath left me; it was everything I'd ever wanted. The photo was now rich with colors that were usually mine alone to see, including the aura that had been around Cassius. Tears sprang to my eyes.

"Sakes alive." Mrs. Whitlock put in the picture of Larkin next.

I didn't object. It was magnificent to see.

While we waited, I realized something. "You weren't wearing your goggles!"

Mrs. Whitlock smiled. "The whole world can see *all* the colors now. Just think about what else we can capture with your photos and my colors."

When the photo of Larkin came out, I sobbed. There was the little brother I knew, the one I wanted back. The one with the beautiful healthy shades around him and the pink in his cheeks.

"Just look how we put the colors right into his photo, right into *him*," Mrs. Whitlock mused.

My photos now had the colors, but Larkin didn't. My eyes blurred with tears and I was no longer able to see the photos. I could show Larkin the photo of Cassius, just like he had wanted, but better. I would show him what I saw every day, but then he would shut his eyes and go to sleep and never see this world again.

Unless....

I wiped away my tears, thinking of what Mrs. Whitlock had said. "We can give him his colors back," I said, shaking with excitement. "Not just in his photo, but in him! Everything is always in the aura first. All illness and all health. If we restore the aura, we give him his health back."

Mrs. Whitlock pursed her lips "It could work. If you're willing to try?"

"Yes!" I nearly shouted at her, overcome with hope.

She went to the central tank and opened a tap. Inserting a clear glass vial, she filled it with the liquid color. It wasn't what I expected. When combined, all the colors made white.

"Don't be fooled," Mrs. Whitlock said, seeing my shocked expression. "All the colors are in there."

"Thank you." I slipped the vial into my pocket along with the photos, then stumbled on my words. "What do you…. What would you like in return?"

Mrs. Whitlock went to a side door I hadn't noticed before and opened it. A blast of icy air shot in from outside, and she pulled her blanket tightly around her shoulders. "A few photos, is all. I'll call for you in time. Good luck, Miss Morgan."

I'd been dismissed.

Before I left, I had to know one thing. "What was it? What did you give Cassius to wake him?"

Ms. Whitlock patted the pouch at her waist. "Smelling salts. The same thing I gave his mother when she swooned."

I went out into the cold night, armed with my color cure for Larkin.

No sooner had I entered the forest than a hand clamped over my mouth, pushing me up against a tree.

"Shhh," Alo warned.

When he took his hand away, I asked, "What is it?"

He pushed his goggles up, his arm still around my waist. He had a finger to his lips, and I remained quiet. In the distance, I could hear footsteps and talking. Mrs. Whitlock and Simi headed to the house. We stood there until we could no longer hear them.

"I need to get home," I whispered, my heart fluttering at the nearness of Alo.

He was all business, though. "Did she give you the color?"

"How did you know?"

"You can't use it. I suppose you think it was your idea?"

I grew hot with anger and pushed against him. "It *was* my idea."

"No." Alo grabbed my arm and dragged me after him, back toward the conservatory.

"Stop," I hissed. "You're hurting me."

To my surprise, Alo let go, rubbing my arm where a fiery color had sprung up. "Sorry. But trust me. I need to show you something."

"No." I backed away. "I have what I came for. I'm leaving."

"Please. It won't take long."

Somehow, I knew I didn't want to hear or see what Alo wanted me to.

"No." I bolted. No one, not even Alo, could stop me from curing Larkin.

I only made it about twenty steps before Alo caught up with me, shoving something over my head, a tight band that squeezed.

I yelped as my hair ripped and raised my hands to ward him off, but still he persisted, bringing the goggles down over my eyes. "Now, *look*," he instructed.

I stopped struggling and opened my eyes.

Around me, the orbs of color I'd seen earlier materialized into tiny beings: fairies, gnomes, and elves. I gasped, watching in silence. They were all so familiar, like something I'd known, but forgotten.

"How?" I gazed around in awe as they flitted to and fro, and farther back, peeking out from a tree, was the horn of a unicorn. "How is this possible?" I reached out, finding Alo's hand. "Is this what she meant when she said the goggles showed so much more?" I gasped. "Is this what she wants me to take photos of?"

"Is that the deal you made?" Alo's voice was stern. "You can't."

I turned to look at him, but now through the lenses he was all black, devoid of light.

"You can't," he said again. "Some things are meant to be unseen. To be left alone."

I pushed the goggles up. I didn't respond to his comment; I already wanted Larkin to see through the goggles, to see the fairyland that existed right under our noses.

"Do you trust me now?" Alo asked, squeezing my hand.

I chose my words carefully. "I trust you, but that doesn't mean I will agree with you."

"Fair enough. But I still have to show you something. You can make your own choices, then."

I allowed Alo to lead me back to the conservatory, but this time he took me to the far side, the dark one. The sky was colorless now, and without the distraction, I could see this side was boarded up and older, unnoticeable because of the bigger conservatory on the front side.

Alo kicked the door open, and boards splintered, allowing us entry.

The inside was the same as the other side of the conservatory, only here everything was dead. There were aisles of brown, withered plants and empty pots, blackened roots, and dried up soil. Everything was caked in a layer of dust devoid of color.

"What happened?" I didn't want to hear the answer.

"All the color was sucked out." Alo took my hand. "And the clock almost stopped."

Horror spread through my veins, as cold as the ice outside. "What happens if the clock stops?" I blinked, numb. "If she stops leaching the colors out of the flowers?"

"She dies." Alo let me absorb that before going on. "She died, but her father brought her back with the colors and kept her alive." Alo took my hand and pressed it to his chest. "If the clock stops, Simi and I will die, too."

I looked to the place just over Alo's head, where the aura was usually the strongest. There was nothing there. The truth dawned on me. "You were already dead."

"Yes."

I swallowed. "She resurrected you—with the colors."

"Yes."

"She *was* going to bring Cassius back, wasn't she?"

Alo nodded. "She thought it was too much grief for one family."

That had been my exact thought. "But he wasn't actually dead."

Alo crossed his arms, leaning against the wall. "Rather ironic, isn't it?"

"Why didn't she just tell me the truth?"

"Don't you see, Tillie?"

I did, I just wished I didn't. Everything was a balance. Dark and light. Life and death. If you stole from one, you paid for it in another. Mrs. Whitlock could raise the dead, but she'd kill the world doing it. The conservatory was only the start. She had good intentions, but everything comes with a price. To stay alive, one required constant color, continuous energy.

I squeezed my eyes shut, gripping the vial in my pocket.

"I'm sorry," Alo whispered.

I leaned against his chest, knowing what I had to do. "So am I."

We remained like that long enough to last a lifetime, and then Alo pulled away.

"Where are you going?" I asked.

Alo kissed my forehead. "To bed. It's time for me to sleep."

I went back in the main conservatory, alone. It was quiet now, the tubes silent for the night. I made my way to the door in the wall and used the tube that ran from the red dahlias, to smash the lock. *Billanga* (or red to most) splattered on everything.

Inside, the vats gurgled, still mixing rare colors. After studying them, I went and turned the largest brass dial. A warning light blinked red, but I kept going. Sure enough, white liquid began gushing from a spout underneath into buckets, and clouds of color began to rise. It would take a while, but by morning all the color would be drained.

I had only one thing left to do, and I grabbed a full pail and went to the wall behind me. With tears on my cheeks, I climbed the winding staircase that led to the heart of the clock. Opening the mechanical chamber, I raised the bucket.

"Sweet dreams, Alo," I whispered, and tossed the contents.

The liquid sizzled and bubbled, and the minute hand made its last tick.

Larkin was still when I returned, too still, and I knew he was gone.

In the corner, Mama was asleep in the chair, unaware. I stood in the doorway, my body numb, until I remembered the vial in my pocket.

I went over and let a few drops drip from the vial onto Larkin's cool forehead.

He stirred and I breathed a sigh of relief.

I nudged Mama. "Go on to bed," I told her. "I'll stay."

She nodded and left, patting my arm.

"Did you make the picture, Tillie?" Larkin's voice was scratchy. "Of the boy who didn't die?"

"I did." I pulled the photos from my pocket and brought the oil lamp over. Larkin's face was flushed, sweat beaded on his forehead. I showed him Cassius in all his glorious color.

Larkin's eyes grew wide. "You made color, Tillie? The ones you can see?"

"Sort of. Look." I showed him the photo of himself, surrounded by his aura. "This is how beautiful you are to me."

He reached out a shaky hand and took the photo, pressing it to his chest. "I love you, Tillie."

I swallowed past the lump in my throat and settled into the chair beside him. "I love you, too, Lark."

I held his clammy hand until he fell asleep again.

Near dawn, Larkin's breathing became more labored. He made tiny gasps in his sleep, and I clutched the vial in my pocket.

I still had enough to give us one more day, a good one, before his Last Sleep. Quality was better than quantity.

I poured the rest of the liquid over Larkin's forehead, and it flowed out and glowed around his body.

His eyes popped open, and he started laughing.

"What are you laughing at, love?" I cupped his face and kissed him on his cheeks, over and over. This was where time should be stopped.

"Your goggles." He ducked, trying to escape me. "Can I see them, Tillie, please?"

I'd forgotten all about them. I pulled the goggles off, smelling citrus. I eyed Larkin, thoughtfully. "You can, yes, but not here. There's something in the forest that I want to show you."

About Sarah Van Goethem

Sarah Van Goethem is a Canadian author who resides in southwestern Ontario.

Her novels have been in PitchWars and longlisted for the Bath Children's Novel Award. You can read another of her short stories, ACCIDENTS ARE NOT POSSIBLE, in Grimm, Grit and Gasoline.

Dieselpunk and decopunk are alternative history re-imaginings of (roughly) the WWI and WWII eras: tales with the grit of roaring bombers and rumbling tanks, of 'We Can Do It' and old time gangsters, or with the glamour of flappers and Hollywood starlets, smoky jazz and speakeasies. The stories in this volume add fairy tales to the mix, transporting classic tales to this rich historical setting.

Sarah is a nature lover, a wanderer of dark forests, and a gatherer of vintage. You can find her at auctions, thrift stores, and trespassing at abandoned houses.

Sarah is represented by Dorian Maffei of Kimberley Cameron & Associates Literary Agency.

Follow her on Twitter: @Sairdysue

"The things you say may feel like truth, but I assure you they are lies."

His location is impossible to pinpoint, the voice whipping viper-like from the blackness. When I first arrived, this sort of onslaught made me flinch; I am long past that level of feeling now. I have shed my fear of empty words, though their echoes haunt my future.

"You see, gentlemen, that the subject continues to resist. Even after several doses of the treatment for his—"

In the two seconds the healer pauses, the weeks I'd lost in the throes of the drug slam into my brain like a locomotive. The restraints at my wrists rattle, and I try to turn my head away from the cascade of images, but the ribbon of metal across my lower jaw keeps me locked to the headboard.

"—condition," he continues, unperturbed by the spasm of flesh behind him. I cannot see my audience, but I hear them shift and murmur, and a scrabbling like the needle-claws of the rats that rule the asylum at night.

"Excuse me, Doctor Yilmaz." A voice to my right; a wheezing as if he's just climbed a flight of stairs. The aroma of cardamom and coffee interweaves with the staleness of his breath when he speaks. "Maybe you should start with some background information about the subject."

My speech is slurred by the restraints on my jaw. "There is nothing wrong with me. I am not one of them! It's a mistake!"

"Actually, his is a most unusual case. It was only when we started to employ the tattlers that we found him at all."

"No previous signs of violent behavior?"

The disembodied voice of Yilmaz chuckles. "Well, as you can see from the restraints, there has been some violence. He'd managed to conceal that part of his nature until after his arrest."

"My parents were human. I *remember* them!" I grit.

Another voice, deep and full of authority. "You employ the straps in order to keep him from hurting himself?"

"Of course. It is our job to keep all of our patients safe, even if they are Travelers." A glob of spittle lands on the floor, and I feel the dust around my bare feet eddy in its wake. "The tattlers are never wrong; we'll crack him yet."

"Please, listen to me." My own pleading disgusts me, but I have to gamble that the owner of the deep voice has not cut out his heart like Yilmaz.

"There are never mistakes in the detection process?"

"I assure you, the Travelers always show themselves. Eventually." His tone drips with revulsion. "We have never had one of them sent to us that did not present symptoms. I have every confidence in the new methods we have been employing for both detection and treatment." A rustling sound as Yilmaz retrieves something from his pockets. "Would you like to see?"

The aroma does not just attract me; it propels me across the arid landscape. My footprints are erased as soon as I take the next step, the shifting sands swallowing any trace of my existence. The wind carries the promise of sustenance, and I am compelled to follow the scent until long after the moon has chased the sun from the sky.

As I approach, the sweet tang washes over me. The honeyed fragrance tunnels into my nostrils and clutches at my throat, its barbed fingers urging me to go faster despite my weariness.

I take a moment to bask in the conclusion of my long journey before thrusting my face into the pile of rotting flesh. It is clear that some of the air creatures have already had their turn at the carcass, but plenty remains for me. After so many weeks without food, there is nothing sweeter than sinking my teeth through the layers of muscle and sinew as putrescence dribbles down my pebbled chin, and the feel of the meat as it slithers down my reptilian throat.

What do you see, Traveler? A memory of your animal form?

Nothing, Dr. Yilmaz. I see nothing. Just like all the other times. I told you, there has been a mistake.

My claws grapple against the hide and find purchase in the taut skin of the bloated abdomen. As I tear at the slit, the guts slop out, and the corpse of the antelope sighs a final, fetid breath.

The men before me stumble, blinded by the effects of the aetheric tide flashing through their goggles' tinted lenses. The static crackle of the resonator dissipates, and the sickly green glow recedes into my skin. My skull still vibrates from the waves of energy that surged through it moments before.

The dark man is the first to regain his composure. He slams his body into the others and they fall into a heap on the floor. He is by my side and loosening my restraints. All I can do is stare and urge him to haste with my splutters.

He unbuckles the final strap at my ankle and wastes no time darting to the door. As he looks up and down the asylum's long corridor, I flex my hands to get the blood flowing again. I try to rise, but the long hours of immobility leave me stiff, and I fall hard onto my hands and knees. The dark man is at my side again, helping me to my feet. He pushes his shoulder under my bulk and drags me to the door. The anguished cries of my captors recede into the background as we proceed, but there is no sign an alarm has been raised; their shrieks are but a few among many in a place such as this.

As we round the first corner, I crack through my shock enough to ask, "Why are you helping me? What do you want?"

I am startled by the gentleness in his voice, the fleeting tinge of sorrow.

"All you need to know right now is that you are not alone."

"Fascinating!"

The cardamom man shuffles a few steps closer and his stink washes over me. It has been so long since I have had a taste of spice, I would bathe in the stench of his decaying teeth for even this fleeting reminder of home.

His reedy voice sounds close to my ear. "Can we remove the headgear? I'd love to get a closer look at that skull!"

I do not dare to hope, but soon there are fingers fumbling at the back of my head. The buckle pinches and digs into the base of my neck, the skin raw and crusted where the razor had cut too deep. Some part of my brain tells me to close my eyes, to save myself the shock of returning to the light, but a stronger part craves a glimpse of the world outside the wooden box too much to heed it. My eyes sting and stream, making blurry smudges of my surroundings.

I still can't turn to look at Cardamom as he examines me, but I feel the dull coldness of his instruments. The shadows in front of me are coalescing into the solid masses of three more bodies. I can't make out their features yet, but there is something terribly wrong with their faces. The light from the window—an artifact of the ideals that nature held the cure for everything—glistens wetly on their bulbous eyes.

"It is quite obvious now, of course." The voice of Yilmaz comes from the splotch on the left. "But he was above suspicion; there was no way he would be subject to the same checks as everyone else."

The deep voice booms from the figure straight ahead of me. "Indeed. And these—tattlers you called them?—are simply amazing! To actually *see* the way they disrupt the aether? It's incredible."

Yilmaz's sanguine face, so young and out of place for the medical robes he is wearing, is the only one I recognize. The willowy man at his side continues his endless scribbling, his jugular twitching while he speaks to himself in hushed tones. A final dark figure is slouched causally in the corner, and the steady regard of his eyes, the only human eyes I can see, never leaves my face.

"If you would like, you could stay for the exercise period later. The way the aether swirls around them when they move is almost beautiful enough for poetry. The patients are kept on a bland diet, to keep from inflaming their livers, but the food the cook makes for the staff is quite good. You are welcome to stay for lunch if you'd like."

"That sounds lovely, thank you," Scribbler simpers.

A sharp jab behind my ear from one of Cardamom's instruments pulls my focus from the pleasantries. I cry out and convulse against the vice that holds my head still. My vision fills with red and my heart begins clawing its way out of my chest as panic surges.

"I trust you now believe me about the advantages of using my chair."

"Will you administer an anesthetic first?" asks Scribbler, his manner academic.

The goggles that dominate Yilmaz's face give his head an insectile quality. I am half-surprised that I don't see antennae bob as he shakes his head. "If we give him something, it could skew the results. I want a clean experiment. We'll manage." A pause. A sardonic chuckle. "Or, he'll die, and then we can drain his humors and study them. An exciting prospect in itself, hmm? After my demonstration of the Western techniques to the medical board, we have been granted certain… liberties. Either way, science will be advanced by what we do here today, gentlemen." He is puffed up with pride and gives Scribbler a pat on the shoulder, but he just grunts and *scritch-scritch-scritches.* The dark man consults his pocket watch—the very picture of nonchalance. I can't shake the idea that he is much less idle than he seems.

Cardamom moves around the back of my chair and begins his gentle prodding on the other side of my head. His mutters only come to me in snatches. "…Obvious now… and the distance from the secretiveness node… destruction converges here…" This time when he marks the spot behind my ear with his scalpel, I am prepared for it and do not shy away.

"You see?" Yilmaz claps his hands like a child. "Already inured to the pain.

Remarkable creatures, really, in their way."

Scribbler nods sagely. "It's one of the reasons Travelers are so well suited for labor. They work much longer hours than we can."

"Well," Cardamom interjects. The soft clicks tell me he is putting away his instruments as he speaks. "We've never tested the machine on a living body, but based on the way the current makes the dead ones dance, the results will be… stimulating?" The rising inflection of a joke. The light chuckle of fleeting revelry between colleagues.

"And on that note," Yilmaz says airily. "Let's get started."

"This is your last chance, my friend." Yilmaz affects an air of concern. "This facility, not to mention me, has a reputation to maintain. I have a perfect record to this point, and you are not going to spoil it."

With the help of the treatment, I take a deep breath of the clean desert air. My lizard-self of the memory flicks out a long black tongue and tastes something strange on its currents. A rumble below my feet sends the sand dancing and shifting all around me. Before I can flee, a purple ball of flames bursts from a point in midair only inches from my face. My body is engulfed and my vision turns to a wash of amethyst and mauve.

"You're going to force me to take drastic measures."

The sensuous flavor of my decomposed meal turns to chalk—the aftertaste of the drugs they use to try to loosen my tongue. The horizon comes streaking at me from all sides, and in a blink, I leave the desert behind. I do my best to keep the muscles in my face relaxed as I stare into the uncaring void of Yilmaz's eyes.

"What about your oath, Doctor? Didn't you swear to 'do no harm'?"

"That only applies to God's creatures," Yilmaz says with a shrug. He rises from the wooden stool he always brings on his rounds. Dragging confessions out of his drug-addled victims must be tiring. He straightens the ludicrous hat that marks him as a government official and knocks on the door to alert the orderly he's finished. "The rifts are an affront to God, they invert his design and anything that touches a rift bears its taint."

"You and I both know you don't believe that." I lie back against my cot, the dizzying effects of drug still asserting itself. "I never would have hired you if that was the case. Our job is to *study* the effects of the rift, not hunt down the Travelers who accidentally cross the threshold."

"And that is exactly what I am trying to do," Yilmaz replies. "I tried the methods you developed, but as they are *your* methods, I suppose it should not surprise me that you have found a way to circumvent them."

I grimace and rub my throbbing head. "What I remember is you coming into my home as a welcome guest. You complimented my wife's cooking, played with my daughter, and showed us a new device you had developed. Then, you tore away everything I loved."

"Don't be so dramatic. We each have our own side to that story, my friend." Yilmaz smiles indulgently and wags a patronizing finger. "The difference is my word can be trusted."

When the orderly arrives, he trades Yilmaz a wooden box for his stool. The doctor's upper lip curls into the mockery of a smile and he beckons the burly man outside the room to enter. The door swings open, and the orderly wheels in a sort of throne.

"Do you like it?" Yilmaz asks of the wicked assortment of iron, wood, and leather that hulks before me. "A splendid piece of craftsmanship from all the way across the sea." I try to keep the terror from showing on my face, but my apprentice is too versed in my expressions for me to hide. Years of working side by side will do that. "You must admit you saw your true memories from the treatment, or it's into the chair for you."

The canvas of my cot creaks in protest as I turn to face the wall. "I saw nothing."

He sighs, and for a moment even I am almost fooled into thinking he really feels remorse for what is about to happen. "You do not belong here, Traveler. You should have kept wandering."

"Before we begin, can you tell me a bit more about what I should expect to see?" Scribbler asks. He has become a four-eyed monster, his goggles now resting on his forehead. "Our readership has exploded lately, especially with the low-folk, so I need to be able to explain the science even to a child."

"Of course. Let me think." Yilmaz ponders for a moment as he unscrews the top of the vice. Cardamom is standing at the ready, inexplicably holding a fruit bowl. "I suppose you could explain it this way. Everybody knows that something called aether surrounds us, but is not affected by us. I like to think of it as the 'fibers' in the universe, but that isn't entirely accurate."

Yilmaz finishes unscrewing my upper restraint, but my chin is still held by another strap. I do not move, but luxuriate in the release of pressure I had ceased to feel. He gestures to Cardamom, who hands him what turns out to be a helmet. As he scrapes it across my stubble, I see the bundled cables leading away like a long and hideous tail.

Scribbler waves off his concern, hanging on his every word. "I can work with a fabric analogy. Please, continue."

The screw squeaks meekly as he lowers the top of the vice again. "For a long time, we believed that there was something about aether's crystalline structure that left it unaffected by anything other than very powerful vibrational forces. More recently, special lenses—not unlike the ones you are wearing—showed us that the Travelers actually have the power to cause disruptions wherever they go. We have known for generations about the inherent dangers of their kind, but we still do not have a suitable explanation as to exactly what links them to the aether."

His work finished, Yilmaz leans away. My eyes flash to the dark man, his white teeth almost glowing against the florid wine of his lips. Incredibly, his wild smile broadens as he dips his chin in recognition of my regard. These men are sick.

Yilmaz's didactic tone falters as he is swept up in the excitement of his favorite subject. "My theory is that it has something to do with this node here," Yilmaz explains, and places a finger on Scribbler's head, an inch or so behind his ear. "This is the place where destruction and combativeness meet on the skull, and our studies have found that when examined, the Travelers show a marked propensity for exaggeration of this node, which has been linked to their violent behavior—"

"That is why we began our prep with draining away some of the problem humor," Cardamom interjects helpfully.

"Indeed." Yilmaz silences him with a glare and the dark man chuckles. "I suspect there is something particular about Traveler blood, if it is like our blood at all, and its interaction with the planet's magnetic field—"

This time Scribbler interrupts. "The what?"

"Oh," Yilmaz replies sheepishly, "am I getting too technical?"

"It's quite all right," Scribbler placates. "I think that is probably enough of the science. Just one more question before we begin, though? Fine. I know you can't be precisely sure, but what are you *hoping* to see during this experiment?"

"We will watch it all unfold through our goggles so we can monitor the shape of the aether around the subject. We are going to polarize his cranium, and we are hoping to see the aether around the subject return to alignment. If we are successful, it will give us further insight into the nature of the Travelers, and greater control over the aether problem. Not to mention some of their more unique… talents."

"And the subject? How will he be affected?"

"When electricity is applied in small doses to people like us, the effects can be quite beneficial. The resonator is based on a complementary principle so it is possible that he will see an improvement, but he may see no result. This *could* be the boost his mind needs to access the memories of his passage from the other side, or perhaps he'll hallucinate something completely new." Yilmaz pauses for a thoughtful second and mumbles to himself. "There is some risk to the memories he already has, I suppose. They could become disjointed. But that also means he'd be more likely to reveal the truth…" He considers the possibility for a moment, but dismisses it with a shrug.

A short delay while Scribbler's pen catches up with Yilmaz's words, then,

"Great. That is exactly what I needed."

"Then, without further delay, I suggest you put your goggles on and step back!" Even the dark man puts on his glasses this time, and the four figures retreat as far as they can in the confines of my cell.

This is it, my last chance. I can tell them to wait, that I see the visions of my other self when they feed me the drug. If I speak up, they may halt the experiment and just send me to a workhouse. I won't be able to see my darling girl again—all bright smiles and skinned knees—but I realize for the first time that there was never any chance of returning to that life. Once a person is marked, there is no going back. But if I tell them now, they will come for her, too. Not today, but someday. If I am tainted, then so is my beloved. Yilmaz is regarding me, his expression smug as he takes in the indecision in my face.

I grit my teeth and close my eyes, the pell-mell scamper of my daughter across my eyelids the only thing I wish to see.

He pulls the lever.

The dark man props me against a windowsill and peers around the next corner. When he returns, he stoops to take my weight again, but I wave him off. The tingling in my extremities is subsiding, and I know we can move faster if he is not dragging me along. A run is too much to ask, but we continue down the hallway at a brisk stumble.

I know the way by heart, even had a hand in the building's design, and I lead us to the right at the next fork. We reach a stairwell and I lean hard against the railing as we make our way down. The weight of the dark man's hand on my shoulder brings me to a halt, and we can both hear the echo of approaching footsteps ahead of us. He takes a quiet step back the way we came, and there is another chorus of thuds from the ingress above us. There is nowhere to run.

When our pursuers reach us, their actions are surgical and without mercy.

My would-be rescuer shows them his empty hands, and I watch in horror as the orderly smashes a cudgel across the dark man's cheek. His blood mists across my face, the wall, and then he is tumbling down the stairs. As I turn and reach for him in a futile attempt to stop his plummet, there is a sharp crack at my temple, and I sink from the artificial darkness of the stairwell to the true dark of unconsciousness.

I am restrained again when I wake, or at least, I believe that I have woken. It is difficult to know for sure when the world is black. If I try to fill the void with anything, all I see is the pattern of droplets that painted the wall. The man risked everything for me, probably even sacrificed his very life, and I did not even know his name.

Despite my immobility, I call out as loud as I can through my gritted teeth. There is no way to tell time inside my void, no play of light and shadow to signify the hour, just me and the endless loop of the dark man as he plummets down the stairs. Spittle oozes down my chin and pools at my collarbone as I wheeze and choke against the straps. I almost miss the soft jingle of keys and hushed pleasantries as they approach in the midst of my moans. Once I realize someone is in the corridor, I redouble my pleading. Relief washes over me when I hear the scrape of the door.

"Thank you!" I relax as much as my bondage allows. "You finally heard me."

The familiar voice of Yilmaz answers. "Why so eager to get started again?"

"Please," I rasp. The baton strikes the dark man over and over in the emptiness before my eyes. "The other man. Is he dead?" All that I get by way of reply is a long-suffering sigh and a few clicks of his tongue. The doctor can't see them through my mask, but a pair of frustrated tears roll down my face. I whisper again, "Please."

A few tense moments pass before I realize he has already left the room. He calls to someone down the hall before crossing back over my threshold and clearing his throat.

"My assistant is on his way," Yilmaz answers imperiously. "Along with a reporter. I already told them you can't be trusted, so don't bother trying to convince them of anything."

"No. Don't do this!" My world is somehow tilting, even inside the blackness. "You know I'm telling the truth."

The sound of the other men's voices grows louder as they approach. The doctor lets out an exasperated noise, followed by a savage whisper. "I am tired of all this 'other man' nonsense. There never has been another man! You will not mention it again. Is that clear?"

The vision of the dark man shatters, but the splinters make no sound as they cascade—nothing to break your fall in a void.

"I don't blame you, all right? It's a byproduct of the treatment, and you've been lying so long, it probably all feels the same to you," Yilmaz panders.

The two men he is waiting for are about to arrive, so he adds one final remark before I become a "subject" again.

"The things you say may feel like truth, but I assure you they are lies."

About Phoebe Darqueling

Phoebe Darqueling is the pen name of a globe trotting vagabond who currently hangs her hat in Freiburg, Germany. In her "real life" she writes curriculum for a creativity competition for kids in MN and edits academic texts for non-native English speakers. Though her first love when it comes to writing is Steampunk, she dabbles in a variety of speculative fiction genres.

Her nonfiction book entitled *The Steampunk Handbook* is available for free download for her newsletter subscribers (sign up at bit.ly/Steampunkhandbook). Her novels include *Riftmaker: A Steampunk Portal Fantasy* and the Mistress of None Series (*No Rest for the Wicked (2019)*, winner the Pencraft Award for Best Gaslamp Fantasy, and *Nothing Ventured, Nothing Gained* coming in 2020). You can find her short stories in the *Chasing Magic, The Queen of Clocks and Other Steampunk Tales, Harvey Duckman Presents Vol. 2 and Vol. 3*, and *Taught by Time* anthologies.

Find out more at PhoebeDarqueling.com.

The Last Automaton of Doctor Jubal Varva by K. A. Lindstrom

Noon came, but no church bells marked the time. Bells never chimed. Doctor Varva was thinking about the bells nonetheless.

I could always tell. He never noticed anything when he thought about the bells. The Bombardment rattled spare parts on his desk, a spring falling to the floor from the vibrations. He stared at a sheet of note paper.

These times were a problem for me. I needed to get his attention, yet he could no longer hear anything else. After five minutes and twenty-eight seconds, he finally heard me.

"The king is here to see you, Doctor."

"Hmm, what?" he said, blinking at me in confusion.

"The king is here to see you, Doctor."

"How many times?"

"Eighty-three, Doctor."

"Forgive me, Hortensia. I was thinking about the bells again."

"I know, Doctor."

Hortensia was not my name. He often called me that those days. I no longer corrected him. It upset him when I did.

"Where is the king?"

"He is in the atrium, Doctor."

He struggled out of his chair, leaning heavily on his cane. Several bones cracked from the movement. Nurse wanted him to exercise. It would ease his pain. I often urged him to comply. I knew it would be better for him, but he did not like to leave his chair.

The doctor entered the university atrium and stopped, confused again. I went to assist. The king was also used to the doctor's peculiar behavior.

"Over here, Doctor Varva."

The doctor did not recognize the man before him and stared. He wobbled unsteadily on his feet, so I took his elbow and escorted him towards the king.

"Who are you?" the doctor asked.

"Your king. We have been over this. My father, King Hynek, died over a year ago. You put him in a Commander."

"Oh." Doctor Varva's brow wrinkled. He did not remember the old king's death. He did not remember the Conversion. He did not remember the new king at all.

"Where are my automata?" the king said abruptly. He would not let the doctor's forgetfulness hamper his business. There was too much at stake.

The doctor did not respond; he had forgotten where his new automata were kept. But I knew where they were held.

"One is in the machine shop awaiting your approval, Your Majesty."

"Show me." The king gestured for me to lead the way. He refused to look at me as always.

"Yes, Your Majesty."

I held the doctor by the arm as we proceeded slowly. He would remember the new automata as soon as he saw them.

The machine shop included a housing facility for Doctor Varva's larger mechanisms. The new automata were the largest yet. The one that was to be demonstrated to the king took up a third of the space.

"We already have armored vehicles," the king said. His tone indicated he was displeased.

"Yes, but not like this one. It is like nothing you have ever seen, Your Majesty," Doctor Varva replied. "It will change the war."

"I am guessing it moves?"

"Brilliantly, Your Majesty. If I may?"

The king nodded.

The doctor hobbled up to the machine. With his cane, he tapped on the front. "Good afternoon. Are you awake?"

The machine responded with a series of clicking noises. It was awake. A jet of steam issued from the boiler as it came to life, stretching out the long limbs that had been folded beneath it. It gained its footing and rose towards the ceiling as the mechanical legs straightened.

"Will you demonstrate your capabilities for the king, please?"

Gears turned and steam hissed as the automaton complied. It moved about the machine shop. Several of the doctor's other machines in progress were crushed beneath its feet. The king was watching as Doctor Varva directed it around the room. I watched Doctor Varva.

He was pleased. His machine operated as it should. He had designed it after a cockroach he had living in his office. The low, nimble body had given the doctor the idea for his new design. It would make the other armored vehicles obsolete. They could only cross flat terrain, and no flat terrain existed anymore. They had wheels and treads. The new automata walked on many sturdy legs. They could go where others could not.

The King approved.

"With a only a few hundred of these, we could end the war!" The king grinned. I had never seen him so happy. "How many do you have done?"

"Unfortunately, Your Majesty, less than a dozen. They take a long time for the Thoughtless Ones to construct, and we are low on parts—"

"I will get you the parts. We will salvage the scrap in no man's land."

"You will lose many soldiers in The Bombardment—"

"We will send automata. They will be able to haul in the larger parts easier, anyway. The factories are spitting out Drones as quickly as they are destroyed. Soon, they will outnumber the human soldiers. It will be glorious when we march into the city. How fast does it take to make one of your…what do you call them?"

"This series will be called Crawlers. This particular machine is General Bronifac."

"Excellent. Bron was a superior general. Good choice, Varva. Send him to the front immediately."

"I would like to test him further—"

"Nonsense! He is excellent. We will put him to use in the charge tomorrow. See if we can retake the salient on Winter Hill. He will be an intimidating sight for those traitors."

"And a tempting target," the doctor said, but the king did not notice. He had the same faraway look as the doctor when he thought about the bells. Reality was lost to him.

When the king left, Doctor Varva sat at his desk, lost in thought again for the rest of the afternoon. He stared at his designs spread out across his desk, but did not see them. The Thoughtless Ones took General Bronifac to the front. With it out of the shop, they began work on a new Crawler. It was easy enough for the automata to build the exoskeleton once parts started coming in from the front. Until the doctor inserted the consciousness, no supervision was needed. The Thoughtless Ones' programing would ensure constant function.

While they worked, I built a brain.

I was the only one Doctor Varva trusted with the brains. He no longer had the hands steady enough to adjust the fine clockwork. I sat in the workshop assigned to me and started a brain. It took me thirty-seven hours, twenty minutes, and fifty-two seconds to complete one when uninterrupted. Rarely was peak efficiency achieved anymore.

"Number One, the doctor is not in his office."

I turned towards Nurse. I was only eighteen percent done with the brain.

"Is he in the shop?"

"He is not."

I stood to go look for the doctor. I sent Nurse to check the second floor, whose rooms functioned as storage, containing old remnants from when the university was open. It would not be unusual for the doctor to be there, searching for parts or new ideas.

I checked the other workshops. The doctor planned in his office, his blueprints covering most surfaces, but most of his machinery was crafted in the workshops on the lower levels. They were easier for him to get to in his old age.

Doctor Varva was not in a workshop. He was in the auditorium, which we did not use for building automata. The roof had collapsed in an air raid, ruining the seating area. Much of the room was damaged by weather, and it frequently flooded. Only the stage remained intact and undamaged. It was here that the doctor sat. He had found a machine I had never seen before. It was old and rusty, and I gave it little thought.

"It is time for dinner, Doctor."

"I will get to it later, Hortensia." His voice was weak. I moved in front of him and noticed tears on his face. It was unclear what had caused his sorrow.

"It has been done for thirteen minutes and twenty-eight seconds, Doctor. It will get cold."

The doctor's face turned angry. He wiped away his tears and glared at me.

"Leave me be, Number One," the doctor said with a peculiar irritability that I had not heard in his voice before.

"I must insist, Doctor. You must take your medication."

"Ha, those pills that useless Nurse keeps giving me are as helpful as an umbrella in The Bombardment."

"I do not understand, Doctor. How would an umbrella help in The Bombardment?"

"It wouldn't, which is the point."

"Your dinner is getting cold, Doctor. It has been ready for—"

"Oh, stop it with your numbers. I am coming."

Doctor Varva set down the machine and stood, leaning heavily on his cane. I approached to help, but he waved me away. I followed him from the auditorium. Once he was seated at his desk, his now cold meal in front of him, I went to fetch Nurse.

"The Doctor is eating dinner. He was in the auditorium with an old machine."

"I will bring him his medication."

"He seems to think it is 'as useful as an umbrella in The Bombardment.' I believe he meant that the medicine is ineffective."

"I shall check his vitals and increase the dosage as necessary."

"Let me know if changes are made."

"Yes, Number One."

Something peculiar was happening to the doctor. I had completed eight brains before Nurse brought news of his odd behavior to me.

"He spends all day in the auditorium."

"Is he building a new automaton in there?"

"It is unclear. He is building something, yet I do not know what it is. He has six Thoughtless Ones assisting."

"I will inspect his creation. Perhaps the king requires a new machine."

"The king has sent letters asking for more Crawlers. No new machine was requested."

I did not know what the doctor was creating. He usually asked my assistance. Yet he had left me alone to build brains. I found him on the stage once again.

"What are you building, Doctor?"

"Ah, Hortensia. Glad you could join us. Will you help these gentlemen with the gears? I am afraid their fingers are just too indelicate."

"Yes, Doctor." The automata stepped out of my way. "What do you need me to do, Doctor?"

"I need those wires fed through the gears and the teeth lined up with that camshaft."

"What are you building, Doctor?"

"The last automaton we will ever need."

I asked what he meant, but he would not elaborate. He was too focused on his creation. I had helped him with many others, but I could not decipher what he was building. It was unlike any other automaton. There were rows of wires that seemed to hold no function. Metal plates of various sizes were visible, but they were placed inside the machine instead of outside, so they were not meant as armor. The automaton's construction was illogical. I told the doctor so.

"Give it time, Hortensia. It will serve its purpose."

While Doctor Varva built his device, the king grew anxious for his new Crawlers. Several were irreparably damaged on the front. The salient at Winter Hill was reclaimed for forty-seven days before it was lost again. The doctor had not put a consciousness in a machine since General Bronifac. I had no choice but to ask the doctor to stop working on the new machine.

I returned to the auditorium. The doctor's machine had grown. It now took up half the stage. It did not appear to have any legs like the Crawlers or wheels like the Commanders. The rusty machine I had seen him holding seventy-three days previously had now been polished and attached to the strange automaton. A tube ran from one end and disappeared into the inner workings. I could not decipher its purpose. I did not ask what it was for as I had more urgent matters to address.

"New consciousnesses need to be uploaded, Doctor."

"They will not matter once this is finished."

"The king demands it, Doctor."

"The king is a fool. He is more bloodthirsty than his father." His voice was bitter. I waited. He sighed and turned to me. "Nevertheless, I will show you how to upload the consciousnesses, Number One. It will be important."

"Yes, Doctor."

He showed me the process. It turned out to be quite simple to take the containment vessel and plug it in to the brain stem. I uploaded sixteen consciousnesses into Crawlers in the first twenty-four hours. Crawlers that had been stored in a damaged hangar until activation were finished and sent to the front. The King sent back a letter of approval. The doctor ignored it and continued his project.

It did not look like an automaton. It did not look like anything I could identify. It was almost as large as a Crawler, but its function continued to be a mystery. The doctor still refused to explain. I stood at his side as he admired his machine, Thoughtless Ones busy at work. All he said was, "Not much longer now, Hortensia."

I continued producing machines for the king. News from the front suggested that while the Crawlers were outperforming our previous armored vehicles, they were being targeted by aerial attacks and destroyed as fast as we could build them.

I created brains. I plugged them in. I uploaded consciousnesses. I sent the machines to the front. I only saw Doctor Varva when he came looking for parts.

"He is more alert than he has been for six months," Nurse said during her weekly update. "He is moving more and recalls more details. He is improving while working on this new project."

I let him be. Nurse came to me on day two hundred and ninety-two. The doctor had finished with his project and wished to see me. He was not well, but would not let Nurse administer aid.

"I could not attach the instruments to test his vitals. He refused my assistance."

"I will see him."

His machine had grown. It now jutted from the open hole in the ceiling. I recognized the transmitter. Though I did not know the full purpose of the machine, this part was meant to signal another automaton. Perhaps multiple automata. He had said it was the last automaton we would need.

"Nurse says you are refusing aid, Doctor."

Doctor Varva said nothing. He sat in a crooked auditorium seat, staring up at his machine. It hissed gently as Thoughtless Ones fed the boiler. It was ready.

"Are you refusing aid, Doctor?"

"Do you remember the bells, Hortensia?" he asked.

"I have no memory of any bells, Doctor. Why are you refusing Nurse's treatment?"

"No, I suppose you wouldn't. I made you perfect. Your clockwork body, your steel casings. I could never make another quite like you."

"What about your treatment, Doctor?"

He winced as he shifted. Despite his pain, he continued as if he had not heard me. "You loved those bells. Such a jolly sound amidst all the dark rumors. We *thought* they were merely rumors, anyway. Yet here we are. The town is ruined. Those merry bells are now probably shrapnel scattered across no man's land. And you have no memory of them at all."

"The bells serve no purpose, Doctor. What matters is your health. Nurse wishes to treat your pain."

"She can do nothing for me now," Doctor Varva said, acknowledging my enquiries at last. "I must be uploaded."

"Doctor, you must not—"

"I am old and tired, Hortensia. I do not want to continue. I told you how to upload consciousness. Now you have to do so with me. You must upload me into my machine."

"What is your machine, Doctor? Is it a formidable weapon?"

"In a way." He looked at me. He was sad. "I hope you will forgive me for what I have done to you. I did not know how far my grief would take me. I hope this will make it right."

"I do not understand, Doctor."

"I know you don't," he said with a sigh. He stood slowly, leaning heavily on his cane. He shuffled towards his machine. Cables extended from the side, connecting to a consciousness cylinder already installed within the machine. Doctor Varva settled himself beside it and began attaching the cables.

"Help me with these, Hortensia."

"The king will be unhappy to lose you, Doctor."

"The king will have other things to worry about."

I did not understand Doctor Varva's smile. "Nurse will give you a sedative, Doctor."

"No. It will weaken the connection. Plug me in now."

"It will hurt you, Doctor."

"I will not notice for long."

I helped him attach the cables to his spinal cord and brain. He groaned as I inserted the needles. When I attached the main cable at the base of his skull, he whimpered. I continued despite his pain. I had been given orders.

"Things will be well, Hortensia. I hope you remember how much I love you."

I did not know how to respond to the doctor's sentiment. He closed his eyes and leaned back against his machine.

"Do it," he said solemnly. I obeyed.

The transfer was slow. Doctor Varva had many years of data stored in his brain, and it was not pliant and flexible as in the soldiers. Transfer was easy on the youth. Nurse came in as the process was underway. She saw what was happening and accepted with a single question.

"Was a sedative administered?"

"No."

Her own programming did not allow for sentiment, as mine did not allow it. My only thought was that I must now inform the king that he would get no new machines. Nurse's thoughts would be on what to do with the body when transfer was complete. It would be her last task. She had no other purpose than to care for Doctor Varva.

Transfer completed, Nurse tended the body, unplugging the cables and cleaning up the fluids. I went to the control panel at the back of the machine. A jet of steam escaped. A Thoughtless One adjusted a valve, increasing pressure within the boiler.

"Doctor, are you integrated?"

I received no response. I inspected the consciousness cylinder. It was active, but needed manual integration. I locked the cylinder into the brain stem. I watched the doctor's consciousness stream through the nervous system. The usual pale green tinge that colored the liquid mercury was darker than usual, but still within normal parameters. The rate of flow was normal for the automaton's size. A spike in pressure within the boiler normalized as the consciousness reached full integration. The machine was operational.

I did not know if the doctor would be able to understand me as his other automata did. This machine had few of the usual mechanisms. "Doctor?"

A strange sound came from the machine, like a loose screw falling onto scrap metal. It continued, the pitch changing as if Doctor Varva experimented with what sounds he could make.

When the metallic sounds stopped, a new style started, low vibrations that echoed in my chest cavity. I had never felt anything like it. Again, he experimented with pitch. The odd machine the doctor was so fond of released a blast of sound from a horn of some kind. It too changed pitch. The doctor's machine was some sort of sonic device. I waited.

The sound paused for a moment before a specific pattern emerged—a low, drawn-out vibration on what I had identified as a wire under tension accompanied by the tap of metal on metal. Another vibration on the wire, this one higher pitched than the first. A low blast from the horn.

I listened intently as the machine varied between types and pitches in this pattern. It varied slightly as if the doctor were trying to find a specific set. The pattern sounded almost like speech.

"Hor-ten-si-a."

It was wobbly and strange, but I gathered his meaning.

"Yes, Doctor. I am here."

After several tries, he found the sounds he needed to continue. "Flip switch."

On the transmitter, a switch stood out prominently.

"What will it do, Doctor?" I asked. It was not my place to question the doctor. But I wanted to know.

"Help." I did not know what he meant, but I obeyed. Help meant something good. I did not doubt the doctor.

The transmitter activated. The boiler hissed and gears spun. The electricity they generated crackled. It was fully functional. I stood back and observed. The doctor was silent for a moment. Then he began to send out his message.

It was garbled at first. He was still learning what sounds worked best. But as his familiarity grew, the sounds came faster and faster. The vibrations that penetrated my exoskeleton created strange feelings within my gears. I waited to see what this machine the doctor had created would do.

The doctor's consciousness took time to work out the right configuration of sounds. I do not know how long it took. I stopped registering time and let myself feel the vibrations, the sounds echoing in my metallic skull.

I do not remember powering down. I merely remember reactivating and no longer being Number One.

Music. I remembered what that was now. The doctor was playing music. But he was not just Doctor Varva anymore. I remembered him as a young man, carrying me on his shoulders as we went to the church, the bells ringing joyously. I remembered him playing with me in a wheat field, chasing me through the stalks rippling in the autumn breezes. I remembered laughing as he tickled my fleshy stomach. I remembered when he was my father.

I also remembered the moment he no longer was. The war came to our town, and in the first bombardment, I was crushed by the collapsing stones of our home. He had been a proper human doctor then. He fixed me as best he could, but I was irreparably crippled. He played the violin for me as I cried. There was so much pain. More pain than I could ever register in my artificial form. The music could not distract me from it.

I was weak. The army had taken all the medical supplies, so my father could do little for me. But the university, they could perhaps help. With the machinists at the academy, he began to build a new body, one that would let me live. One that would not feel pain.

The first was imperfect. I was still mostly flesh, and the agony of the attached metal limbs made me almost as useless as my fully human form. So they tried again. Nerves were severed to ease my pain, and more of my flesh was replaced with machinery. Movement was possible, but not easy. Many times they tried to fix me, but I begged for death.

My father would not let me go. He put me to sleep one night, promising the morning would be better. He sang me to sleep. He hoped the music would soothe my agony, if only a little. That was the last time I heard music.

I woke, but was no longer myself. I was the first automaton. Though I was sentient, I was not Hortensia. My consciousness let me move about, to control my limbs, but it did not give me access to memories. My father wanted to fix me. He wanted Hortensia back. But soon the old king heard of his work. He was ordered to build more of me. And I remained Number One.

Somehow, my father found the secret to unlocking full consciousness within his machines. Decades of research and experimentation, perhaps, had given him clues. The harmonic vibrations were what did it, stirring the consciousness in unusual ways until it flowed freely. But I like to think it was his music, the beautiful, haunting music. Music that had not been heard since the war took away everything pleasurable.

I listened to my father's music, wishing I was still human enough to cry. I could hear them. For the first time in over fifty years, I heard bells. They were different. They had been fabricated from scrap metal rather than forged for a decadent churchyard, but the happy tinkling sound was clear through the music my father played. Through the rumbling of the drums and the braying of the horns, I listened for those imperfect bells.

Time had no meaning anymore. I only knew it passed because other automata arrived. Drones, Commanders, Crawlers, every model soon filled the auditorium. The sounds of machinery halting outside the building indicated that more were arriving. They filled what was left of the university grounds. All of them were just listening, listening to my father's music.

The sounds of The Bombardment stopped as the automata left the front. There was nothing left to fight. The artillery shells had no targets. The only sound remaining was the growing crescendo of mechanical parts echoing around the university, blending perfectly in sync with the music my father made. Perhaps the automata were singing, joining in the music the only way they knew how. Somehow, my father had done what he never could as a man. As an automaton, he had managed a moment of peace, a moment of beauty in a time of war. Pride surged through me as I joined the automata in their song. We all stood together, listening to the drums and the strings, the horns and the bells.

About K.A. Lindstrom

K.A. Lindstrom is a nomad masquerading as a writer. Raised in the hills overlooking Cornell University in the Finger Lakes region of New York, she has a degree in International Affairs and has used it as an excuse to travel. She has lived of-and-on for almost two years in the South Pacific and Oceania, working in pubs, orchards, and on tall ships. She has written short stories, ghostwritten novels, and published serials in order to supplement her travel budget. Much of her writing is inspired by the people and places she encounters on her adventures.

A Skies of Fire and Lightning Story

Jackson Shrike leaned back in his chair and shifted his manacled hands. He had to admit that the room was a good deal nicer than any other interrogation room he'd ever been in. It had to be the warm wood paneling and the brass fixtures. A benefit of being caught by the flagship of the Royal Sky Navy here in the Caribbean, he supposed. Shrike had been in the room for about an hour, and he wasn't concerned for himself so much as he was for the rest of his crew. He hoped they were being treated at least half as well as him.

The door opened, and a man in vice admiral's uniform walked in carrying a file. The man nodded at Shrike before putting the file down on the table and sitting down across from him. A Naval MP Sergeant walked in behind the admiral, and the officer gestured to the manacles around Shrike's wrists, saying, "I think we can do away with those." The MP nodded, then stepped to Shrike's side and removed the manacles. "Thank you," the admiral said. "Do go and see about a bit of tea for myself and our guest, won't you?"

The MP Sergeant saluted and walked out of the room.

The admiral opened the file and began reading through it. When the tea arrived a few minutes later, he looked up and said, "Please, help yourself, Captain." Shrike made a cup of tea for himself and one for the admiral. Taking the cup with a muttered thanks, the admiral closed the file, took a sip, and gave Shrike a considering look. "Now then, Captain Shrike," he said. "Allow me to introduce myself. I am Vice Admiral Robert Ballymore, commander of Her Majesty's Sky Navy forces here in the Caribbean."

"Pleased to make your acquaintance, sir," Shrike said, giving Ballymore a respectful nod.

"Likewise, Captain," Ballymore replied. "You've had quite the varied career, haven't you? From a promising officer in the Sky Service to a mountebank near the top of Her Majesty's Most Wanted List in just under four years. An impressive accomplishment, really."

"I'm not sure if you meant that as a compliment, but I thank you," Shrike said, unable to contain a slight smirk.

"Half a compliment, at least," Ballymore replied with a smirk of his own. "As a matter of fact, it is your skills as a freebooter that interest me, and what I would chiefly like to discuss with you today."

"When your marines boarded my ship and clapped us all in irons, I rather thought you had a bit more than a conversation in mind, Admiral," Shrike said, taking a sip of his tea.

"Normally, quite a safe assumption, I assure you. However, today we find ourselves in a rather unique situation, and I invited you aboard the *Intrepid* to discuss it with you. Where we go from here will depend entirely on where that discussion leads us."

"Well then by all means, say on."

"I invited you aboard because I have a proposal to present to you."

"I assume that your proposal doesn't involve imprisonment, hanging, or Transportation?" Shrike asked.

"None of the above. Not for today at least," Ballymore replied, absently moving the file back and forth on the table. "I pray you hear me out before you make your final judgement. As ludicrous as it may sound, I'd like to hire you and your crew. You see, something of crucial importance to the Crown was stolen here in the Caribbean by one of your, shall we say, colleagues. I'd like you to steal it back."

Shrike couldn't help himself, he threw his head back and laughed. To his credit, Ballymore didn't become angry. He simply sat there with a slightly indulgent smile on his face, sipping his tea and waiting for Shrike to compose himself. Once under control, Shrike said, "I apologize, Admiral. No offense intended, I assure you. Your proposal is downright Swiftian in its modesty,

I dare say."

"Only on the face of it," Ballymore said with a thin smile. "What we have before us is the epitome of the old saying, 'Send a thief to catch a thief.' In this case, send a pirate to best a pirate. I believe that this will be the best way to get this done quickly and with the least noise, shall we say? I have looked over the records of your…exploits…and your time as a freebooter is marked with a certain creativity, a certain effectiveness, and a very respectable unwillingness to spill blood when it isn't absolutely necessary. If only you had been able to continue your Royal Navy career, who knows to what heights you could have risen. Oh, make no mistake, you are rightly considered to be a dastardly villain. However, your skills are beyond question, and I regret that we lost a damn fine officer when you were drummed out of the service."

"Again, I thank you. If we could avoid talking about the circumstances of my discharge for now, I would be very grateful to you."

"Understandable. That is not what I am interested in. As I said, I need you to steal something back for the Crown, I know you and your compatriots have the skills to do it, and I am fairly confident that you will be a good deal more receptive to my proposal when I tell you that your target will be Rejik Helgarsson."

Shrike's smile dropped off his face like a stone. Through gritted teeth, he asked, "Rejik?"

"Rejik the Red himself," Ballymore confirmed with a nod of his head.

"Is it going to put you out too terribly much if I bring back his corpse along with whatever it is he stole?" Shrike growled.

"I would prefer that you not bring him in at all. The item he stole is of primary objective… But if you do bring him in, I would prefer that he was still among the living, yes. There are a number of other crimes that Helgarsson must be brought to book for," Ballymore replied.

Shrike's voice was deadly quiet. "I make no promises, Admiral."

About an hour later, Shrike walked down a corridor towards the *Intrepid's* general detention area. He needed to get Willow out and take her back to *The Wild Rover* so they could be away from here to discuss Ballymore's insane proposal. The admiral had ordered the rest of the *Rover's* crew confined to the ship in the docking bay, but had brought Willow aboard and into the detention area. With her also aboard as a "guest," Ballymore had quite rightly assumed that Shrike would be more likely to agree to the stunt. It was an extremely effective button to push, and Shrike didn't like how much the admiral seemed to know about him. He took no comfort knowing he was on the other side of the law from a man who was as intelligent and capable as Ballymore was proving himself to be. Shrike decided that at some point he was going to have to do something about that situation, but for now he had a job to do.

Following the same MP that had taken his shackles off in the interrogation room, Shrike walked into the detention center and looked around. While not quite as nice as the room where he'd met with Ballymore, it was a good deal nicer than any other brig he'd ever seen. It was certainly nicer than the brig they had on the *Rover*. Apparently, Ballymore believed in treating all his prisoners with courtesy and civility. Something else to note.

Shrike stepped up to the cell housing Willow, which had bars made of an extremely thick, sturdy mahogany. She wasn't making any attempt to escape, but the cell was obviously meant to keep an Oremancer like Willow from using her talents to refuse the ship's hospitality. Willow sat in a plain but reasonably comfortable-looking chair with a hand of Single Castellan laid out on the small wooden desk in front of her.

"I'd play the Black Rook on the Red Empress," Shrike said.

"And that's why I've never seen you win a game," Willow said without looking up. "You've got no sense of long term strategy." She turned a card and laid the Rampant Chaos card over the Black Duke, then shifted her gaze to Shrike. "How nice to see you, love. Have a nice chat with our gracious host?"

"Oh, very pleasant," Shrike replied with a smile. "But this isn't really the place to discuss it." He nodded to the jailer, who approached with the key. "Unless of course, you'd like to stay and finish your game, oh Mistress of the Castellan?"

"I think I can stand to leave this behind, thank you," she said with a smirk. "Just an exercise to fight off boredom." She stepped through the cell door with a nod to the jailer, and then turned and headed out of the detention center.

Back on board *The Wild Rover*, Shrike called his senior crew together in the ship's war room to discuss the admiral's proposal. "So, we've been given an interesting opportunity. It seems that the commander of Caribbean Naval forces has a broader mindset than we'd normally credit to flag officers in Her Majesty's Royal Sky Navy. Another gentleman of fortune and his crew have hit one of the RSN's cargo shipments and taken something of particular value, and Admiral Ballymore would like us to track down the culprits and steal it back."

"What exactly was taken?" asked Professor Ambrose Wakeridge, the ship's main science officer, sitting off to the right. He was seated next to Annabelle, the sweet-faced automaton girl who was deceptively strong and agile, and a very important member of the *Rover's* boarding party.

"I don't know, the admiral wasn't forthcoming. He simply said that it was a large container, roughly the size of two London taxi carriages end to end, marked with symbols from the Royal Agricultural Society, and secured with an Oremantic lock."

Wakeridge's eyes narrowed at the description of the prize.

"Now," said Shrike. "we come to the biggest point of interest in this job. The one who stole whatever it is that we're tasked with retrieving is an old friend of ours. Rejik the Red." There were a few gasps from around the table. "Trust me, that I feel the same way. We all know what happened the last time that we tangled with Rejik in Kingston, but this is not about revenge. Well, it may be a bit about revenge."

"Well, what *is* it about, then?" asked Oliver Wainwright, the *Rover's* first mate. "What could be the motivation to tangle with that madman again?"

"It's the terms of the admiral's offer. Whatever Rejik stole is so important that we're being offered full pardons for all crimes to this point, provided we get the item back intact."

"And then?" asked Oliver. "We turn the *Rover* into a sky barge and start running cargo for the RSN?"

Shrike replied with a chuckle. "Not in this life. No, we'll just have to take care to stay off of Ballymore's scope in the future."

"And how will we go about doing that?" asked Ciara, the *Rover's* master of arms.

"One thing at a time," Shrike said. "Now, as far as getting back whatever cargo Rejik stole, I've had a couple of thoughts."

It took the crew less than a day of checking with various contacts in the pirate community, along with a wild night and a couple of hundred pounds spent in a bar on St. Lucia, for Shrike and Wakeridge to find the cargo that Rejik had stolen from the RSN. It was sitting in The Red's private island lock-up, the location of which they learned from some former *Basilisk* crew members plied with too many rum cocktails.

As luck would have it, the day was a particularly cloudy, so Ollie was able to hide the *Rover* close to Rejik's island warehouse. Wakeridge and Skuttle, the ship's engineer, had managed to rig up a periscope that rose out of the cloud bank. Someone on the *Rover* would be able to see when the landing party shot off a signal flare, and the ship would sweep in and snag the cargo.

Shrike decided to keep the landing party small, giving them the best chance to get to the cargo without being spotted. From their drunken intelligence gathering, the crew knew that with most of Rejik's forces out raiding, the guard contingent was likely to be modest. However, no sense taking chances.

Shrike, Wakeridge, and Annabelle set off in one of the professor's most useful inventions, a small landing craft they referred to as the Zep-Launch.

The airship could only hold five people, but had the advantage of being quick and quiet, making it perfect for a clandestine intrusion such as this one. They landed and moored the Zep-Launch on the far side of the island and slipped ashore without being spotted. Luck continued to be with the trio as they found the warehouse they sought relatively unguarded. If the pilfered cargo was in there, the large platform out to the shoreline would allow the *Rover* to swoop down and take the booty on board.

Shrike, Annabelle, and Wakeridge entered the warehouse through a loose vent, then waited a few moments, getting their bearings.

"Which way do you think it might be?" asked Shrike.

"Well, knowing how lazy some pirates can be, I'd imagine they'd leave the cargo as close as possible to where they unloaded it. My guess is it's still sitting near the door at the back." Shrike pointed in the direction of the shoreline. Shrike looked around to see the warehouse was pretty standard. Large open areas for storage, and a series of metal catwalks running under the rafters where guards could patrol, blessedly free at that moment. "Someone should get up there and give us some high cover. What do you say, Cap?" Wakeridge asked.

"Sounds like a good idea to me, Wake," Shrike replied.

Wakeridge grinned and said, "Annabelle, make sure our captain here doesn't get himself into too much trouble, eh?"

Annabelle nodded as he began to climb, then she smiled brightly at Shrike, bowing and gesturing in the direction that he had just indicated. Shrike returned the automaton's smile, then with one hand on his cutlass and the other on his pistol, they headed further into the warehouse as quietly as possible.

They made it a good twenty yards before they ran into a sentry. The pirate grimaced at them, then gave a piercing whistle. Several more pirates arrived, climbing around crates and shelves. All of them were angry and armed.

The first pirate drew a Mjolnirium cutlass and started to advance. Shrike drew his own cutlass and set his stance. The impending fight was interrupted by a loud boom and a flash of light, and Shrike's opponent was staring at a smoking hole in the center of his chest. Wakeridge crouched on the catwalk above Shrike, with Vorpalier, his custom-made Albionium rifle, at the ready.

The Red's men took aim at the professor with their pistols, but never got the chance to pull the triggers. In a blur of white, Annabelle kicked one man in the stomach, who folded up with a "whuf" of displaced air. She grabbed the pistol out of another mans hand and smashed him across the face with it, rendering him unconscious in a single blow. She pirouetted to her right, just ahead of a third man pulling his trigger. As they were packed in like sardines, the pirate only succeeded in shooting one of his compatriots before Annabelle twirled up to him, firing a knockout punch to his jaw.

Two more pirates dropped after being shot by Wakeridge, and Annabelle took out the few who remained. Shrike smiled as he returned his blade to its scabbard, unused, then stepped up to Annabelle as she came to rest in a fifth position plie, smiling brightly. Shrike turned and snapped off a salute to Wakeridge, got one in return. Shrike took the automaton's hand and planted a kiss on it. "Thank you, my dear." The clockwork girl's eyes sparkled as she curtsied, then gestured further into the warehouse, tilting her head in a questioning manner.

"By all means, let us proceed." Shrike offered her his arm. He then raised his voice and said, "If you could keep an eye on things from up there, Wake, I'd be most grateful."

"That's why I got this beauty out of storage," Wake said with a smile, patting the stock of his rifle. "Lead on, you two. But please keep in mind we're here to burgle these miscreants, not attend a spring cotillion."

"Don't be jealous of my manners, dear Professor," Shrike said with a smirk. They both chuckled and headed deeper into the warehouse.

They found their prize sitting exactly where Shrike thought it would be, almost flush with a large door big enough for two cargo barges to fit through side by side. The crate itself was also large; at least the size of two London carriages. Thankfully, there were a couple of mindless service cargo automatons standing by, each over eight and a half feet of gleaming brass and gears. Shrike and Wakeridge activated them, while Annabelle found the door controls.

After getting the cargo out on the loading area and dismissing the automatons, Shrike loaded a flare and shot into the sky.

A few minutes had passed when the door behind them opened. Shrike shot a quick glance at the others and motioned for them to take up positions close to the crate, hoping the pirates wouldn't want to risk a wild shot damaging their prize. Shrike's heart sank. At the head of the group strode a mountain of a man twice as massive as Shrike, with the red hair and beard of a Norse god of old. Rejik the Red.

In his heavy northern accent, Rejik said, "Ah, Captain Birdy. So nice to see you again. Would you mind telling me just what it is you think you are doing with my property?"

"Rejik, a pleasure as always," Shrike gritted. "I'm afraid you're quite mistaken. You see, this piece of property belongs to the Royal Sky Navy. The commander of Caribbean forces was missing his goods, so he asked me to get them back for him, and that's precisely what I intend to do."

"Oh, ho! The Bird man makes a joke! Tell me. Just how will you accomplish this? I see your odd clockwork girl standing with you, but other than her, just you and that scientist we almost made an example of in Kingston. You cannot move that container, so why don't you just stand away from it before I order my men to shoot you? Then, we can all have a nice *chat* before I turn you over to some warrant officer who might offer me a small reward for you, nasty pirate that you are."

Thankfully, Shrike was spared from the need to reply to Rejik because at that moment, the *Wild Rover* arrived from around the headland, the cargo bay door already open, the crane extended, and several of the ship's guns pointed squarely at Rejik and his men.

Shrike's smile held no humor. "I don't believe that we're going to be able to accommodate you, Captain Helgarsson. So sorry. I realize that this is just terrible manners, but I'm afraid we have an appointment to keep, and we really must dash. You understand, press of business and all that."

Shrike pulled his pistol and aimed it at Rejik's head, keeping the fuming pirate chief at bay while Wakeridge and Annabelle hurriedly attached the shipping container to the grapples from the cargo crane.

"Captain, we are ready to depart!" Wakeridge said, crouched atop the container. His rifle tracked back and forth between several of the pirates. "Annabelle, my dear, would you be so kind as to help the captain?"

"This isn't over, Shrike," Rejik bit out. "We went through a lot to acquire that item. You had best believe that we are going to come for it. That, I can promise you."

Annabelle leapt lightly down from the top of the shipping container and wrapped a hand around Shrike's shoulder. Then she jumped back up to the top of the container, carrying him with her.

Shrike stepped to the edge and offered a mock salute to Rejik. "Oh, I know. But you know as well as I do that my ship is much faster than yours. Catch us if you can."

Shrike flashed another smile at Rejik and waved as the container was drawn into the cargo bay. When the door began to close behind it, he jumped down from the container, strode over to the wall, and activated the speaking tube to the bridge. "Ollie, we're aboard. Get us out of here."

"Aye aye, Captain."

After the crate was secure in the cargo hold, Shrike called Willow, Annabelle, Wakeridge, and Skuttle together.

"I want to hear opinions," Shrike said, looking at the crate. "Should we open this thing, see what's in it, and possibly put ourselves in a stronger negotiating position with the admiral, or should we just leave well enough alone?"

Wakeridge looked at the crate with an expression alternating between curiosity and anger. "I recognize those markings."

"What, the registry number?" Shrike asked.

"Yes, the registry number. I've seen registries like that before." Wakeridge rubbed his chin.

"Where?" Willow asked.

"I saw them in my occupation before I joined the crew of *The Wild Rover*."

"So, we finally get to hear the Mysterious Origin of Professor Ambrose Wakeridge, man of piratical science?" Skuttle cackled and rubbed his hands together. "This should be fun!"

Wakeridge glared briefly at the engineer, then sighed and said, "Before I came out here, I was a member of the Ministry of Peculiar Science."

Everyone was silent for a moment, except for Skuttle, who was chuckling and pumping his fist in the air. When the others looked at him, he smiled and asked, "What? I had a bet with Oliver. I told him that Wake used to be a Peculiar. He owes me a week's pay."

Wakeridge rolled his eyes. "I know what everyone thinks of the Ministry, that we were a bunch of unethical monsters perverting the laws of nature to create massive and dangerous weapons that could destroy the world three times over without so much as breaking a sweat."

"Are you telling us that's not true?" Shrike asked.

"For the most part, no, it's not," Wakeridge replied. "Obviously, there was weapons research and military applications to some of the things we did. We worked on weapons and armor research, but also ways to improve crop yields, the occasional treatments for diseases, things like that. These projects fell under the Ministry of Peculiar Science mainly because we were using things like Mjolnirium, Albionium, Oremancy, some of the other exotic materials. Most of it was really quite dull. At least it was after you'd gotten used to the fact that you were working almost exclusively with unearthly metals and elements that could blow you to smithereens if used incorrectly."

"There had to be more to the Ministry than that," Willow said. "There are just too many stories about the preposterous bollocks you Peculiars get up to for all of them to be lies."

"You are right about that," said Wakeridge. "From time to time, there would be those dark projects that should have never been conceived of, let alone made. And from time to time, those projects would be sent from one facility to another under disguise." He gestured at the shipping container's markings identifying it as property of the Royal Agricultural Ministry. "That was always the favorite disguise. And that shipping number. I don't know exactly what's in there, but I do know what that type of code indicates."

"And what does PSM01SPEX mean?" asked Shrike.

"Well, the PSM denotes Ministry of Peculiar Science. The 01SP indicates a Special Project, Level 1. That's the highest level of importance at the Ministry. The E is a substitution. E is the fifth letter of the alphabet, so that means that whatever's in this container is one of at least five other objects of the same type. And the X, well, that means it is considered to be one of the most dangerous projects the Ministry works on. Only a Zed level project is considered more dangerous."

"They don't use Y?" Skuttle asked, chuckling again.

Wakeridge smirked back. "No, the Peculiar higher-ups dislike using Y for their special projects. They think it makes it sound like there's no point to them. Like someone is actually asking why they would do this." Wakeridge shrugged. "Scientists. What can I say? We're an odd bunch."

"All right then," Shrike said, looking over at Willow. "You think you can get that thing open so we can get a look at what's inside?"

"Of course, I can," Willow snapped. "It's just a matter of figuring out the lock and applying the proper counter force. Though I will say that this looks like a strong one. You had all better clear out and let me do this. It might take me awhile."

Willow shambled into the mess. She slumped into a chair, looked balefully around the room, and croaked, "Coffee."

Shrike walked over with a large, steaming mug. "How did it go?"

Willow removed the cup from Shrike's hand and proceeded to drain it with a series of large gulps. She held the mug out, shook it, and said, "Again."

Shrike complied. He opened his mouth to ask a question, but Willow held up her hand, shook her finger, and pointed at the mug while taking another series of sips.

Shrike stood quietly for a few moments, then crossed his arms and tapped his foot in impatience. "What hap—"

Another small, aluminum mug levitated into the air, flew across the room, and pressed itself firmly to his face, covering his mouth. Willow pointed a finger at him, her eyes glowing a bright, cobalt shade of blue as they always did whenever she used her Oremancy.

"Darling," she said. "I do love you, but if you don't stop nattering at me until after I've finished my coffee, I will strip an armor plate off the bulkhead and wrap it around your head."

Shrike nodded and sat down as Willow went back to savoring her coffee. The mug fell from Shrike's face and clattered to the table.

After a few minutes, Willow sighed with pleasure and put her mug down. "Now then, what was your question?"

"How did it go with the lock?"

"It took a good deal more energy and effort than I'd anticipated, but I got it open in the end. The crate is unlocked."

"And what's in it?"

Willow shrugged. "Not a clue. You're going to have to have Skuttle and Wake look at that thing."

Oliver joined them. "Anything at all you can tell me? I mean, you must have formed *some* kind of impression of it."

Willow fixed the XO with an icy stare. "I said I don't know what it is, and I meant it, Ollie. But gun to my head? Fine. I can't say what it's meant to be used for, but I can tell you that it's made from both Albionium and Mjolnirium."

"How the hell could they have done that?" asked Oliver. "That's not even supposed to be possible."

Willow shrugged. "Not my field. Ask Wake. No doubt he'll have some idea about how the Peculiars get up to what they do."

"It's a bloody flying machine," Wakeridge said several hours later, sitting in a chair across the desk in Shrike's office. "I'm not sure what the hell the Ministry is playing at, but that thing is a bloody flying machine."

"But how the hell can it be a flying machine?" Shrike asked. "It's got no airbag. Are you telling me that those protrusions on either side of the thing are actual *wings*? They crafted a metal bird?"

"Yes, that's how it looks to me, Captain. It has wings, though how it's supposed to remain aloft without the ability to flap them is beyond me." Wakeridge looked thoughtful for a moment. "It does have an Oremantic engine in the, well, beak I guess is as good as any description, and those two nozzles at the back along the tail, I suppose they could channel that energy to create thrust, like Oremantics do with steam in any sane airship design."

"What about those tubes that are embedded into the wings?" Shrike asked.

"I think those are meant to be guns, Captain. There's another power reserve in that thing. Unlike the engine, which is made of Mjolnirium, like any other engine. Though Willow told me it's a grade of Mjolnirium purer than anything she's ever seen. No, the other reserve is pure Albionium, like what powers handguns, ship's guns, land artillery. At least the British version of all those things. But again, this Albionium seems much purer and much stronger than anything I've ever seen. If this thing actually works, Captain, it will change the game of war forever. I really don't like the look of it. Not at all."

"Well, the question now is do we crate it up and take it back to Ballymore, or—"

The blaring of alarms and Oliver's voice over the speaker tube interrupted him. "Captain! This is the bridge! We have a confirmed sighting of the *Basilisk*, sir. I repeat, the *Basilisk* has found us! Please report to the bridge immediately!"

"On my way," Shrike replied into the tube. "Damn, that was fast."

The *Basilisk* descended from the clouds looking as menacing as the serpent it was named for.

"Well, that's not good news, is it?" Olliver said, staring out the forward viewport. "Orders, Captain?"

"For now, we'll bob and weave. Keep us out of her firing line.."

"And when that plan stops working?"

"Hopefully, I'll have another plan ready to go at that point," Shrike said grimly.

Olliver moaned. "Please think fast, Captain."

"Doing my best, XO."

Shrike's mind raced until a thought struck him. He weighed the risks and the possible benefits, but really they had no choice. It had the potential to go horribly wrong, but it could also save all their skins. "Professor?" he called to Wakeridge. "A moment of your time, please?"

Wakeridge looked up from his station, nodded, and then walked with Shrike to the back of the bridge. "What can I do for you, Cap?" he asked.

"That contraption we took from Rejik. Do you think that it will actually fly?"

Wake's eyes widened for a moment, and then he said, "In theory, yes. But I have to say that I'm not 100% certain of that. As far as I can tell, that thing contravenes just about everything we know about aero-gation."

"No one's ever 100% sure of anything, Wake," Shrike said. "I just need to know if you think that thing will fly and whether or not Skuttle agrees with you."

"He has a rosier view of the thing than I do, so yes, he agrees that it should fly and, possibly, even fly quite well."

"Perfect. Go get him, hunt down Ciara, and meet me in the cargo bay. Quick as you can, please."

Wakeridge nodded and headed off. Shrike stepped back over to Ollie and asked, "XO, do you think you can keep us out of the teeth of that behemoth for a bit longer?"

"No question, Captain. They may be big and terrifying, but they move like a drunken, three-legged cow compared to us. Plus, Rejik's gunners have never been known for their accuracy. A definite case of quantity over quality, sir."

"Still, be careful," Shrike said. "That's a whacking great lot of quantity he's got packed on to that monster." Shrike nodded to Willow over where she was keeping an eye on the ship's Oremantics, and motioned for her to walk with him out of the bridge.

As Willow fell into step beside him, she said, "All right. I know that look. You're planning something stupid and ridiculously dangerous, aren't you?"

"Could be," said Shrike with a smile. "I want to try and use that contraption we took from Rejik."

Willow sighed and put her hand over her eyes for a moment. "Hoy. That really doesn't sound like a good idea, love. Who are you going to try and dupe into getting behind the control stick of that thing?"

"Well, I figured that I'd ask Ciara if she wants to fly it and take a crack at the *Basilisk*. If she doesn't want to, well then…"

"You're going to fly it." Willow rolled her eyes. "You magnificent idiot. I suppose you won't be talked out of it, will you?"

"Most likely not, love." "Thought as much. So why am I here then? Want me to grow faint and fall into your arms at your foolish bravery and total lack of sense?"

"Wake said that the thing uses some kind of advanced Oremantic engine. I figured that we might need you to try and get the thing started."

Willow smirked. "Ah, so I get to mess about with a totally unknown bit of Oremantic technology that for all we know is just as likely to blow up in my face as it is to actually work properly. You always come up with the most fun outings for us, dearest."

When they got to the cargo bay, they saw that the contraption had already been rolled out and almost seemed to be stooping near the cargo doors looking like a gigantic metal hawk preparing to take flight. Skuttle was rubbing his hands and cackling at the thought of unleashing this thing. Wakebridge stood on one of the wings, fidgeting and talking Ciara through the process of operating it.

"As far as I can tell, you use that stick and those pedals at your feet to steer. I imagine the button on top of the stick fires the weapons housed in the wings, and I would guess that that iron sight on the front there is your aiming point." He gestured towards the end of the device, a circle of metal with a needle-like protrusion extending from the bottom up into the middle of it.

As Shrike stepped up to the side of the thing and opened his mouth, Ciara cut him off. "Don't even bother, Captain. I know the risks, and I'm willing to accept them. I'm taking the *Peregrine* out, and I'm taking down Rejik with it."

"*Peregrine?*" Shrike asked, smiling despite himself.

"It fits, don't you think? A lovely, gleaming bird of prey!" Ciara said with a wide grin.

"If anything seems about to go wrong—"

"That's what the parachute is for, sir." Ciara gestured towards the pack she was wearing. "I promise that I'll jettison at the first sign. Now you had all better get out of here so I can take this lovely girl out for a spin." With that, pulled the glass canopy forward, cutting off any further discussion.

Not certain of any other way to get the *Peregrine* up into the air, they had devised a rather odd strategy for launch. Once everyone had cleared out of the bay, leaving the doors open, they grabbed hold of something as Ollie put the *Rover* into a steep climb for a few moments. There was a sound disturbingly like an explosion, and then, just like its namesake bird but with lightning blazing from its tail, the *Peregrine* came soaring up in front of the *Rover*. It waggled a touch as Ciara got used to the controls, but after a few moments, the craft was soaring like Ciara had been born to fly it. Everyone held their breath as the craft flew much faster than any airship could ever manage towards the giant bulk of the *Basilisk*. A few of the guns on Rejik's ship attempted to hit the *Peregrine*, but it was moving far too fast for that. By the time the shots got to where the gunners were aiming, the craft was no longer there. Deftly avoiding any further volleys, Ciara brought the *Peregrine* on a straight on run at the *Basilisk's* bow, firing the small craft's weapons as she came.

No one was prepared for the results. Wakeridge had vastly underestimated the power of the Albionium ammunition store aboard the *Peregrine*. The blasts ripped through the *Basilisk* like bullets through parchment, leaving gaping exit breaches all along the hull. With several of its steering rudders destroyed, the giant airship listed badly to port. There was no question that the *Basilisk* was going to go down, but that wasn't enough for Ciara.

Ciara banked and took one more run at the giant airship, this time targeting the general area of the ship's Oremantic engines. She scored several hits, causing several large waves of destructive electricity to come sparking out from the areas where the engines had been, setting several fires, and even melting parts of the ship's hull before one of the engines actually exploded, taking another one with it, ripping the giant airship to pieces in a cataclysmic wave of destruction..

For a long moment, no one on *The Wild Rover* said a word. They all stared out the viewport, dumbfounded by what they had just witnessed. The rules of the air had changed forever.

The *Peregrine* banked away from the *Rover*. Heading straight towards a smallish, barren island in the distance.

Shrike turned from the forward view port to Wakeridge. "Wake, did you and Ciara go over a theory of how she could bring that thing down safely?"

In a shaky voice, the professor replied, "Yes, sir. Those struts just under the wings have wheels in them. It should land on a flat field just fine." No doubt she's going to attempt a landing there, Captain."

"Very well," Shrike replied in an odd tone. "Well, let's head after her. We need to make sure she's all right above anything else. Then, I think we had better find anything suitable nearby and do what we can to cover that thing up. We'll leave Ciara and a few of the crew behind to stand guard until we can come back and pick them up. Make note of that island's position, if you please, Mr. Wainwright."

"Come back?" asked Willow. "Where are we going?"

"We have an appointment to keep, remember," Shrike replied. "The admiral is waiting."

"What are you going to tell him?" Wakeridge asked.

"I'll think of something."

Heading into the *Intrepid* the second time was a good deal different than it had been on their last visit. This time, they weren't dragged in under guard, the rest of the *Rover's* crew wasn't confined, and neither Shrike nor Willow were incarcerated. Instead of the interrogation room, they were shown to Admiral Ballymore's office.

As Shrike would expect from the commander of Caribbean forces, the room was more like a pleasant study in some English country estate than the commander's office on board a military vessel; just another indicator of the type of man Ballymore was. Even so, Shrike couldn't help but be apprehensive. He knew from their last meeting that Ballymore was no fool. That didn't mean they were just going to turn the *Peregrine* over to the RSN. Nothing for it but to forge ahead and hope that Ballymore was in the proper mood to be deceived.

"Ah, Captain Shrike, Miss Aberdale. Do have a seat." The admiral rose from his desk, gave a brief bow, and gestured to two over-stuffed chairs in front of his desk. "Would you like a cup of tea before we begin our discussion?"

"Thank you, but no, Admiral," Shrike replied. "I'm sure you have many things to do, as do we, so if it's all the same to you, we'd just as soon have our discussion and be on our way. No offense intended, of course."

"None taken. I completely understand." Ballymore sat down, took a file out of his desk drawer, and scanned its contents. "Now then, how fares the job I hired you and your crew to perform, Captain? I note with some interest that our deckhands are not, in fact, unloading anything from your vessel. Also, there has been word of a rather large airship disaster occurring a day or so ago, quite near to where we believe that Rejik Helgarsson has his headquarters. Would I be incorrect in assuming that these two facts are related?"

"No, sir, you would not be," Shrike said, affecting an air of regret. "We did locate the stolen cargo that you sent us after. However, when we were about to go in to where we thought Rejik had stashed it, his ship appeared and maneuvered to attack us."

"Mmmm. That must have been a nerve-wracking turn of events. The *Basilisk* was definitely a ship to be feared. Even many of our own RSN vessels would think twice about taking it on. At least taking it on alone."

"Understandable. It was a rather, ah, shall we say, formidable vessel."

"And yet, here you are, here is your crew, and I note that there is very little sign of damage on your own vessel. Would you care to explain how you managed to escape Helgarsson unscathed? Surely, you are not about to tell me that you managed to take out the *Basilisk* all on your own?" Ballymore gave Shrike a pointed look.

"Nothing so fanciful," Shrike said, waving his hand. "No, it's not a thrilling tale of how we concocted some insanely clever plan and managed to destroy the great evil. Such things are the stuff of the Penny Dreadfuls and Pulp novels. No, sir. Our deliverance was an entirely fortuitous happenstance."

"Would you care to tell me what exactly happened?" Ballymore leaned back in his seat.

"Certainly," Shrike said. "You are quite correct in thinking that my ship would have had no real chance at destroying Helgarsson's. At least, not without considerable damage and loss of life on our own side. To undertake such a gambit, even if we had won, would have been an unacceptable Pyrrhic victory. No, sir, as much as I'd like to thrill you with a tale of our cleverness, bravery, and skill, the simple fact is that we had nothing to do with what happened to the *Basilisk*."

"Explain, if you please, Captain."

"Gladly. The reason that we have no lost crew and suffered so little damage is that we never actually engaged Helgarsson directly. While the *Basilisk* was a very powerful and terrifying ship, ours was much more maneuverable. He would most likely have caught us eventually, but we managed to stay out of the path of his gunners, ducking and dodging. We were actually preparing to make a full-speed burn to try and get away, when… well, it's hard to describe, but there was some sort of massive explosion on board the *Basilisk*. That explosion caused her own Oremantic engines to explode. When that happens, there's really not much to do but plan the funerals, sir. I can only assume that whatever they stole from you was something very dangerous indeed, they had it aboard, tried to use it, something went wrong, and they paid the price."

"And how would you reason that out?" Ballymore raised an eyebrow. "I never told you what it was that you were going after."

"That may be true," Shrike said steadily. "But there's really no other explanation, is there? At least not to someone willing to spend more than a moment of thought on it. The size of the Oremantic explosion made it obvious."

Ballymore didn't speak for a long moment, staring off into space. Finally, he looked back at Shrike and said, "So, you made no attempt to investigate the wreckage of the *Basilisk?*"

"You hired us to recover a shipping container. We did that, though granted the item is no longer inside. Unfortunate, but unavoidable. After seeing what happened to the *Basilisk*, I wanted to go and look for anything salvageable, or perhaps any survivors, but—"

"I wouldn't let him," Willow broke in. "An Oremantic explosion of that size? Such massive discharges tend to have lingering effects. Effects that any sane person should wish to avoid."

Ballymore sighed, heavy with regret. "No, you are both quite correct. Still, I was hopeful. Well, I suppose that concludes our business for now. You did indeed perform the task we sent you out to perform. Just a shame that it came to the finish it did. Still, you kept your word, Captain, so I shall keep mine." Ballymore reached into another desk drawer and took out a rolled parchment affixed with the seal of the RSN Admiralty. "As promised, here is your Mark of Pardon. As you know, this absolves you of all past crimes against the Crown. It does not, however, do a thing about any *future* crimes you might consider committing." The admiral gave Shrike a shrewd look.

Shrike returned a slight smile. "Yes, Admiral, I know how Marks of Pardon work, and I quite understand."

"Mmmm," Ballymore rumbled. "Well, I wish you good luck. I trust that you will now be doing your best to remain somewhat more inconspicuous?"

"You are absolutely correct. In fact, I don't expect you shall hear from us again," Shrike said.

"I doubt that," Ballymore replied with a small smile of his own. "Still, there are many things that demand my attention, minor yet annoying piracy not necessarily being one of them. Do try to keep out of trouble, Captain Shrike. I realize that a return to the RSN would be out of the question. But have you ever considered the Privateer Corps?"

Shrike chuckled. "I really don't think that would be a good fit either for me or the Corps itself, sir."

"Perhaps not. Still, keep it in mind. In any event, I am sure that you and your crew have much to attend to, as do I. I thank you for your time and your efforts on our behalf." Ballymore stood and extended his hand.

Shrike rose and took the Admiral's hand to shake, not prepared for the speed with which the grip tightened to iron. The pleasant expression never left the admiral's face, but there was a new steel behind Ballymore's eyes as he said, "Farewell for now, Captain Shrike. Do try and stay out of trouble, won't you?"

Shrike met the Admiral's gaze with a steely one of his own. "Oh, I will do my level best, sir. One can but try."

"Of that, I have no doubt," Ballymore replied with a chuckle. "Until we meet again. Godspeed, Captain."

"And to you as well, sir," Shrike replied.

"Well, do you think the Admiral believed you?" Wakeridge asked when Shrike stepped into the cargo bay.

"I think he's going to accept what I had to say and take the fact that Rejik's been removed from the board, so to speak as a victory. But as to whether or not he actually believed me? No, I don't expect he did. At least, he's somewhat suspicious, and he's going to be much more on his guard from here on out."

They both stood looking at the machine they'd dubbed the *Peregrine*, sitting on the deck and gleaming like new. Shrike had seen it and still couldn't quite believe what it could do.

"So, you say that there must be at least four more of these infernal contraptions, yes?" Shrike asked.

"Without a doubt," Wakeridge replied. "And if the Ministry is anything close to what it was when I was there, I would say it would be a safe wager that there are more." He gestured to the Peregrine. "Something like this is going to change everything about air combat, Jack."

"I agree. I think we need to take a more active role in this."

"What will that entail?" "If it's not too much trouble to you, I'd like you to head back to England for a while. Assuming you still have some, see if you can get in touch with some of your old Ministry contacts and find out if they know anything about these machines."

"A tall order," Wakeridge said, stroking his beard. "But yes, there are some individuals I might be able to contact. No idea if they'll be of any help, however."

"Perhaps not, but at least it's a place to start. I assume you'll be taking Annabelle with you?" Shrike asked.

"Oh, without question," Wakeridge said. "I'll need to visit some seedy places, and she'll be a great help keeping me breathing. So, I guess you'll have to adjust your boarding tactics if you decide to take any prizes when we're gone."

"You'll both indeed be missed," Shrike said with a chuckle. "But this is important, Wake. We need to get some kind of a handle on this thing. I don't like the idea of anyone having something with that kind of power, let alone many things."

"I'll go collect Annabelle and get my things together. We'll leave as soon as I can arrange passage."

Shrike extended his hand. "Good. I appreciate it, Wake."

"No thanks needed," Wakeridge said, shaking the captain's hand. "I completely agree with you that something needs to be done about these things. But I have absolutely no idea what that will be."

"Nor me. I expect we'll just have to burn that particular bridge when we get to it, eh?"

Wakeridge laughed. "Yes, that does rather seem to be our style, doesn't it?"

Shrike nodded at Wakeridge and headed back to his quarters. As he walked, the events of the past few days and their implications for the future washed over him. He wasn't sure what was going to happen, but he had a sinking feeling that before too long, things were going to get a good deal more interesting in the Caribbean, and not in a good way.

Shrike sighed, then smiled as he walked into his quarters and saw Willow sitting at their shared desk with another hand of Single Castellan laid out in front of her. Like he'd told Wake, they would indeed burn that bridge when they got to it. But with the crew of *The Wild Rover* at his side, doing what they did best, he was certain that they would find a way to muddle through. They always did.

About Drew Carmody

Drew Carmody is a writer of strange fantasy and science fiction.

He is currently working on the first novel in the Skies of Fire and Lightning series, a Steampunk universe shared with this story. When not writing, Drew can be found engaging in all manner of nerdy pursuits in the general vicinity of Charlotte, North Carolina with his fiancé, his almost-stepson, three dogs, three cats, and a ferret. He is also on a lifelong quest to find the perfect cheeseburger.

Also by Phoebe Darqueling: The Mistress of None Series

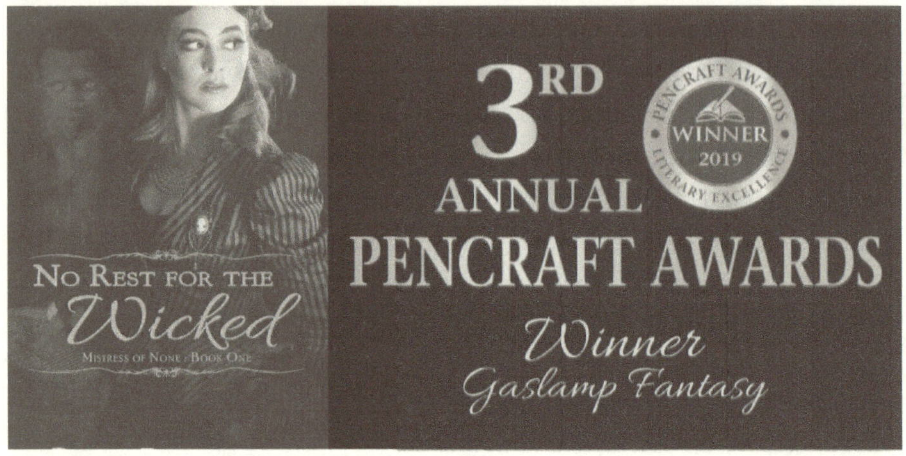

Other people just think they're "haunted by the past." In Vi's case, it's true. Clairvoyant Viola Thorne wants to forget about her days of grifting and running errands for ghosts. The problem? Playing it safe is dull. So when a dead stranger begs for her help, Vi jumps at the chance to dust off her hustling skills. The unlikely companions are soon tangling with bandits, cheating at cards, and loving every minute.

Then she finds out who referred him, and Vi has to face both a past and ex-partner that refuse to stay buried. Though she betrayed Peter, his spirit warns her of the plot that cost him his life. Vi's guilty conscience won't let her rest until she solves his murder. Though she's spent her whole life fighting the pull of the paranormal, it holds the key to atoning for the only deception she's ever regretted—breaking Peter's heart.

Available in print, e-book, and audio formats. Find them all at bit.ly/ViolaThorne

Nothing Ventured, Nothing Gained: Mistress of None Book 2 is coming Aug 2020.

Save his boy, uncover a conspiracy, and master opposable thumbs—a dog's work is never done.

Buddy's favorite thing is curling up for a nap at the foot of Ethan's bed. Then he stumbles through a portal to a clockwork city plagued by chimeras, and everything changes… Well, not everything. Sure, his new human body comes with magic powers, but he'd still rather nap than face the people of Excelsior, who harbor both desire and fear when it comes to "the other side."

He discovers Ethan followed him through the portal and underwent his own transformation, and it becomes Buddy's doggone duty to save him. Buddy finds unlikely allies in an aristocrat with everything on the line, a mechanic with something to hide, and a musician willing to do anything to protect her. Using a ramshackle flying machine, the group follows the chimeras deep into the forest and uncovers a plot that could reshape the worlds on both sides of the rift.

Available in e-book and print formats. Find them at www.bit.ly/Riftmaker

Also by Phoebe Darqueling: The Steampunk Handbook

Get your e-book for FREE when you sign up to receive Phoebe's e-newsletter at bit.ly/SteampunkHandbook

The Steampunk Handbook is a collection of articles by Steampunk author and lecturer, Phoebe Darqueling. It covers topics such as the history of steam power, the philosophical roots of punk and punk literature as a whole, and the history and evolution of the Steampunk fandom. In addition, you will find information about the historical and cultural underpinnings behind twelve of the most popular tropes in Steampunk. Enjoy pages of recommendations for books, movies, and television shows that are perfect for fans of Steampunk both old and new.

Coming to print May 1, 2020.

Thank You

This book and it's companion, *Gears, Ghouls, and Gauges*, came to life thanks to the generous backers of a Kickstarter campaign. Our deepest gratitude goes to:

Aaron Turko
Abiran Raveenthiran
Alex Chapman
alicat
Allison Payne
Alyssa
Andi Newton
Andrew Parsons
Andy and Ali Prudom
Anna Kaling
Anonymous
Arielle Wasiak
Barb and Carl Kesner
Barbara O'Dell
Baronessa Arts
Beth Culp
Brandy A. Melville
Brittany Nock
Carol Gyzander
Cryptic Creative
Crysta Coburn
Cynthia Fry
D

Dale A Russell

detly

Dianne Nicholson

Dianne Nicholson

Donald

Emma & Simon Gelgoot

Eli Weaverdyck

Engel Dreizehn

Erik T Johnson

Faye Ringel

Gaslamp Fancier

Gevera Bert Piedmont

Gordon Emrick

Grady Hess

Hel broisha

Hilary Anderson

Hisham Barazi

Ian Glover

Ian McFarlin

Ib Rasmussen

Irina Marinescu

James Jester

James Lucas

Javed Mawji

Jen Linton Carvahlo

Jennifer L. Pierce

Jess Gisler

JL Merrow

Joe Dubé

Joshua C. Chadd

Joshua Whitaker

Karen J Carlisle

Kathleen Burns

Kati Hamilton

Kevin Drew

King

Kirasha Urqhart

Kristi Fox

Kristin Anne Danko

Leigh Smith

Linda

Lisa Kruse

Madeleine Holly-Rosing

Mandy Burkhead

Mark Carter

Mark Featherston

Mark Lukens

Matthew Karpinski

Megan K. Ward

Melanie

Melissa Williams

Mercy J Meilunas

Michael the Horologist

Michelle Mishmash

Mike Bundt

Mitchell A Johnson

MoMo

Nathan Lueth

Nicholas Eng

Nicolas Aguirre

Olivia Montoya

Paul Hiscock

Rie Sheridan Rose

Robby T. Tatom, G.GiftGuru

Robin Komarica

Robinette Waterson

S and A Hudson
Saga Albright
Sarah Van Goethem
Shannon M.
Shannon O'Neill
Shawnee M
Sheldon Rock
Stephanie Gonzales
Steve Lemanski
Steven Peiper
SwordFire
thatraja
The Fryer Family
Tim "Buzz" Isakson
Tracy 'Rayhne' Fretwell
Zoltan Deathspawn

www.ingramcontent.com/pod-product-compliance
Lightning Source LLC
Chambersburg PA
CBHW030738110726
47900CB00008B/2362